Skin Deep

MJ Howson

ENGINE ❶❸

Previously published as *Skin Deep (Episodes 01-22)* on Kindle Vella.

Published by Engine Thirteen

ISBN: 979-8-9864583-1-1

Library of Congress Control Number: 2022911398

Cover design by MJ Howson

Other books by MJ Howson

Dawn of Eve

The Tallow Series:

Tallow – An Urban Legend (Book 1)

Tallow – Rosemary (Book 2)

Tallow – Time to Pay (Book 3)

Co-Authored by MJ Howson

FASTER (with Alex Schuler)

I dedicate this story to my niece Stephanie. Her youth and joyous spirit gave me the idea to craft a tale aimed at a younger generation.

Prologue

Body Dysmorphia Disorder

"Body dysmorphic disorder is a mental health condition in which you can't stop thinking about one or more perceived defects or flaws in your appearance — a flaw that appears minor or can't be seen by others. But you may feel so embarrassed, ashamed and anxious that you may avoid many social situations.

When you have body dysmorphic disorder, you intensely focus on your appearance and body image, repeatedly checking the mirror, grooming or seeking reassurance, sometimes for many hours each day. Your perceived flaw and the repetitive behaviors cause you significant distress and impact your ability to function in your daily life.

You may seek out numerous cosmetic procedures to try to "fix" your perceived flaw. Afterward, you may feel temporary satisfaction or a reduction in your distress, but often the anxiety returns and you may resume searching for other ways to fix your perceived flaw."

Mayo Clinic (n.d.) Retrieved from https://www.mayoclinic.org/diseases-conditions/body-dysmorphic-disorder/symptoms-causes/syc-20353938

One

Where's Emily?

Monday, April 22, 2019

Kaylee furrowed her brow as she gazed at the selfie staring back from her phone. Despite the bright smile, all Kaylee could see was the acne and chubby cheeks that seemed to define her look. Even her hooped gold nose ring did little to bring life to her pale complexion. The cackling of voices outside the high school bathroom stall rattled her concentration. Kaylee used her thumb to flip through a dozen pictures taken over spring break. She stopped and studied a nighttime photo of her and her older sister Hailey. Their mom had gotten them a fire permit for the local Orleans beach at the Cape Cod National Seashore. They were bundled in jackets, the flickering flames of the campfire doing their best to keep the two girls warm. She couldn't help but wonder why Hailey looked so photogenic. So perfect.

"Why do I bother?" Kaylee said, her voice barely a whisper.

She closed her photos and allowed her thumb to pause over a nearby app called *SkinDeep*. The bright lime-green icon with the offset white letters "SD" sat nestled between her Instagram and TikTok apps. Kaylee opened the app and launched the front-facing camera. She smiled and snapped a picture. Her image appeared on the screen, along with a list of sliders and control options. Kaylee opened the eye controller and immediately changed her blue-gray eyes to a brighter shade. The app's ability to target and alter specific areas was impressive. There were times she always found her eye color to be a bit depressing. She briefly played with the controls labeled complexion until her acne vanished. As Kaylee debated what to change next, a pounding on the door startled her.

"What the hell is taking you so long?" Hailey yelled from the other side.

Kaylee sighed, closed the app, and slipped the phone into her skirt's pocket. She grabbed her school-issued iPad off the floor. The tablet's navy case had her name and student ID listed in bold print. She opened the door and stepped out of the stall just in time to see her sister leave. There were only a few other girls in the bathroom. They ignored Kaylee as they bumped past her on the way to the exit. Kaylee stopped briefly at the mirror to adjust her shoulder-length wavy brown hair and inspect her somewhat ill-fitting clothes.

Engel Academy's mandatory dress code required everyone to wear the same uninspiring uniform. The girls wore pleated knee-length navy skirts, white blouses, and black leather shoes. The boys wore navy slacks, white long-sleeved shirts, and brown leather shoes. If it wasn't for everyone's varying heights and hairstyles, the students would be almost indistinguishable. Kaylee groaned as she stared at her puffy face, turned, and left the bathroom.

The din in the private school's hallway was deafening as students slammed locker doors closed and talked loudly over one another. Hailey was standing across the hall with her three best friends – Allison, Jade, and Paige. These were Hailey's best friends, not Kaylee's. The foursome, all standing at the same height, made a striking combination of contrasting styles. Allison's bobbed curly red hair and piercing blue eyes always seemed to glisten, even in the darkest of shadows. Her freckled cheeks somehow made her look younger than most her age. Paige, meanwhile, always appeared a bit gaunt and tired. Her long blonde hair cascaded past her bony shoulders. No matter how trim, Paige's clothes always seemed to be a size too big. Highly self-conscious, Paige routinely twirled the pearl necklace clutching her neck. And then there was Jade, one of only half a dozen Black students in the school. Jade routinely pushed the limits of what the school's strict rules would tolerate. Most notably, her thick afro raised several eyes of some of the more traditional-biased teachers. But Jade's mother made it clear that her daughter could wear her hair however she pleased.

Kaylee found herself envious of the four seniors. They were all thin, pretty, and popular. Everything she wasn't. Yet, a part of Kaylee was thankful to have them around. Being a loner, Kaylee preferred getting to know a new book or streaming series rather than making friends. If it wasn't for Hailey, she'd have almost nobody at school to talk to. Her big sister wasn't only her best friend, but also her fiercest defender.

The students ambling through the hallway forced Kaylee to snake her way over to the other four.

"We have to hurry," Paige said. Her eyes darted back and forth as she spun a few of the pearls around her neck. "I don't want to be stuck sitting near the juniors." She glanced at Kaylee and added, "No offense."

Everyone followed Paige's lead as they entered the sea of students, all headed in the same direction.

"Does anyone know what this assembly's about?" Jade asked. She looked around, loudly snapping a piece of peppermint gum. Jade's afro softly bounced as she walked. "Kaylee, you must know."

"I . . . I think it's about Emily," Kaylee said.

Paige stopped, causing everyone to skid to a halt. She looked at Kaylee and said, "That new trash girl?"

"Paige!" Kaylee glared at Paige and then the other three girls. "It's been a week."

"Whatever," Allison said as she rolled her eyes. "As long as it gets me out of class."

Paige laughed and put her arm around Allison. They turned and continued down the hallway. As they all made their way to the gymnasium, Kaylee drifted toward the back of the group. She gently tugged on her sister's elbow.

"What?" Hailey asked.

"Do you think they know?" Kaylee asked.

"Does who know what?" Hailey replied. She stopped as the crowd around them came to a halt. They'd reached the gym, and people were waiting to enter. Hailey's eyes widened as she stared at her sister. "Do you mean the video?" When Kaylee nodded, Hailey took a moment to survey the crowd. "Should it matter? I mean, nobody got hurt. Right?"

"I . . . I don't know." Kaylee crossed her arms across her chest and nervously looked around. "I guess."

"Relax." Hailey put her arm around her sister, pulled her close, and smiled. "If anything happens, we're fam."

The gymnasium's bleachers were packed. As usual, the students were sitting almost exclusively by class. The seniors had staked out the prime seating closest to the exit. Although Kaylee was a junior, she stuck with her sister and followed her, Allison, Paige, and Jade to a bench mid-way toward the top.

As they sat down, Hailey whispered into Kaylee's ear, "There are some cute boys a few rows back. Juniors. We need to get you a boyfriend."

Kaylee briefly glanced behind her. She recognized two of the guys Hailey was talking about. The pair sat behind her in Spanish class and routinely made fun of her. Kaylee sighed and returned her focus to the main floor.

A half-dozen chairs sat perched atop a small elevated stage in the middle of the gym. Several adults, including two police officers, stood at the edge of the platform, watching the students get seated. A camera crew from a Boston television station sat off to the side.

"Is this a press conference?" Hailey asked.

"Why are the cops here?" Allison nervously spun her bright red hair through her fingers. "What happened?"

"Do . . . do you think it's Emily?" Kaylee asked. "She hasn't been here since the video."

"Who cares," Jade said. "I mean, nobody really knew her. New students starting mid-year always have a rough start."

Kaylee suddenly felt nauseous. She remembered the day Emily Mason first arrived at Engel Academy. It was the Monday just before spring break. In the weeks leading up to her first day at school, Emily had posted on the school's online bulletin board about how excited she was to be starting a new school in a new town. Once Jade and the others had her full name, they'd tracked her down on different social media apps.

Emily loved to post everything everywhere. Her online persona was loud, bold, and beautiful. But when she showed up for that first day of school, she looked nothing like her pictures. Jade, Allison, and the rest had taunted her for how radically different she appeared.

"You never got to know her," Kaylee said to Jade. She quietly studied Allison, Paige, and Hailey. "None of you gave her a chance."

"She kind of asked for it," Paige said.

"We'll know soon enough," Hailey said. After giving Kaylee a reassuring smile, Hailey's eyes scanned the gym. "Has anyone seen Noah?"

"What did you expect, Kaylee?" Allison asked. "I mean, Emily obviously used SkinDeep to change her appearance. But c'mon. It's one thing to tweak your skin tone or go extreme with a crazy look."

"That girl made herself look twenty pounds lighter," Paige said. "She changed her eyes. Her skin. Everything. That's all she'd post!"

Kaylee opened her mouth to weigh in, but realized her opinion was in the minority.

"We taught her a lesson," Jade said. She blew a bubble before loudly snapping her gum. Her eyes widened as they settled on the stage. "Hailey, isn't that cop Noah's uncle?" Jade tapped Hailey's shoulder and pointed toward a tall, broad-shouldered Orleans police officer standing on the corner of the stage. Detective Lane stroked his long silver beard as he surveyed the students entering the gym. His bright blue eyes darted back and forth as he studied each person's movements and actions.

"I think so," Hailey said. She put a comforting hand on Jade's knee. "Don't worry. I don't think this has anything to do with your family." Hailey grabbed her phone to check for a text from Noah. She looked out into the crowd. "Where the hell is my boyfriend?" Hailey sighed and quickly sent Noah several text messages telling him where they were seated.

Several more minutes passed as everyone got settled. Soon, the clang of the main door closing echoed throughout the room. As Principal Torres walked to the microphone, her trademark pink high-heels clacked against the floor, and the whispers and chatter died down. She took a moment to adjust the bobby pins holding her ink-black hair in a tight bun. The principal lowered the pole to put the mic closer to her mouth. Her deep brown eyes briefly settled on the men seated behind her. She cleared her throat and, in a vaguely Latin accent, said, "I know the rumors are already swirling, so let me cut to the chase. Detective Rick Lane of the Orleans police department is here to discuss the recent disappearance of Emily Mason. For those of you who may not know Emily, she started at Engel Academy two weeks ago and went missing over spring break. I'm sure you've all noticed the news crew in the corner. We've notified your families about the details of this assembly. Some are even here."

The voices in the stadium rose as the students began to whisper to one another. Principal Torres frowned as she surveyed the crowd, and then she tapped her fingertips on the microphone. The loud thumping resonating through the speakers silenced everyone. She said, "I don't have to remind you we do things differently here at Engel Academy. Your parents put you here for a reason. No sugar-coating. No babying. You live by school rules while here." A small smile spread across the principal's thin pink lips. "I'll turn this over to Detective Lane."

Detective Lane shook hands with Principal Torres before approaching the microphone. He immediately adjusted the height by a foot and pressed his scraggly beard against the mic.

"Thank you, Principal Torres," Detective Lane said. He paused briefly to survey the crowd. "Emily Mason disappeared on Saturday the thirteenth, exactly nine days ago. Cell data puts her last known location here at the school at eight o'clock that night."

"This is old news," Jade whispered to Hailey.

"Quiet!" Kaylee hissed.

"We've had little to go on since her disappearance," Detective Lane said. "Until yesterday."

Jade, Hailey, Allison, and Paige all exchanged glances. Undecipherable conversations began to break out throughout the gymnasium. Principal Torres stood up and clapped her hands once. As she sat back down, the murmurs faded away.

"As you may know, we never received a ransom note," Detective Lane said. "So we were never sure what could have happened. Did she run away? Was she abducted? Maybe she had an accident somewhere." A gentle tap on the detective's back caused him to turn around. Principal Torres glared at him and then nodded toward the tall, middle-aged man sitting a few seats away. His head was hung low, and his shoulders slumped. "Sorry," Detective Lane continued. "Well, all of that changed this weekend. We received an envelope at the police station. Inside was Emily's necklace. And . . . it was covered in blood."

Voices erupted from the student body, and a handful of people screamed.

"Please, everyone," Detective Lane continued. "I need you to all calm down. Right now." He waited several seconds, but the commotion continued, albeit at a lower volume. "We've confirmed that both the necklace and the blood belong to Emily. There was also a note with two words." Detective Lane leaned closer to the microphone and said, "It begins." He raised his hands to calm the outbursts from the crowd. "Now, the fact that her last known location was at this school . . . well, it changes everything. All of you need to be on high alert. At this point, we must assume Emily was forcibly abducted. Whether or not she's still alive, well . . . ." Detective Lane turned and looked back at the solemn-looking man behind him. "Mr. Mason? Is there anything else you'd like to add?"

Silence quickly fell across the gymnasium. One by one, all eyes turned to the man sitting at the end of the row. The cameras aimed at the detective pivoted and focused on the other man. Slowly, Mr. Mason stood up and approached the microphone. His hollow eyes reflected a man in pain - a man who hadn't gotten a good night's sleep in days. Mr. Mason's brown wavy hair, gray at the temples, appeared unkempt. His shoes dragged across the stage as if he didn't have the strength to lift them to walk. Mr. Mason's hand shook as he gently gripped the mic.

"I just want to thank everyone for their support," Mr.

Mason said, his voice quivering. "We've been here less than a month. My Emily, she . . . she was my world. If any of you know anything . . . anything at all, please let us know. Please." He paused and wiped the tears now rolling down his face. "I can't believe my baby girl is gone."

Mr. Mason briefly stared at the students packed into the bleachers. He turned, lowered his head, and returned to his chair. Paige and Allison briefly looked at one another before lowering their heads.

Principal Torres spent the next ten minutes talking about increased security around the school and the need to cancel several nighttime events. Each announcement was met with quiet frustration from the crowd. Detective Lane closed the assembly by warning everyone to stay vigilant.

Kaylee and the others stood up and waited to make their way down to the main floor. She tapped her sister Hailey on the shoulder and said, "I feel awful. Don't you?"

"I can't believe that cop," Hailey replied, her face buried in her phone. "He's trying to scare us with the bloody necklace. I'm texting Mom."

"Emily's dad's so . . . broken. I didn't know they'd been here less than a month."

"Why do you care? We barely knew her."

"That's the sad part." Kaylee stared at the back of her sister's head, waiting for some type of emotion to emerge. All she got was silence. As they descended the stairs, Kaylee watched Emily's dad collapse into Principal Torres's arms and weep. "We shouldn't have been so mean to her."

Jade spun around, snapped her gum, and said, "Would you drop it, Kaylee? It's not like we killed her."

Kaylee lowered her head and followed everyone out into the hallway. Deep down, her blood boiled. She found Jade to be just as insensitive as the rest of them. Times like these made Kaylee wonder if she needed to get a new set of friends. There was only one nice one out of everyone that Hailey spent time with.

"Noah!" Hailey cried.

Kaylee lit up when she saw Noah approaching them. Her sister's boyfriend was tall enough to play on the school's basketball team, but his interests were in math and science. Noah's skin tone hued a few shades darker than Jade's, and his smile was infectious. He scratched his buzz-cut head as he walked up to Hailey.

"Where have you been?" Hailey asked. She craned her neck up and kissed Noah on his cheek. "Didn't you get my texts?"

"Sorry, I was busy," Noah said. He glanced at the students still leaving the gymnasium. The crowd thinned, and Principal Torres and Detective Lane emerged. Noah locked eyes with the cop. "I need to go. I'll text you later."

"Where are you going?" Hailey asked.

Noah didn't respond and pushed his way through the other students until he reached the detective. Noah, his uncle, and the principal all walked away together.

Paige, Allison, and Jade stood against the wall watching everyone walk by. Kaylee couldn't hear their whispers but knew they were being judgmental. Suddenly they stopped talking as Brittney, by far the most popular girl in school, strutted by. With her short auburn hair, flawless skin, and piercing green eyes, Brittney looked like a fashion model. Unfortunately, she knew how good she looked and Brittney often bragged about her privileged life.

"Hi, Brittney," Allison said, her voice uncharacteristically shy.

Brittney flashed her a side-eye but didn't bother to stop to talk to her. Once she was out of earshot, Jade said, "You know she doesn't use SkinDeep."

"Right?" Allison replied. "She's perfect."

Allison and Paige began to walk down the hallway, and Kaylee and the rest followed. Principal Torres had scheduled the assembly for late morning, just before the first lunch block. Kaylee's stomach growled as they made their way toward the cafeteria. She did her best to ignore the trash-talking happening between Allison, Paige, and Jade. Kaylee was glad her sister wasn't participating, but that was because she was too busy playing with the *SkinDeep* app on her phone. Kaylee watched as her sister adjusted the sliders to darken her pale skin tone and narrow her nose.

"If you ask me, I'm not surprised Emily got bagged," Jade

said. "She was so fake. Liars like that end up getting what they should."

Jade turned the corner and slammed into Detective Lane. When she realized who she'd hit, she screamed and jumped back.

"Oh, did she?" Detective Lane asked. He folded his arms and glared at Jade. "Given your family's history with the law, maybe I should make you my top suspect?"

Jade was about to reply when Principal Torres appeared from behind the detective. She looked at Jade and said, "We're going to want to talk to you." She raised her eyes and looked at the rest of the girls, adding, "All of you."

"What?" Jade cried. "I was just mouthing off."

"We've gone through Emily's social media posts, including those of other students," Detective Lane said. "We know what you girls did. How you treated her."

"Bullying is not tolerated at this school," the principal said, her voice seething with anger. "I've already alerted your parents." She clasped her hands together and let her eyes take rest on each one of them. "If it were up to me, you'd all pay the ultimate price for what you did. I just hope your parents teach you a lesson." Principal Torres spun on one of her high heels and bellowed, "Follow me."

Kaylee, Hailey, Jade, Paige, and Allison spent the next two hours being individually questioned by both Detective Lane and Principal Torres. Their phones were seized to prevent them from coordinating their stories. When Hailey objected, the principal reminded her that school policy allowed the staff to take a student's phone away as punishment for breaking any rules. Jade's mom was the only parent to be present during the questioning. Once dismissed, the five girls were sent back to class, and their phones returned. Kaylee found the entire experience rather traumatizing. Her mind remained numb, and her eyes spent the rest of the afternoon focused on the clock as she waited for the school day to finish.

When her last class ended, she bolted to her locker, collected her belongings, and rushed to meet Hailey. Cool, damp air, hovering around fifty degrees, greeted them as they left the school. The late afternoon sun brought a smile to

Kaylee's face as she and her sister descended the stairs toward the parking lot.

"Are you okay?" Hailey asked. She stopped at the curb and tapped Kaylee's shoulder. "You've been so quiet."

"I keep thinking about Emily and all those questions in the principal's office," Kaylee said. She let her eyes wander as she studied the students leaving school. "Do you think we need to worry?"

"About what? The principal? That cop?" Hailey's confusion quickly turned to annoyance. "We didn't do anything, Kaylee. That video meant nothing." Hailey smiled and put her arm around her sister. "Relax."

"No, I'm not worried about the cops or Torres." Kaylee sighed and pulled herself away from her sister. "I just wonder, well, could . . . could one of us be next?"

"Disappear like Emily?" Hailey shook her head and added, "No." After noticing her sister's stress, she put her arm around Kaylee again and said, "I . . . I think we'll be okay."

A chime rang out from Hailey's pocket. She grabbed her phone and checked the screen.

eChat: 1 New Message

"What's eChat?" Kaylee asked.

"Stop looking at my phone." Hailey angled the screen away from her sister and unlocked her phone. "Noah likes to use it to chat with me. It's encrypted. Super private."

Hailey launched the eChat app and frowned. The encrypted message wasn't from Noah but rather someone named Dr. Ed. Messages on eChat appeared as a blood-red bubble masking the text, with shimmering white pixels inside. The app required you to slide your finger across the message to expose the text. The text would then vanish seconds later. She ran her finger across the text bubble to expose the message from Dr. Ed.

Knock Knock

"What's Noah want?" Kaylee asked. She tried to look at her

sister's phone, but Hailey kept the screen tilted away. "Is it about the assembly? His uncle, the cop?"

"Mind your own business, Kaylee!"

Hailey lowered her phone as she searched the parking lot for Noah. She hadn't heard from him since he vanished after the assembly. The phone soon chimed again. Hailey nervously ran her finger across the encrypted message.

Are you ready to meet yet?

Hailey frowned and quickly sent a reply.

I told you to stop bothering me.

Dr. Ed's reply appeared a few seconds later. Hailey slowly slid her finger across the blood-red bubble to reveal the hidden text.

Do you like who you see in the mirror?

The message vanished. Hailey lowered the phone. Her eyes glazed over as she looked off into the parking lot. Kaylee stepped closer and casually glanced at the blank screen. She frowned at the lack of information. Glare from the sky obscured the ID of the person texting her sister.

"Well?" Kaylee asked. "Who was it?"

Two

Dr. Ed

Kaylee stared at her half-empty dinner plate. Chunks of her mom's meatloaf rested in a pool of packaged gravy smeared with bits of mashed potatoes. A pile of steamed broccoli sat untouched. The scent of garlic and butter filled the dining room. Kaylee grabbed the nearby bowl of potatoes and scooped a fresh pile onto her dish.

"Put that away," her mother, Lesley, said.

Kaylee looked across the table at her mom. Although in her mid-forties, Lesley Jones looked like she could have been an older sister to her daughters. All three shared the same hair color, dull blue-gray eyes, and distinctive nose. Kaylee soon realized her mother wasn't talking to her. She glanced at Hailey to find her sister engrossed in the *SkinDeep* app.

"No phones while eating," Lesley said. "Hailey?"

"Sorry," Hailey said. She sighed as she tucked her phone between her legs.

"I was shocked when I got that email from the school about today's assembly." Lesley tugged at the tips of her shoulder-length brown hair. "I tried to clear my schedule to be there, but I had too many showings today." Lesley took a moment to stare at her daughters. "And then getting called into the principal's office? Principal Torres told me there was a video I needed to watch. Something on Instagram? Did you know this girl who went missing? What was her name? Emma?"

Kaylee waited for her sister to respond. After several awkward seconds of silence, Kaylee said, "Emily. Her name

14

was Emily. We . . . we didn't really know her." She stared at her sister, hoping she'd join in on the discussion. "She was new at the school and, well, didn't make the best, um, first impression."

"First impression?" Lesley asked. "I'm not following." She moved her gaze to Hailey. "Well?"

"Why are you looking at me?" Hailey asked. She sighed and retrieved her phone, and launched the *SkinDeep* app. "Emily was a fake. There's this app, and you're supposed to use it to make small changes to your appearance." Hailey smiled as she scrolled through her most recent altered selfies. She handed the phone to her mom. "See how I fixed my nose?"

Lesley frowned as she looked at the photo of Hailey. Her eyes darted back and forth between the screen and her daughter. All three women shared the same hook-shaped nose. The picture in the *SkinDeep* app displayed Hailey with a slimmer, flatter nose. The change was subtle but noticeable. Lesley shook her head, handed the phone back to Hailey, and said, "There's nothing wrong with your nose."

Hailey didn't bother to argue her case and went back to playing with the *SkinDeep* adjustment tools, tweaking the photo she'd just shared with her mom.

"So, what did this Emily do?" Lesley asked Kaylee.

"She went extreme," Hailey replied, not realizing the question was meant for her sister. "She made a lot of full body changes. I mean, she was almost unrecognizable when she showed up at school."

"What is it with your generation?" Lesley asked. "Your obsession with selfies and how you look it's. . . it's unhealthy." Lesley reached across the table and snatched the phone from Hailey's hands. "I was just reading about how body dysmorphia is becoming a real—"

"Can I have my phone back?" Hailey asked.

"No." Lesley placed her daughter's phone beside her plate. "Principal Torres promised to send me a transcript of the meeting in her office with that detective. You do know she recorded it, didn't you?"

The two sisters stared at one another in disbelief.

"You should have been there, Mom," Hailey said. "It wasn't

fair to have that cop asking us—"

"I've told you both before, Hailey, that Principal Torres acts as my eyes and ears when I can't be there." Lesley folded her arms and glared at her oldest daughter. "Why do you think we send you to this private school? I'm not letting my children run around some public school with their lazy rules. I can't believe you were both called in." Her tone softened as she leaned across the table. "Hailey, you're Kaylee's big sister. It's your job to keep her safe."

"I didn't get her into trouble," Hailey said. "Honest. That cop was just being a jerk."

"Was he from the Orleans P.D.?" Lesley asked. When Hailey didn't reply, she looked at Kaylee and raised an eyebrow.

"Yes." Kaylee quickly swallowed another spoonful of mashed potatoes and wiped her lips dry. She said, "Detective Lane."

"Isn't that Noah's uncle?" Lesley asked.

Hailey nodded quietly and went back to eating her dinner.

"Emily kind of got in this argument with Jade," Kaylee said. "And we were all there when it happened. And, well, that was the last day that Emily was at school."

"I don't understand," Lesley said. "Did they think you were somehow involved in her disappearance? What did they ask you?"

Kaylee suddenly felt sick to her stomach. She felt her face become flush as she recalled the endless questions she'd been asked by the principal and Detective Lane. She cleared her throat and said, "It . . . it was just a bunch of dumb questions. Like how long we knew her and if we talked with her after the fight."

"Fight?" Lesley's jaw slowly fell open. "There was a fistfight? Is that the video?"

"No!" Hailey said. "It wasn't like that. Just a lot of yelling."

"Yelling can be just as hurtful." Lesley's voice now simmered with anger. "Did you see this girl after the fight? What happened next?"

"Next?" Kaylee asked. "Nothing. None of us saw her again. We didn't really know her. Everything we knew about Emily was from what she'd put on social media before arriving at school."

Lesley leaned back in her chair and sighed. She stared at both of her daughters. Hailey refused to look up, sulking as she ate her broccoli. Kaylee stared back at her mom and frowned. Lesley asked Kaylee, "Do you use that app?"

"SkinDeep?" Kaylee replied. "Um, well, sort of. I . . . I play with it."

"You're just a teenager," Lesley smiled and leaned forward. "Your body is still changing. That acne will clear up. I told you I had it at your age." Lesley paused and let her mind drift back decades to when she was in high school. A wry grin spread across her face, and she shook her head and sighed. She looked at Kaylee and said, "Don't be in such a rush to grow up."

"The app's fun," Hailey said. "I plan to get a nose job someday."

"What?" Lesley's jaw fell open in disbelief. "I won't allow it."

"You can't stop me once I'm over eighteen." Hailey pointed at her phone resting near her mom. "I can use SkinDeep to show him."

"First of all, you can't afford it," Lesley said. "Second–"

"There are cheaper options," Hailey interjected.

"Second," Lesley said, her voice raised. "You still have a lot of growing up to do. Let your body take the shape it's meant to. Then, after college, you can decide."

"Whatever," Hailey said. She took a moment to calm down and then asked, "Did you talk to Dad today?"

Lesley's composure visibly stiffened, and her face became pale. She glanced at her plate of food and asked, "Why?"

"Well, with everything that happened at school today, I just figured he'd want to know what was going on," Hailey said. "Wouldn't the school contact him, too?"

Kaylee sighed beneath her breath and glanced at the subtle smile and arched eyebrow on Hailey's face. Part of her wanted to lean over and smack her sister. Hailey knew how to push their mom's buttons, and bringing up their dad was the biggest one.

"It's not my job to keep your father informed on everything that's happening in this house," Lesley said. She tugged on her hair and added, "He needs to be checking in on you." Lesley stood up, picked up her plate, and headed toward the kitchen, adding, "That's his job."

Hailey smiled and leaned across the table to retrieve her phone.

"Why did you have to bring up Dad?" Kaylee asked.

"What?" Hailey unlocked her phone and went back to the *SkinDeep* app. "Mom might like this dumb family nose, not me."

"I heard that," Lesley said from the other room. She stuck her head into the dining room and said, "I will need you two to do clean up tonight. I've got that office birthday party thing I have to go to."

"No problem, Mom," Kaylee said.

Kaylee stood up and began collecting the plates from the table. Her sister pocketed her phone and soon joined her. As they carried everything into the kitchen, Lesley kissed each one on the cheek before heading upstairs.

Cleaning the kitchen didn't take long. Kaylee soon found herself upstairs in the bathroom, brushing her teeth and staring at herself in the mirror. She looked at the acne medication on the counter and then back at her reflection. Her mom's words from earlier, telling her not to rush things, repeated in her mind. She frowned and ran her finger along the bridge of her nose and then over to her pock-marked cheeks. She sighed and mumbled, "I hope you're right."

Hailey's bedroom popped with color. The deep red carpet and bright blue bedding complimented the pinstriped white and pink wallpapered walls. Mirrors of different shapes, sizes, and materials hung at varying heights, making the room appear much larger than its actual size.

She lowered her phone and glanced at the bathroom door. The two sisters shared a single connecting bathroom, and Hailey always kept the door closed. She could hear Kaylee on the other side, loudly brushing her teeth. The running water stopped, followed by a gentle knock on the door.

"What?" Hailey asked.

Kaylee opened the door, stuck her head inside, and asked, "What are you doing?"

"Chatting with Noah."

Kaylee walked across the room and sat on the edge of the bed close to her sister. She tried to look at the text messages, but the screen was blank. Soon a blood-red pixilated text bubble appeared, floating against the bright white screen. Hailey slid her finger across the encrypted message from Noah.

> *Hold on*

"Do you two always use eChat?" Kaylee asked.

"Most of the time. It's fun. And private." Hailey held the phone up so her sister could see the message fade away. "Gone forever."

Hailey tossed her phone onto the bed and began playing with the silver charm bracelet on her right wrist. There were four charms – a heart, a teddy bear, a four-leaf-clover, and a key. Hailey flicked her hand back and forth and said, "Noah's late getting me another charm."

"Another one?"

"He buys me one every month on our anniversary." Hailey's phone chimed with a new notification. "He's been weird lately. Like he doesn't have time for me." Hailey grabbed her phone and slid her finger across the message from Noah.

> *My uncle is here*

"The cop?" Kaylee asked.

"He only has one uncle." Hailey turned the phone away from her sister. "And stop reading my screen."

Hailey wrote back to Noah.

> *Your uncle is a dick and Jade hates him*

Two blood-red pixilated bubbles appeared a few seconds later.

> *I know*
> *Can't talk rn*

Hailey stared at the now blank screen and closed the eChat app. She looked up at her sister and asked, "Did you want something?"

"Oh, I called Dad."

"Did you tell him what happened today? What did he say?"

"I got his voicemail."

"Figures." Hailey shook her head in disgust and opened the *SkinDeep* app. "He's probably away on business. Again."

"I left him a message and told him about Emily." Kaylee waited for her sister to say something. After a few seconds of silence, she continued. "He'll call back tomorrow. He always does."

"That's all he does, Kaylee." Hailey lowered her phone and looked at her sister. "He just phones it in."

Kaylee sighed, stood up, and walked toward the bathroom door. She stepped through the doorway, turned, and asked, "How much longer will Mom and Dad stay separated?"

"It's been six months," Hailey said. "You need to prepare yourself."

"You . . . you don't think they can work it out?"

"Work what out? All they ever did was fight. All Dad does is travel for work. All those stupid business trips. You know he's cheated on her."

"I know Mom said that but . . . ." Kaylee's eyes welled with tears. "Dad denies it."

"I just don't see them getting back together. Besides, Mom seems happier without him here." Hailey buried her face back in her phone. "Can you close the door?"

"Oh. Okay. Well, goodnight."

"Night."

Once Kaylee was gone, Hailey returned to playing with the controls in the *SkinDeep* app. She'd gone through multiple iterations of reshaping her nose. After making one final tweak, she posted the picture to her Instagram account with a message saying, "Can't wait for college!"

Hailey closed the *SkinDeep* app and placed her phone on the nightstand. She yawned and stretched her arms. The charms on her bracelet sparkled in the dimly lit bedroom. Suddenly the phone chimed. Hailey grabbed her phone and inspected the screen. It indicated a new eChat message was waiting for her. She opened the eChat app to find a message from Dr. Ed.

Knock Knock

The message only lasted for a few seconds and then disappeared. Hailey shifted uncomfortably in her bed. She and Dr. Ed had been texting back and forth the last few days. Hailey would usually block someone trolling her, but this person intrigued her. A second encrypted message emerged.

R U ready, Hailey?

Hailey went to Dr. Ed's profile, but, like always, it had no detailed information other than the word "Private." Even his account name was a series of random letters and numbers. But the external-facing profile name was labeled "Dr. Ed." She closed her eyes and recalled their past exchanges, including the promises made. Hailey quickly sent a reply.

How do I know I can trust you?

Hailey fiddled with her charm bracelet. After what felt like an eternity, Dr. Ed wrote back.

I helped Brittney
I can help you

Hailey's eyes widened. She whispered, "I knew it!" Then she replied back to him.

What did you do?

Dr. Ed's response soon appeared.

It's painless

Hailey's gut told her she should block him from ever texting her again. She remembered her mother telling her to wait for her looks to change. Another blood-red bubble appeared, the mystery text inside hidden behind the shimmering white pixels.

Do you like who you see in the mirror?

The text faded away. Hailey glanced at the mirrors covering her wall and sighed. The screen flashed with three more encrypted messages.

I can change your life
Trust me
You'll never look at yourself the same way again

Hailey walked to the nearest mirror and looked at her reflection. She ran her finger against her nose, frowned, and said, "Change my life."

☺☹☺

Kaylee stood before the pantry's open doors and stared at the stacks of cookies, crackers, and chips. The setting sun cast a warm glow throughout the kitchen. The nearby microwave showed the time to be 7:05 p.m. Her mother had left shortly after dinner for her work party. A creak from the nearby staircase caused her to flinch. She spun around to see Hailey zipping a bright pink and white checkered jacket closed.

"Where are you going?" Kaylee asked.

"Are you already snacking?" Hailey asked. "We just had dinner."

"I'm just looking for later." Kaylee stepped closer to her sister. Hailey's normal look of confidence was nowhere to be found. "Well?"

"I'm. . . I'm meeting Noah."

Kaylee glanced out the window, expecting to see Noah's car. She turned to her sister and asked, "Why isn't he here?"

"I'm. . . I'm riding my bike to his place."

"Your bike?"

"My car's still in the shop!" Hailey groaned and shook her head. "That stupid repair is taking forever."

Kaylee rolled her eyes as she recalled the day her sister drove up a curb on the way to school. Her parents had bought a Lexus CT200 when Hailey had turned sixteen. The car was meant for the two sisters to share, although Hailey continued to refer to it as "hers." The damage to the vehicle required a new rim and replacement of half the front suspension.

"But Noah always comes and gets you."

"Well, he can't!"

"But–"

"Don't tell mom," Hailey said.

"But why–"

"I'll tell her you're raiding the pantry again."

Kaylee frowned and watched her sister quietly open the front door and leave the house. She went back to the pantry, grabbed a package of chocolate chip cookies, and went back upstairs. Kaylee spent the rest of the night in her bedroom, doing homework, watching Netflix, and playing on her iPad. Unlike her school-issued tablet, which was heavily locked down for curriculum use only, Kaylee's personal iPad allowed her to install any app she wanted. The tablet's dull black case lacked any personalization.

When Kaylee awoke the following day, the first thing she saw was the empty bag of cookies resting beside her. Guilt washed over her as she sat up and rubbed her eyes. She grabbed her phone and looked at the time. "Shit. I overslept."

Kaylee flung the sheets off and crawled out of bed, causing the crumbs surrounding the bag to tumble to the floor. She went to her window and snapped the shade open. The morning sun filled her bedroom. Unlike her sister's colorful room, Kaylee's bedroom cast a more somber tone. Almost everything in her room tended to be some shade of gray – the carpet, bedding, curtains. The wallpaper's dull white background had half-inch round pale red and blue balloons in a repeating diamond pattern. The wallpaper had been there for decades, and the tiny bits of color had faded over time. The dark walnut furniture did little to brighten the space.

What little color that popped in the room came from the half-dozen posters hanging on the walls. Kaylee had bought them during different family vacations. Hawaii. Mexico. California. Her favorite was a poster of Universal Studios Orlando showcasing the Wizarding World of Harry Potter. Orlando had been the last vacation the family had taken together before her parents separated.

Kaylee snatched the cookie bag from the floor, crushed it into a ball, and went into the bathroom. The door to Hailey's room was closed. Kaylee dropped the bag into the trash and gently knocked twice on the door. After a few seconds, she twisted the handle and stuck her head into her sister's bedroom.

The morning sun framed the lowered window shades, casting a dim light throughout the bedroom. Kaylee entered the room and looked around, somewhat confused to find Hailey wasn't there. Why hadn't her sister bothered to wake her? Hailey always woke Kaylee up whenever she overslept. The door to the hallway was closed. Kaylee walked to the door and reached for the handle, but the door suddenly opened. Her mother was standing in the hallway.

"Where's your sister?" Lesley asked.

"I . . . I don't know." Kaylee looked back at the messy bed. "Isn't she downstairs?"

"No. I've been calling for both of you. You're going to be late for school." Lesley pushed her way past Kaylee and looked around the empty room. "Well? Where is she?"

Three

Two Down

Kaylee sat quietly in the living room, her head hung low. She kept her eyes raised just enough to watch Detective Lane's polished black boots scuff and drag across the faded floral wool carpet. The house phone rang in the background every few minutes, but her mother refused to answer it. Kaylee wondered if it was her dad or possibly the school. She was already two hours late for her first class. Detective Lane's pacing stopped. His boots were positioned directly in front of Kaylee.

"Okay, let me see if I've got this straight," Detective Lane said. His voice didn't have the calm tone of a concerned member of law enforcement. Instead, he sounded annoyed that he was here this morning. The detective let out a heavy sigh as he flipped through the small notepad in his hand. "You last saw your sister around seven last night. She said she was heading out to see Noah. You went up to your room and never left the rest of the night."

"Right," Kaylee said. "I had a lot of homework. When I was done, I watched some videos and went to bed."

"And the only person she talked with was Noah?" the detective asked.

"I saw her texting with him."

"Mrs. Jones, we're going to want to go through Hailey's social media and devices," Detective Lane said.

"Of course," Lesley said. Her lips quivered as she struggled to keep herself composed. She slowly walked to the living room window and parted the curtains. "Anything to find my daughter. I . . . I gave you the description of her bike, right?"

Detective Lane nodded and said, "We're already looking for it."

Kaylee watched her mom look back and forth through the window, desperately hoping to see Hailey return home. She briefly closed her eyes and replayed last night's conversation with her sister.

"What were they texting about?" Detective Lane asked.

"I don't know," Kaylee said.

"I can ask Noah. Or just have the records pulled."

"You can't." Kaylee glanced up at the cop. "They use eChat."

"What's that?"

"It's a chat app that deletes everything you text."

Detective Lane sighed and shook his head. He made a few more notes and asked, "Is this the latest app all you kids are addicted to?"

Kaylee didn't answer. She wanted this interrogation to end. Her eyes suddenly widened. She looked at the cop and said, "Oh, wait. Hailey said that Noah had been distant. So, I don't know, maybe they had a fight or something. Maybe that's why she went to see him."

"A fight?" Detective Lane closed his pad and smiled at Kaylee. "Thank you for your time." He walked over to Lesley and handed her a small business card. "This is my number, along with the Case I.D. I'll be in touch."

"Thank you," Lesley said. "Do . . . do you think this could be related to that girl's disappearance?"

"Emily?" Detective Lane scratched his beard and shook his head. "It's too soon to say."

Lesley walked the detective to the door and locked the deadbolt once he was gone. She leaned back against the door and began to sob. Kaylee stood up, walked over to her mom, and placed a comforting hand on her mother's quivering shoulder.

"I have a bad feeling about this," Lesley said. She threw her arms around Kaylee and pulled her close. "You know my intuition's always right."

"It'll be okay, Mom." Kaylee hugged her mother, but deep

down, she knew to trust her mother's instincts. A sense of dread washed over her. She took a deep breath and closed her eyes. "I . . . I should probably get to school."

Lesley kissed the top of her daughter's head and asked, "Would you rather stay home? I already told them you'd be late. I can just tell them you're staying home. It . . . would be safer."

Kaylee pulled herself from her mother's embrace and said, "No. I want to go. I'm sure everyone's wondering what's going on."

She kissed her mom's cheek and walked over to the kitchen. Kaylee's phone was resting on the counter. She glanced at the screen, expecting to see a bunch of text notifications from everyone asking where they were. There was only one. She unlocked the phone to see a message from Noah.

U OK?

Kaylee spent a long time staring at the text, debating if she should respond. She couldn't think of what to say, so instead raced upstairs to finish getting ready for school. As she rushed to get her things, all she could think about was how the only person to reach out to her was Noah. A part of her felt angry that the other girls didn't check in with her. And what to make of Noah? Did he know his uncle was headed over to question him? Was Noah the last one to see her sister? Could he be involved in Hailey's disappearance? Kaylee shook her head and shrugged off the notion.

As Kaylee made her way back downstairs, the doorbell rang. She heard the deadbolt unlatch and the hinges quietly creak.

"Stephen," Lesley said flatly.

Kaylee struggled to keep her balance as she rushed down the last few steps. She smiled when she saw her dad standing in the doorway. Her father looked rattled, his unshaven face a departure from his normally clean-cut appearance. Even his typically polished bald head looked overdue for a close shave. Stephen's navy blazer hung poorly over his protruding stomach.

"Why did I have to hear about our daughter's disappearance from the cops?" Stephen asked. "Why didn't you call me?" He pointed at the house phone in the kitchen. "Or answer the damn phone?"

"I've been busy," Lesley replied. She kept one hand on the doorframe and another on the door, blocking her husband from entering the house. "The cops just left. When . . . when did you talk to them?"

Stephen looked past his wife's shoulder and smiled when he saw Kaylee standing at the bottom of the stairs. She smiled back and nodded.

"They called me earlier," Stephen said. "I told them I hadn't heard or seen Hailey in over two weeks."

"Of course you haven't."

"I've been traveling." Stephen ran his fingers through the scruff on his cheeks and sighed. "I'm heading to the police station this morning to talk with them."

"What do you want, Stephen?"

"Are . . . are you okay?" He looked back at Kaylee. "Both of you?"

"Hey, Dad," Kaylee said. She walked to the front door and moved her mother's arm so she could hug her father. "I'm okay. Just a bit rattled."

"Hey, Pumpkin." Stephen held Kaylee and kissed the top of her head. He looked up at Lesley and asked, "What did the police say? Any leads?"

"Noah was the last person to see Hailey," Lesley said.

"Who?" Stephen asked.

Lesley didn't respond. Kaylee could feel the tension in her father's embrace, so she pulled herself away and took a few steps back from her parents. Kaylee looked at her mom and allowed herself to feel a glimmer of hope. Her dad was obviously reaching out. If there was ever a time to put differences aside and come together as a family, this was the moment.

"Noah's been Hailey's boyfriend for the past five months," Lesley said. She put her hands on her hips and glared at her husband. "You'd know that if you took an interest."

The spark of optimism inside Kaylee vanished, replaced by

anger over her mom's endlessly defensive attitude. Her dad jammed his hands in his pockets and frowned. Kaylee hated being in the crossfire between her parents. She'd been in this position far too many times. Kaylee looked at her backpack flopped at the bottom of the staircase. As she turned and walked away, she said, "I need to get to school."

"Are you taking the car?" Stephen asked. "You've got your license now, right?"

"The Lexus is still in the shop," Lesley said. "Hailey's little distracted driving incident. Remember?"

"Oh," Stephen said. "I can give Kaylee a ride." He looked at Lesley and added, "If that's okay with you?"

"Sure," Lesley said. She turned to Kaylee and said, "But stay away from Noah. I don't want you talking to him."

"What?" Kaylee didn't hide her shock. "He's been driving Hailey and I to school for weeks."

"And now he's a suspect!" Lesley shook her head and crossed her arms. "You said they were fighting."

"I didn't say–"

"I've heard Hailey complaining about how he's been treating her. He's always seemed like an odd boy to me."

"Mom, I think–"

"We're done. Go with your father. I'll pick you up after school today. I don't want you out late."

The ride to school felt a bit surreal to Kaylee. She couldn't remember the last time her dad had driven her to school. Even when he still lived with them, his business trips always came first. During the drive, Kaylee told him what she had told the cops and what had happened the night before. Her dad stayed positive and asked Kaylee to keep him in the loop. Once her father's silver Mercedes sedan pulled away from the curb, Kaylee found herself alone in front of the school.

Engel Academy, founded in 1922, stood two stories high. The blocky building contained a maze of interconnecting hallways. A white shingled clock and bell tower rose above the main entrance. The clock hadn't worked reliably in several months, and the bell only rang sporadically. Sand and gray colored stones formed the main foundation of the building, with traditional red bricks making up the rest of the structure.

White framed windows matched the clock tower's siding.

Cool air whipped Kaylee's black windbreaker against her cheeks. She couldn't think of the last time she'd entered Engel Academy without her sister by her side. Birds from the nearby trees loudly chirped as Kaylee made her way to the main entrance.

Kaylee's arrival at school coincided with the middle of the first lunch block. As she roamed the halls, she found herself doing a double-take on everyone she caught looking at her. Why are they looking at me like that? Did they know what happened? Did one of them know who took her sister? Or worse, did one of them take Hailey?

Kaylee turned the corner and stopped dead in her tracks. Noah was in the middle of the hallway, towering over the surrounding students. He began walking directly toward her, his eyes locked on hers. Kaylee found herself unable to move as if her feet were cemented to the floor. Her mouth went dry when Noah stopped in front of her.

"Hey," Noah said. He moved within inches of Kaylee, easily standing over a foot taller than her. "Are you okay?"

Kaylee remained silent and stared up into Noah's deep brown eyes.

"You didn't answer my text this morning," Noah said. Students pushed their way past the pair, now blocking the middle of the hallway. Noah put his hand on her shoulder and guided her to the side of the hallway. Once out of the sea of students, he shoved his hands into his pockets and asked, "What's going on?"

"You . . . you tell me," Kaylee said as she tried to compose herself.

"My uncle pulled me out of class. He said Hailey's missing. I've been trying to reach her all day, but she's not returning my texts."

Kaylee felt her nerves subside. The concerned tone in Noah's voice somehow put her at ease. She said, "Did . . . did you see Hailey last night?"

"Last night? No. We just texted. My uncle asked me the same thing."

"Hailey told me she was meeting you last night. Then this

morning, well, her room was just like when I last saw her. She . . . she never came home."

"That's what my uncle said. Shit." Noah looked up over the crowd of students walking by. He shook his head and said, "No. No, I never heard from her again."

"I . . . I believe you."

"Thanks." Noah frowned and crossed his arms. "But, why wouldn't you?"

"My mom. She, well, she's just worried that you know. You . . . ."

"Kaylee, you know I'd never hurt your sister."

"I know."

"Wow. Wait. So, your mom thinks I'm involved?"

"No. I mean, well, she's. . . ."

"She's never liked me, has she?"

"She's just upset, Noah." Kaylee couldn't help but notice everyone now staring at her and Noah as they passed them by. "Hailey said she was going to see you. That's what she told me. So, that's what my mom believes."

"I swear I never talked to her again. I told my uncle the same thing. He asked to see my text messages, but I told him we used eChat. There was nothing to show him."

"Did . . . did he believe you?"

"Of course he did. He may be a cranky old white cop, but he's my uncle."

The two shared a brief nervous laugh. Noah sighed and asked, "How are you handling all of this?"

"I'm just, well, in kind of a fog."

"Me too."

"Do the others know?"

"They know Hailey's not here. I ran into them this morning before my uncle showed up. We all started texting Hailey's phone. But I haven't said anything to them since my uncle questioned me. I knew the minute I told them, the entire school would know."

"I . . . I think we need to talk. All of us. But later. When school ends."

The rest of the school day felt like a blur to Kaylee. Her paranoia over everyone staring at her subsided as she realized nobody knew of Hailey's disappearance. She told a couple of people her sister was home sick, which seemed to end the few questions she'd gotten. She and Noah had gotten word to Paige, Allison, and Jade to meet up near the bike rack after school. When Kaylee finally got there, she found all three girls busy playing with the *SkinDeep* app. Noah stood there, his eyes fixated on Kaylee as she arrived.

"So, what's this all about?" Jade asked. "What's with all the secrecy?"

"Is it Hailey?" Paige asked. "How sick is she?"

"She's not sick," Noah said. He turned and looked at Kaylee.

"Hailey's missing," Kaylee said. She fought to suppress rising tears.

"What do you mean missing?" Allison asked. The confusion on her face quickly turned to shock. "Do you mean like Emily?"

"I . . . I don't know," Kaylee said, her voice now quivering. "She went out last night. I saw her leave. But she never came home. And then this morning, her bedroom was just how she left it."

"Did she say where she was headed?" Jade asked as she anxiously chewed a piece of gum.

"She said she was coming to see me," Noah said. "But she lied. We weren't planning to meet."

"No?" Jade asked. She placed her hands on her hips and stepped closer to Noah. "Why should we believe you?"

"I don't have to answer to you!" Noah said. "The cops already questioned me."

"The cops?" Jade said. "You mean your dirty uncle?"

"Look, Jade, I know you hate my uncle, but–"

"He beat my dad and shot my brother dead!" Jade's voice echoed off the nearby brick walls. A few people, busy collecting their bicycles, backed off and quickly pedaled away. "Your uncle's dirty, Noah."

"Everyone, just calm down," Allison said. She positioned herself between Noah and Jade with her arms raised to separate them. A clunky diamond ring hung loosely from Allison's middle finger on her right hand. The jewel glistened in the late day's sun. Allison waited for Jade to visibly back down. She lowered her arms, turned to Kaylee, and asked, "Are you okay?"

Kaylee didn't know how to respond. She found herself taken aback by Allison's concern. Kaylee always felt like an afterthought within the group. She was junior to all the other seniors, with her sister firmly in charge. All eyes were now on her. Kaylee said, "I'm okay. I'm. . . I'm trying to stay positive. The cops really don't know much. They haven't even found her bike yet."

"Bike?" Paige asked.

"Hailey said she was going to bike over to Noah's."

"And she's never done that before," Noah said. "None of this makes sense."

"If it's connected to Emily, I mean, who could have done this?" Paige asked.

Allison looked up at the row of windows on the school's second floor. The janitor the students called "Rat" was staring at her. Tall and lanky, his bulging pale green eyes and severe overbite seemed to pierce the dust-covered glass. Allison glared back and waited until Rat disappeared into the darkness. "What the hell are you looking at?"

Kaylee and the others followed Allison's gaze toward the second-story windows.

"Who did you see?" Paige asked.

"Rat," Allison replied.

"He creeps me out," Paige said as she nervously twisted her pearl necklace.

"Hey, at the assembly yesterday, didn't they say Emily's phone was last pinged here at the school?" Allison asked.

"I think so," Jade said.

"Rat works here after hours," Allison said.

"Works here?" Paige asked. "He lives here."

"What?" Jade asked. "But he's Principal Torres's cousin. What do you mean lives here?"

"I heard some teachers whining about it the other day," Allison said.

"I heard that too," Noah said. "He's been kicked out of the last three places he's lived. So he's here until he can get back on his feet."

"I knew the principal was a bitch, but you'd think she'd at least open up her own home to her cousin," Jade said.

Kaylee suddenly noticed Principal Torres marching across the yard, heading their way. Her mouth fell open, and she said, "Shit."

The group remained quiet as the principal walked up to them.

"Well, isn't this an interesting gathering," said Principal Torres. "Didn't I just have five of you in my office yesterday?" She looked up at Noah and added, "And you were there earlier today, weren't you?" Noah lowered his head and didn't respond. "But today's a bit different, isn't it?" She looked at Kaylee. "We're one short today, aren't we?" Principal Torres clasped her hands behind her back and began to walk in a slow circle around the group. Her pink high-heeled shoes struggled to keep their balance against the cracked blacktop. "We now have two missing girls. First Emily. Now Hailey."

"That's what we were talking about," Noah said.

"Talking about?" Principal Torres stopped and looked up at Noah. "Aren't you the prime suspect?"

Kaylee stared at the principal in shock. Jade shot Noah a look of disapproval, opened her mouth to say something, but lowered her head and looked away. Allison and Paige appeared stunned by the principal's statement.

"Me?" Noah jammed his hands into his pockets and glared at Principal Torres, his temples throbbing in anger. "You were there when my uncle questioned me. I never saw Hailey last night! All we did was text."

"Yes. You texted using an app that doesn't keep your text messages. How convenient."

"What's that supposed to mean?" Noah asked angrily.

"Check that temper." Principal Torres crossed her arms and cast a piercing gaze at Noah, her brown eyes dripping with judgment. She turned to face the others. "You should all get home as quickly as possible. This is where Emily disappeared. For all we know, Hailey too." The stern look on her face softened when she glanced at Kaylee. The principal turned and headed back toward the school's main entrance.

"What an asshole," Allison said. She looked at Noah and added, "She's just trying to get under your skin. Ignore her."

"We know you didn't do it," Kaylee said.

"What did she mean about Emily disappearing here?" Paige asked as she pointed at the ground. "Did she mean this spot right here? Can they trace the phones like that?"

"I don't think so," Allison.

"I think it depends," Kaylee said. "Like if you're using an app to track someone, then yes."

"Right," Noah said. "They ping the cell towers or something like that. To track a phone. The cops."

Allison stepped away from everyone and began to pace back and forth, anxiously twisting her diamond ring. Her finger soon became red due to the severe pressure she was applying. Allison stopped and looked up at the second-floor windows. Rat was once again looking down at the group. Allison kept her eyes locked on his. Her glare faded when Principal Torres appeared beside Rat. She said, "We should go."

As the group disbanded, Kaylee said, "Wait!" She waited for everyone to look at her. "We . . . we all need to keep in touch. And stay alert."

"For what?" Jade asked.

"Anything," Kaylee said. "First Emily. Now Hailey. I . . . I just have a bad feeling that this is only the beginning."

Kaylee spent the rest of the week in a haze. Every phone call or text startled her. Sleep became erratic as she would wake up in the middle of the night and then find herself unable to fall back to sleep. Jade and the others continued to spin theories that only added to her dismay. Jade was convinced Detective Lane was involved. Allison and Paige believed the principal and Rat should be investigated. The endless texts only added to her angst.

When the Thursday school day came to a close, Kaylee found herself shocked it wasn't Friday. She had to replay the past events in her head. Hailey had disappeared Monday night, and the cops had come on Tuesday. How could it only be Thursday? Kaylee grabbed her belongings and rushed to escape the building's confining walls. A smile spread across her face as she noticed Noah standing at the bottom of the stairs just outside the front doors. As she approached him, her cellphone buzzed with a message from her mother.

> *I can't pick you up today. But you need to get home ASAP. Uber? Or get a ride? Not Noah!*

Kaylee sighed and replied.

> *K*

She pocketed her phone and walked toward Noah. Suddenly Jade pulled up on her Super73 electric bike. Bright red arrows dotted the jet-black bicycle's sturdy frame. Jade slowed to a stop beside Noah.

"Nice bike," Noah said.

"This was my brother's," Jade said as she ran her fingers across the arrows. "It's all I have left of him."

Noah glared back at Jade and briefly clenched his fists. He took a deep breath and said, "I've told you I'm sorry."

"I have my doubts about you." Jade slowly blew a bubble and snapped the gum back into her mouth, leaving behind a hint of peppermint. "With Hailey."

"I know you do."

Kaylee joined them and asked, "What's going on?"

"Nothing," Jade said. "I was just leaving."

"Do you have room for me?" Kaylee asked.

"What?" Jade replied. "I can't carry you."

Kaylee inspected the bicycle's elongated seat and debated asking Jade why not. Before she could say anything, Jade backed her bike up, turned, and drove away.

"You should wear a helmet," Kaylee yelled.

Jade responded with a dismissive hand. Kaylee sighed and briefly looked up at Noah.

"Everything okay?" Noah asked. His bright smile comforted her. "You look upset."

"My mom needs me home. Like, now."

"I can give you a ride."

Kaylee looked around the parking lot, hoping to see Allison or Paige. There were so many students walking around, and none whom she felt she could ask for a lift home.

"What?" Noah asked.

"It's just that my mom, well, she . . . she . . . ."

"She still doesn't trust me." Noah chuckled and shook his head. "I hope you trust me."

"I do." Kaylee felt taken aback. "Of course I do."

"Then, let me take you home. I'll drop you off a block away so your mom doesn't freak out."

Kaylee laughed and nodded. She said, "Thanks."

The ride home was brief. Noah and Kaylee exchanged theories about Emily's disappearance and if or how it could be linked to Hailey's. Neither could think of a single connection, and they both dismissed the crazy ideas the rest of them had. After a tense few days, Kaylee felt a bit of relief spending time with someone as level-headed as Noah.

Noah's 2015 bright red Chevy Camaro came to a halt around the corner and several houses away from Kaylee's home. *No Tears Left to Cry* by Ariana Grande drifted from the stereo. Noah lowered the volume, put the transmission into park, and put his arm behind Kaylee's seat.

"You're nothing like your sister," Noah said.

Kaylee briefly stared at Noah, a blank expression covering her face.

"You're strong," Noah continued. "I mean, your faith that she's alive is, well, inspiring. You know?"

"You . . . you don't think she's alive?"

"Of course I do."

"Good." Kaylee felt her eyes well with tears. She allowed one to roll down her cheek before quickly wiping it away. Kaylee nervously clasped her hands together and rested them on her lap. Her eyes widened as Noah's hand gently rested on top of hers.

"It's going to be okay," Noah said. "Trust me."

Kaylee nodded and slowly pulled her hand away. She grabbed her bag and exited the car without saying anything.

She stood and watched Noah do a U-turn and speed away. Kaylee smiled as she made her way down the street. She wondered why her mom didn't trust Noah. Jade also needed to calm down. Noah was a good person.

As Kaylee turned the corner, she came to a halt. Two police cars were parked in front of her house. Kaylee's steps quickened from a casual walk to a nervous run. Before she knew it, she was sprinting across the neighbor's lawn and gasping for air. Panic set in as she reached her front porch, ascended the stairs, and flung the door open.

Her mother was sitting at the kitchen table, surrounded by Detective Lane and two other police officers. All four turned and looked at Kaylee as she came inside.

"Thank God you're home," Lesley said. "I was going to send the cops to get you, but I didn't want to cause a scene." Her cheeks were bright red, and her eyes were bloodshot from crying. She held her arms open wide and motioned for her daughter. "Come here."

"What?" Kaylee asked. She dropped her bag in the foyer and kicked the front door closed. "What's happened? Is it Hailey? Tell me!"

"It's okay," Detective Lane said. "Please, come sit with your mother."

Kaylee slowly entered the kitchen. Her mom pulled the nearest seat closer and patted the chair. Kaylee sat beside her mother and stared at the three police officers as her mom put her arm around her.

"We got a message," Detective Lane said. "About your sister."

"So, she's alive?" Kaylee asked.

Detective Lane didn't answer her question. Instead, he stared at the sealed plastic bag in his hands. Inside rested a single sheet of five-by-seven-inch yellow blue-lined paper, slightly crinkled. The corner of the bag had an evidence label with a date and other information scribbled in ink. The detective cleared his throat and read the typed note.

This town has a disease, and it must be cleansed. Emily was the start. I can't say when it will end, but Hailey was an easy catch. Who's next? Hard for me to say. I have a long list to go through.

"I . . . I don't understand," Lesley said. "Are you sure it's the same person?"

"Both girls are named." He twirled the plastic bag between his fingers. "Forensics will analyze the typeset, ink, and paper, but they appear to match the one we got for Emily. We're also tracing the post office tracking." Detective Lane turned to a nearby officer and raised his hand. "Besides, we got more than just this note."

The officer opened an envelope and slowly retrieved another clear plastic bag. Kaylee gasped when she saw the charm bracelet inside.

"Can you identify this?" asked the detective.

Kaylee grabbed the bag and stared at the small silver bracelet crammed inside. Her eyes welled as she recognized each of the four charms – a heart, a teddy bear, a four-leaf-clover, and a key. She did her best to ignore the splotches of blood smeared inside the bag. Tears ran down Kaylee's cheeks. She looked at her mother and said, "It's Hailey's."

"You're sure?" Detective Lane asked.

Kaylee nodded and said, "Noah gave her those."

The detective took the plastic bag back from Kaylee. He scratched his beard and said, "I hate to say it, but it looks like our little town may have a serial stalker." His eyes settled on the blood-speckled charm inside, and he added, "Or a killer."

Four

Who Can You Trust?

Friday, April 26th

The following day , Kaylee found herself staring listlessly at the digital bulletin board posted in the school's main first-floor hallway. The forty-two-inch screen showed pictures of Emily and Hailey, listing both as missing. The police notice included details such as physical stats, where and when they were last seen, and how to contact the police with any information. Kaylee was still in shock, knowing her sister and Emily were taken by the same person. A hand on her shoulder caused her to jump.

"Hey," Noah said. He gently squeezed Kaylee's shoulder before letting go. Noah glanced at the board and sighed. "Crazy, right?"

"I know."

Jade, Allison, and Paige came around the corner and joined them. All five spent a few moments reading the information about the two missing people. The screen faded to black. A message stating "Announcement" appeared for several seconds before being replaced by a video of Principal Torres sitting behind her desk. Her hair was held up in its typically tight bun. The video had been playing between blocks since school began. The gang walked away, having no interest in watching the principal's message. The overhead speakers started playing the recording.

This is a reminder that a curfew is now in effect per the order of the Orleans Police Department. All students must be home by 7 p.m. unless accompanied by an adult. All after-school activities have been canceled until further notice. Remember, if you see something, say something.

"This sucks," Jade said.

"I can't believe the cops think there's a serial killer on the loose," Paige said.

"Or stalker," Noah said. He shot Paige a look of disappointment and then nodded toward Kaylee.

"Oh, right," Paige said. "Stalker. Sorry."

"The curfew makes sense," Kaylee said. "The note said there was a list. A long list."

"Did the note say what he did with them?" Paige asked.

"No," Kaylee replied. "But there's no reason to think they're. . . ." Kaylee paused to stop herself from crying. She took a deep breath and said, "To think the worst."

"Kaylee's right," Noah said. "We gotta stay positive."

"I'm with you," Allison said. "We . . . ." Allison stopped and watched as Rat slowly passed by, pushing a mop and bucket. The wheels on the bucket rattled and squeaked loudly, and drops of ammonia-scented gray water splashed onto the floor. The janitor kept an awkward gaze on Allison until he reached the end of the hallway. As he turned away, Allison raised her middle finger with the diamond ring and waved it in his direction. She sighed and said, "He's such a creep. Anyway, we need to stick together. And watch our backs."

Paige put her arm around Allison and said, "I don't trust the principal or her creepy cousin."

"Maybe . . . maybe we should all start using eChat," Noah said.

"I've never used it," Jade said. "Why?"

"Everything's encrypted," Noah replied. "And it deletes everything instantly. Even on the servers. Remember when the principal made us show her our texts?"

"Works for me," Allison said. "The last thing I need is Principal Torres confiscating my phone again. I hate the rules at this school."

"I gotta get to class," Noah said. "Later."

As Noah walked away, Jade tugged on Kaylee's elbow to

signal her to stay. She waited for Noah to get out of earshot. Jade spun Kaylee around and asked, "Weren't Hailey and Noah using eChat the night she disappeared?"

Kaylee nodded and asked, "Why?"

"He said it deletes everything. So that means there's no way to know what they were talking about."

"And?"

"Do I have to spell it out for you?"

"Jade still doesn't trust Noah," Paige said.

"Noah's innocent!" Kaylee said.

"C'mon, Kaylee," Paige said. "We know why you keep defending Noah."

Paige, Allison, and Jade put their arms around each other and formed a semi-circle around Kaylee.

"Spit it out," Jade said, a wry grin spread across her lips. "It's obvious."

Kaylee felt her cheeks get flush. Paige, Jade, and Allison were all staring at her and smiling. Kaylee couldn't think of what to say. Her mouth went dry as she tried to come up with a question to ask them.

"You wouldn't be the first girl to crush on her older sister's boyfriend," Allison said. "God, I've done it more than once. Especially now that my sister's in college. She brings the hottest guys home."

"I . . . I . . . ." Kaylee took a deep breath. "Noah's just a friend."

"If you say so," Jade said, rolling her eyes.

The girls broke their embrace, and all four began walking down the hallway.

"Noah's cute," Paige said. "Sort of. I mean, he just looks too . . . ." She looked at Allison and asked, "What's the word? He's tall. Smart. But he looks it, you know? Not, like, athletic. But from certain angles, he can be adorable. Kind of."

"He's like my little brother," Allison said. "My aunt will always tell him how adorable he is. But whenever he does something silly, she waits for him to walk away and then sighs and calls him a dork." Allison squinted her eyes and then smiled. "Adorky! Adorable. Dorky. That's Noah. We need to hashtag him."

"Hashtag adorky?" Paige laughed. "I love it!"

All three girls laughed while Kaylee struggled to think up something witty to say. Instead, she just looked around, bewildered. Kaylee decided not to weigh in on Noah's looks, because, deep down she didn't know how she felt.

"I just hate that Noah's always defending his uncle," Jade said. Her serious tone quickly dampened the mood. She stepped closer to Kaylee and asked, "What do you think of him?"

"Detective Lane?" Kaylee asked. "I . . . I haven't spent a lot of time with him. He had those questions in the principal's office. And then Tuesday morning at my house. I guess if I had to describe him, I'd say he's. . . intimidating."

"Most cops are," Jade said. Her eyes glazed over as she closed them, and suddenly they popped open. "Hey, don't you have a cousin in Truro?"

Kaylee stopped walking, causing everyone to awkwardly stumble to a halt.

"What?" Kaylee asked.

"I thought Hailey told me you had a cousin on the Truro police."

"Truro?" Kaylee sighed and shook her head. Then she remembered. "Oh, wait. We've got like a second cousin or something like that. My mom's mentioned him, but we've never met him."

"Oh," Jade said. "Do you think you could call him?"

"Why?"

"To get a second opinion."

"No!"

"I'm with Kaylee on this one," Allison said. "Your hatred is showing, Jade. Just let it go."

"Sorry, but I don't trust Noah's uncle." Jade crossed her arms, snapped her bubble gum, and shook her head. "I can't help it."

"I'm not dragging someone I've never met into this mess," Kaylee said. "We have to let the Orleans police do their job." Kaylee didn't bother to wait for a response. She turned and headed to her next class. As she made her way down the hallway, she thought about Jade's opinion of Detective Lane.

Kaylee knew why Jade hated him. But they had to trust the detective to find Hailey. Kaylee stopped when she reached another digital bulletin board. She looked at the image of her sister and whispered, "Don't worry, Hailey. We're fam, and I'm going to do everything I can to find you."

☺☹☺

Allison twisted the clunky ring on her finger and sighed. She turned to Jade and said, "I don't know if I could stay as strong as Kaylee." She ignored the other students filing into class as they walked through the hallway. "I mean, Hailey's been taken. Her sister! I just . . . ."

"She's a tough one," Jade said.

"We . . . we probably shouldn't rag on her about Noah."

"That girl seriously needs to come out of her shell. Hailey drags her around like a puppy."

"Do . . . do you think she's okay?" Allison instinctively started to twist her ring. "Hailey."

Jade sighed and said, "I . . . I don't know. It's messed up."

"I think Noah's right. About eChat."

"Why? It sounds shady."

"Think about it, Jade. Do you want Torres reading your text messages? Or Noah's uncle?"

"Shit. I didn't think of that." Jade glanced around the hallway. The crowd from earlier had thinned out. "Let's get to class."

"I'll catch up with you," Allison said.

Allison turned and quickly made her way to the restroom. Once inside, she went to the closest stall and locked the door. She pulled out her phone and downloaded the eChat app. The elite school's robust wi-fi made for a speedy install. The app's blood-red icon had a small white "e" resting below a black eye-shaped graphic. Allison dragged the icon to a folder with her other social media applications.

The installation process asked her to connect her Contacts. She approved. The app then asked if her profile should be public or private. Allison selected private. The app recommended she select public to allow others from social media to automatically find her. She changed it to public. A message appeared, indicating the app was linking to her Instagram and TikTok accounts. Another message appeared, asking her if she'd like the app to notify everyone that she was now on eChat. She said yes, frustrated by all of the questions. After completing some basic profile details and uploading a pic, the app's main screen appeared. She immediately went to eChat's contacts and found Noah. All of her friends were listed, along with their social media links. She sent Noah a message.

> *I got the app!*

Allison's eyes widened as the message vanished. She remembered Noah telling her how the app wiped all chat history. Allison grinned and said, "This is so cool."

She pocketed her phone and left the stall. Allison spent a bit of time staring in the mirror and adjusting the fit of her clothes and hairstyle. Her phone buzzed, and the screen showed one new eChat message. Allison went back to the app, surprised to find the message wasn't from Noah. Instead, it came from a profile named "Dr. Ed." She slid her finger across the blood-red pixilated bubble, revealing the hidden message.

> *Knock Knock*

Kaylee spent the rest of the day trying to focus on schoolwork, but her mind kept filling with too many questions. Was Hailey okay? Could they trust Detective Lane? Why did the other girls think she liked Noah? Did she like him? Her head throbbed as she tried to sort through everything.

When the school day finally ended, Kaylee exited through the main doors and welcomed the damp fresh air on her skin. Her phone buzzed with a message from her mom.

> *Stuck with a client. Can you get a ride home?*

Kaylee replied that she could and then started looking around for Noah. She noticed Allison and Jade laughing a dozen yards away, their faces buried in their phones. Kaylee cautiously walked over and joined them.

"What's going on?" Kaylee asked.

"Oh, hey," Allison said. "We're just playing with SkinDeep."

"The new version came out," Jade said. She giggled as she held her phone up so Kaylee could see the screen. "It's got all these preset controls now. You can tell it to make you look like Beyoncé or Lady Gaga. I mean, it's *so* slick now. See. I made myself into a skinny white girl."

Kaylee stared at the screen but said nothing. The image looked nothing like Jade, save for the subtle shape of her eyes and nose. Even her school uniform had shrunk down, completely changing Jade's figure.

"We're sisters!" Allison said as she burst out laughing. She, too, had the *SkinDeep* app open. She'd just finished changing herself from a redhead to a brunette. Allison posted the pic to Instagram. In her post, she asked if she should dye her hair. Allison looked at Jade and said, "I love this app."

"We need to clip these together and make a TikTok video." Jade's smile faded as she noticed the frown on Kaylee's face. She sighed and asked, "What?"

"Nothing," Kaylee said. "It's just, well, that app seems stupid."

"SkinDeep's just for fun," Jade said.

"You should try it," Allison said.

"You didn't think it was fun when Emily used it," Kaylee said. Jade and Allison both lowered their heads. A part of Kaylee felt emboldened. "Anyway, could one of you give me a ride home?"

"We've got plans," Jade said. "Sorry."

Kaylee watched Allison and Jade make their way back toward the school until they disappeared around the corner. Suddenly Noah came into view. He smiled, waved, and walked up to Kaylee.

"Need a ride?" Noah asked.

"How'd you know?" Kaylee replied. "My mom's stuck at work again."

"Can I drive you? Or does your mom still not trust me?"

"I . . . I don't know."

"Did she forget how many times I drove you and Hailey to school after Hailey trashed the car?" Noah sighed and didn't wait for Kaylee to respond. "Tell your mom I'll bring you home every day. I can even get you in the morning."

"I know. She's being ridiculous. I . . . I will tell her. Eventually."

Noah pointed to the lot's far corner, and they began to head toward his car. He looked at Kaylee and said, "Besides, I'd feel better knowing you were safe. With me."

☺☺☹

Allison waited for Jade to unlock her electric bike from the rack. The wind felt extra harsh as it blasted against her skin. She flicked the collar of her cobalt blue jacket higher to cover her neck. Allison slowly looked up at the second-story row of windows. A part of her felt relieved to find them empty. She grabbed her phone, unlocked the screen, and opened the *SkinDeep* app.

Jade glanced over and said, "You're more obsessed with that than me."

"I can't help it." Allison squinted as she focused on the various slider controls to adjust her picture. She glanced at Jade and said, "I'm making us sisters."

Allison held the phone up to Jade. The image on the screen showed Allison with frizzy black hair, full lips, big brown eyes, and a skin tone identical to Jade's. Jade's jaw slowly fell open.

"Did you just black face yourself?" Jade asked, her eyebrow now cocked.

Allison's smile faded, and her eyes widened. She looked at her screen and cried, "Oh, shit!" Allison quickly deleted the picture, looked at Jade, and said, "I'm so sorry! What was I thinking?"

Jade grinned, shook her head, and said, "It's okay. I still love you."

Allison chuckled. As she went to put her phone away, she received a notification from eChat. Allison went to the app to find a message waiting from Dr. Ed. She looked up at Jade and then returned her gaze to her screen. Allison ran her finger across the pixilated text bubble.

Do you like who you see in the mirror?

"Will you put that away?" Jade asked. "I told you I don't want you trying to text and hold on at the same time. You need both arms."

"Wait."

Allison quickly typed a reply.

You asked me that before
Keep it up and I'll block you

"Who are you chatting with?" Jade asked.

Allison stared at the response from Dr. Ed.

I can change your life
You'll never look at yourself the same way again

Allison ignored her and sent a reply to Dr. Ed.

Prove it troll ! ! ! !

"Allison!" Jade said.

"One second!" Allison replied.

A blood-red text bubble appeared on the screen. Allison slowly ran her finger across the secret message.

Go ask Brittney

"Holy shit," Allison said.

"What?" Jade asked. "Who the hell are you texting with?"

"It's. . . nothing." Allison locked her phone and slid it into her coat pocket. "Okay, let's go."

Jade frowned as she stared at Allison. "Are you sure you're okay?"

"I'm fine. It was just . . . my mom. She's rattled about this stupid curfew thing."

"Me too. I'll be glad when they finally catch that asshole."

Jade hopped on the bike and checked the battery charge. The gauge showed the capacity at half-full. She set the throttle to full electric and inched the bike away from the rack. Allison grabbed the shiny black helmet strapped to the back and secured the safety strap below her chin. She sat down and flung her arms around Jade's waist. The electric motor whined and hummed as the pair quickly zoomed away and left the school property.

Each bump in the road caused the phone in Allison's pocket to thump against her thigh. Her mind no longer wondered who this troll named Dr. Ed could be. All she could think about was Brittney. Could it be that the most popular and most beautiful girl in school had work done? Hadn't Brittney come back last summer looking even prettier than ever? There had been rumors, albeit only a few, that Brittney had work done before starting her final year at Engel Academy. Were the stories true? Was this Dr. Ed the real deal?

Five

Too Many Suspects

Monday, April 29ᵗʰ

Allison stood in the school parking lot, lost in her phone, ignoring the other students filing into Engel Academy. The morning air felt brisk as it whipped her red wavy hair across her face. She'd spent most of the weekend with Jade, zipping around on her e-bike, hitting some small shops, and making the most of the pre-curfew fun they could share. They'd taken dozens of photos, and Allison was busy deciding which ones to post to Instagram. An eChat notification broke her concentration. The message came from Dr. Ed.

Knock Knock

Allison watched the text bubble fade until it disappeared. She debated how or even if she should respond. Dr. Ed had texted her several times over the weekend, often interrupting her time with Jade. She still had no clue who Dr. Ed was but felt intrigued by his messages. Allison kept their chats to herself, never bothering to tell Jade about them. She finally responded.

WHAT?

A few seconds later, a pixilated text bubble appeared. Allison slid her finger across the screen to reveal the message.

Have you talked to Brittney?

Allison watched the message fade away. She'd been debating when and how to confront Brittney. For all she knew, Dr. Ed was some troll. He could have been anyone. But deep down, she thought he had to be the real deal. Why else would he keep bringing up Brittney? Allison sighed and responded.

No

Another encrypted message appeared. Allison stared at the two blood-red pixilated bubbles for several seconds before revealing them.

GO NOW!
Then you'll know you can trust me

Allison raised her finger and watched the message vanish. Her grip on her phone tightened as she jammed it into her pocket.

"Fine!" Allison said.

A few people gave her an odd look as she marched up the stairs, through security, and into the school. Allison made her way to the second floor, walked past the science lab, and turned the corner. She stopped when she saw Brittney standing at her locker. Allison took a deep breath and walked up to Brittney.

"Hey," Allison said, a nervous smile spread across her face.

Brittney ignored Allison and instead rifled through the contents of her locker. After several seconds she turned and asked, "What?"

Allison's smile immediately faded. She studied Brittney's flawless skin and what could only be described as textbook-perfect eyes, nose, and lips. She said, "So, I heard the rumors are true."

"What rumors?" Brittney slammed her locker closed. "What are you talking about?"

"You had work done."

"Work?" Brittney instinctively touched her nose, but only briefly. Her shock soon turned to anger. "I don't know what you're talking about."

"Don't deny it." Allison stepped closer, her confidence growing. "It's just you and me. You can tell me."

"There's nothing I want to tell *you*."

"I . . . I talked to your doctor."

"What!" Brittney looked around as a few people nearby stopped momentarily to see what the fuss was all about. She lowered her voice and said, "I don't believe you."

Allison's eyes widened. She grinned and said, "He was right."

Brittney crossed her arms and leaned against her locker. The two girls stared at one another for several seconds. A wry grin spread across Brittney's face as she looked Allison up and down. She asked, "Why would someone like you even care?"

"Someone like me? What's that supposed to mean?"

Brittney rolled her eyes but didn't respond.

"Was it the guy online?" Allison asked. "Was it painful? What did he do?"

"Guy online?"

"How much did he charge? He . . . he won't give me any details."

Brittney waved her hand dismissively and said, "Based on those cheap shoes, you couldn't afford my doctor. I mean, if I had one. Which I don't."

Autumn and Summer quietly appeared behind Brittney, as if materializing from thin air. The identical twins stood a few inches shorter than Brittney. They styled their blonde hair in a similar manner to Brittney's auburn locks and could often be seen marching a few feet behind the most popular girl in school.

Allison watched as Brittney and the twins turned and walked away. She called after her, "Was it, Dr. Ed?"

Brittney waved her hand again, brushing Allison and her question away.

Allison stood there alone and lowered her head. She looked at her faded black leather shoes. The edges were worn and cracked, and the left heel had a long scrape down the side.

Allison sighed and headed off down the hallway.

The morning flew by for Allison. She tried to focus on her classes, but her thoughts kept ping-ponging between Dr. Ed's claims and Brittney's reaction to their confrontation earlier this morning. She never heard back from Dr. Ed, nor did she attempt to reach out to him on eChat.

Allison would open the *SkinDeep* app and look at her altered photos in between classes. The changes she wanted to make to herself were minimal. Allison loved her vibrant red hair, but her freckled cheeks always looked childish. Deep down, she blamed her family's pure Irish lineage. Dr. Ed had said he could easily make her look like her Instagram posts and get rid of the freckles. Could she trust him?

Allison had over a thousand followers on Instagram. Once Dr. Ed admitted he'd seen her online pictures, she attempted to find him on Instagram, but no profiles with that name could be found. Allison sighed, put her phone away, and headed to the cafeteria. She noticed the gang all sitting together, and after grabbing a slice of pizza and a Diet Coke, she joined them.

"I haven't heard from you all day," Jade said. "What's going on?"

Allison slumped beside Jade and dropped her tray on the table. She said, "I've been . . . distracted."

Allison took a bite of the greasy cold pizza and looked around the table. Noah had a huge bowl of macaroni and cheese in front of him. She had no clue how he could stay so lean eating such heavy food. Jade had pizza, and Paige had a small salad. A half-empty bowl of macaroni and cheese sat in front of Kaylee.

"I figured out a way around the curfew," Kaylee said. "Well, Noah did."

Noah smiled as he swallowed a huge helping of pasta. He cleared his throat and said, "We can use eChat."

"A technical solution?" Paige looked at Allison and grinned. "How adorky."

Allison laughed and said, "You forgot the hashtag."

"What?" Noah asked. He shrugged his shoulders and continued. "The app's got a group video feature. Fully encrypted. Just make sure you enable the camera and mic on the app before we—"

"I hate that stupid app," Jade said. "It's way too much work, sliding your damn finger. Messages disappearing. It's annoying."

"But it'll keep us safe," Paige said. She nodded toward the main entrance to the lunchroom. Principal Torres was standing just inside the doorway, surveying the students. "From prying eyes."

"I kind of like the app," Allison said. "Oh, that reminds me, I have dirt on Brittney."

"What?" Paige asked, unable to hide her excitement.

"She definitely had work done."

"I knew it," Paige said. She used her fork to flip the wilted iceberg lettuce on her plate around. "Her nose, right?"

"She's not saying," Allison said. "But that's why she never uses SkinDeep."

"Enough gossip," Kaylee said. "And enough with that stupid app."

Allison rolled her eyes and said, "Oh, Kaylee, you're just . . . ." She stopped herself, regretting what she might say. Allison had to remember that Kaylee and her family were dealing with Hailey's disappearance. Part of her admired Kaylee's strength. "The app's just for fun."

Noah surveyed the table and frowned. He said, "I already showed Kaylee how to start the group chat. She'll ring everyone tonight at seven. Does that work?"

Paige, Jade, and Allison looked at one another and then, one by one slowly nodded.

"Are we going to have to slide our stupid fingers across the screen to hear each other talk?" Jade asked.

"No," Noah said.

"It's just like the other group video chats," Kaylee said. "Just safer. You can't record or save anything."

The group spent the rest of lunch talking about the latest rumors and information about Emily and Hailey. Everyone still had their core beliefs. Paige had it out for the principal, Allison for Rat, and Jade was convinced Detective Lane was somehow involved. Her distrust of Noah continued. Noah and

Kaylee were the only two arguing that the police would eventually find Emily and Hailey still alive.

The five friends finished lunch and then headed off to their respective classes. Allison stopped just outside the cafeteria door and tucked herself into a corner so she could check her phone. She frowned when she saw she had another message from Dr. Ed.

> *Did you ask Brittney yet?*

Allison looked around to make sure nobody she knew was nearby or could see her phone. She quickly responded.

> *She denied it*

Allison smiled and waited for a response. She felt like she needed to stay one step ahead of this guy, whoever he was. A blood-red pixilated text bubble soon appeared. She slid her finger across the message.

> *Did you believe her?*

Allison frowned and struggled with what to say. Deep down, she knew Brittney's selfishness wouldn't allow her to admit she had work done. But there was no denying how taken aback Brittney reacted to the accusation. Allison connected the dots. Brittney had work done. Dr. Ed knew this. Did that make him the real deal? Why wouldn't Brittney just admit it? What was she hiding about Dr. Ed? Allison twisted her ring in frustration. Two secret messages appeared.

> *You told me what you want*
> *I can help*

Allison watched people file into the classroom. She was running out of time. She knew Brittney couldn't be trusted. But could she believe Dr. Ed? Before Allison could respond, Dr. Ed sent her two more texts.

Trust me
You'll never look at yourself the same way again

Brittney and the twins marched down the hallway. As they walked past Allison, Brittney flicked her hair and smiled. It wasn't a polite smile. Brittney's curled lip and flared nostrils carried an air of superiority. It was a look Brittney had shot Allison far too often. Allison responded to Dr. Ed.

What's the price?

☺☻☹

Kaylee finished stacking the dishwasher and wiped the kitchen counters clean. Her mother was in the den working on her laptop. The clock on the microwave showed the time to be 6:58 p.m. A chill enveloped Kaylee as she realized Hailey had disappeared precisely one week ago. Was that the last conversation with her sister? Ever? Hailey's absence in the home resulted in an uncomfortable silence that blanketed each room. Kaylee headed to the staircase and loudly said, "I'm going upstairs to do homework."

She didn't wait for her mom to respond and hurried upstairs. Kaylee closed her bedroom door and grabbed her iPad. She flopped on her bed and propped the tablet on her legs.

On Noah's advice, she'd installed the eChat app on her iPad. She launched the program and quickly initiated a video call with Paige, Allison, Jade, and Noah. As she waited for them to join the chat, Kaylee couldn't help but stare at the image the front-facing camera showed on the screen. Her acne stared back at her. Kaylee's first pimple appeared when she was eight years old, and it only got worse from there. She closed her eyes and remembered some of the *SkinDeep* edits she'd made to clear up her skin. A loud beep from the iPad startled her, causing Kaylee to lower the volume.

The screen signaled Noah was joining the chat. Noah's face slowly appeared in a red circle. The background behind him was blurred. Kaylee looked at the controls on her screen and wondered how he'd enabled that feature.

"Hey," Noah said. "Is it just us?"

"So far." Kaylee leaned back away from the camera to make her face a bit smaller on screen. She couldn't help but notice how much her eye color matched the wallpaper. "Do you think they forgot?"

"I hope not."

Two pixilated bubbles appeared in the chat room. The circles cleared, revealing Jade and Paige were now on the call, and both looked a bit frustrated. Each ring had its own colorful rim. Dark green surrounded Jade and yellow for Paige.

"Thanks for joining," Kaylee said.

"Can we make this quick?" Paige asked. "I've got too much homework to do."

"We just need Allison, and then we can start," Kaylee said.

"She's not joining," Jade said. "She texted me that she had a spa appointment."

"Spa?" Paige asked. "For what?"

"I dunno," Jade said. "She said her mom was treating her."

"Weird that they went out after curfew," Paige said.

"I think it's okay if your parents are with you," Kaylee said. She tried to smile, but she could tell that Paige and Jade didn't want to be on the call. "Does anyone have any new info? Anyone hear anything?"

After a few awkward seconds, Noah said, "I did."

"Let me guess," Jade said. "From your uncle?"

"He just left," Noah said. "He and my dad–"

"Why can't we see where you are?" Jade asked.

"What?" Noah replied. "Oh, it's just a setting in the app. You can go into your preferences for video and blur the background. It's part of the privacy setting. My room's a mess."

"Whatever," Jade said as she rolled her eyes.

"Anyway, I overheard them talking," Noah said. "My uncle was telling my dad they got Hailey's data."

"What data?" Kaylee asked. "I thought they'd gone through her texts and stuff."

"Her location data," Noah said.

Kaylee shifted and tried to get comfortable. The cops hadn't yet told her or her mom about Hailey's last location. They also still hadn't found her sister's bicycle. That meant Noah had brand new information. Kaylee's throat went dry as she tried to summon the courage to ask Noah what he heard.

"Was she at the school?" Paige asked. "Like Emily."

"No," Noah said. "The last location was a few miles west of the school. Near the bay."

"What's out there?" Jade asked.

"It could be anywhere," Kaylee said. She tried to hide the disappointment in her voice. Like Paige, Kaylee thought the location would be Engel Academy, indicating some sort of pattern to the abductions.

"I'm not done," Noah said. He looked over his shoulder, checking to make sure he was alone. He leaned closer to the camera and said, "My uncle said the phone wasn't far from someone's house. Someone we all know."

"Who?" Paige asked.

"Principal Torres," Noah said.

Six

We Have a Plan

Thursday, May 2nd

A group of three dozen students stood staring at the school's morning announcements. The digital bulletin board showed a reminder that all after-school activities were still canceled. The display changed to a photo of Emily, followed by the police information about Emily and her disappearance. The image faded away and was replaced by Hailey's details. After several seconds, Allison's picture appeared. Several students watching the screen gasped.

Buried within the crowd were Noah, Kaylee, Paige, and Jade. One by one, the other students dispersed until only the four of them remained. Paige struggled to keep herself from crying, her lower lip quivering in distress.

"I can't believe she's gone," Jade said.

"Why her?" Paige asked. "Why Allison?"

"I keep asking myself the same thing," Principal Torres said.

The four friends spun around, shocked to the see the principal standing right behind them.

Principal Torres stepped forward, pushing her way between the students until she stood directly below the monitor. Her bun looked to be wound tighter than usual. A handful of inky-black strands of hair fell across her neck. The principal turned and slowly locked eyes with each of them.

"A month ago, there were 737 students in my school,"

Principal Torres said. "Now we're down to 734. And the three missing girls are all part of *your* little group. Coincidence?"

"Emily was never part of our group," Jade said, her defiance on full display.

"You never gave her a chance," the principal responded. She looked at Kaylee and added, "Even you."

The screen above the principal cycled back to show Emily's picture. Guilt washed over Kaylee as she gazed at the image. She looked to Noah for support, but his head was hung low, his eyes focused on his feet.

"Don't forget there's a curfew in effect," Principal Torres said. "If another one goes missing, it might just be one of you."

Jade glared at the principal and opened her mouth to say something. Paige quickly grabbed her by the wrist. Jade closed her eyes, yanked her arm free, and looked away.

Principal Torres smiled and adjusted the bobby pins securing her bun. Her smile faded as her fingers brushed against the loose strands of hair hanging from her head. The principal pushed through the four students and headed down the hallway, struggling to fix her hairstyle.

"Was that supposed to be a threat?" Jade asked.

"She's just trying to scare us," Noah said.

"Does she even know she's a suspect?" Jade asked.

"Is she?" Kaylee asked. She slowly looked at Noah. "You said the cops pinged Hailey's phone near the principal's house. Did Detective Lane question her?"

"I don't know," Noah said. "Maybe . . . maybe she's a suspect and doesn't even know it. My uncle could have her under surveillance. I'll have to see what I can find out."

"She sure seems overconfident," Paige said. "She's hiding something. Noah, when will they have the location data on Allison's phone?"

"I don't know. Look, I'm doing my best to listen in and see what I can find out without getting caught."

Paige stared at Principal Torres, now standing at the far end of the hallway talking to a teacher. The two of them turned and looked at Paige. The principal pointed to Paige, said something to the teacher, and then chuckled.

"She's always hated us," Paige said. "And what was with her

making Emily part of our group? We barely knew her! Hailey and Allison are the only ones connected."

"It's because of the video," Kaylee said.

Paige shook her head. "Noah, when's your uncle coming over again so you can get more info?"

"You're assuming Noah's telling us the truth," Jade said.

"About what?" Noah asked.

"All the scoops you're getting from your uncle," Jade said. "Seems awfully convenient to me."

"Why would I lie?" Noah asked.

"I don't trust your uncle," Jade said.

"So, you don't trust me," Noah said. "Got it."

"Stop!" Kaylee said. "We need to stick together. Noah, keep doing what you're doing. Get whatever info you can."

"Will do, Boss." Noah smiled at Kaylee, causing her to blush.

"Whatever," Jade said. She tossed a piece of gum in her mouth and then grabbed Paige by her elbow. "We need to get to class."

Jade and Paige walked away, leaving Noah and Kaylee alone at the digital bulletin board. Hailey's picture appeared and seemed to stay onscreen longer than before. Kaylee found it impossible to look away. Her mind drifted back to the night she last saw her sister in the kitchen.

"You okay?" Noah asked.

"Sorry. Just thinking about Hailey."

"She's alive, Kaylee. You have to keep believing that."

"I just wonder if I should have pushed her harder on the night she left. You know? But I had no reason to doubt her."

"Because she said she was coming to see me."

Kaylee nodded and stared at Allison's picture as it appeared on the screen.

"So, Emily's phone was last pinged at the school," Kaylee said. "And Hailey's near the principal. Where does the principal live?"

"She's only a few miles from the school. My uncle didn't give the exact address. He just said it was off Rock Harbor Road. But it doesn't really matter."

"Why?"

"All it means is that's the last ping from the phone. Whoever took her could have smashed the phone and then taken her anywhere. Or taken the phone far away from the abduction and then smashed it."

"I didn't think of that." Kaylee frowned and shook her head. "I was just hoping that, well, maybe there's a pattern with the phone locations."

"Hey, I could be wrong."

"Maybe."

"If it makes you feel better, my uncle's looking for a pattern too."

"Really?"

"You two think alike." Noah grinned and flashed a big smile. "Are you planning to become a detective when you graduate?"

Kaylee laughed and said, "Maybe I should."

Noah looked around the hallway. The few students left were busy filing into classrooms.

"We gotta get to class," Noah said. "Mine's upstairs. You?"

Kaylee didn't respond. She was too busy staring down the hallway. Standing at the far end, holding a grease-covered wrench, stood Rat. The janitor's bulging eyes were fixated on Kaylee. He began to lightly smack the wrench against his palm. A smile spread across his lips, revealing his crooked overbite. Rat licked his lips and slowly moved closer to Kaylee and Noah.

Noah followed Kaylee's gaze. His body stiffened when he saw Rat, and Noah instinctively stepped forward in front of Kaylee. Kaylee grinned but then jutted to the side so she could peer past Noah's arm.

Rat continued his march. With each step, the force of the wrench hitting his palm increased, and his grin widened. He stopped when he reached Noah and Kaylee.

"Shouldn't you two be in class?" Rat asked.

His voice sounded hoarse, as if he'd spent the night screaming. Kaylee wondered if she'd ever heard him talk before. She knew so little about the janitor and was surprised to see he was almost as tall as Noah.

"What's it to you?" Noah asked.

"I gotta repair the shitter," Rat said. He raised his wrench and pointed at the nearby restrooms. "Both of them."

Kaylee grabbed Noah's forearm and pulled him away, causing the pair to head toward the other end of the nearly empty hall. The sound of metal slapping against skin echoed behind them. She looked back to see Rat staring at them, still smacking his wrench against his hand.

"If a phone's last location can't pinpoint the abduction, then couldn't the school still be ground zero?" Kaylee asked Noah.

"I guess," Noah said. "Why?"

Kaylee stopped and stared at Rat. They were now well out of earshot from him. Rat walked to a nearby utility room, pulled a key from his pocket, and unlocked the door. He gave Kaylee and Noah one last glare before disappearing inside.

"So, Rat could still be a suspect," Kaylee said. She looked up into Noah's eyes and added, "Even the primary one."

"Really?"

"Isn't there some rule about the first suspect always being the right one?"

"Where'd you hear that?"

"I don't know." Kaylee sighed and nervously picked at her cheeks. "Probably in some movie."

"But was Rat the first suspect? I thought it was Torres."

"Depends on who you ask." Kaylee stared at the utility room door. "He's had his eye on us since day one."

Noah chuckled and said, "I definitely see you working with my uncle."

"I'm serious. Something about the first suspect. I know I heard it somewhere. Or saw it in a movie."

"You like thriller movies?"

"Totally. You?"

"Definitely. I could never get Hailey to sit and watch a movie." Noah sighed and added, "One of many things we didn't have in common."

Kaylee looked around the empty hallway and said, "We're late for class."

Kaylee closed her bedroom door and ran to her bed. Her iPad, already propped up on a pile of gray pillows, showed the time to be 7:01 p.m. She unlocked the tablet and quickly launched the eChat app. After fussing momentarily with her hair, Kaylee kicked off a group video chat with Noah, Paige, and Jade.

Noah immediately appeared in a red circle, the background behind him blurred. Before he could say anything, two more circles popped onto the screen. The pixilated images soon revealed Jade and Paige.

"Hey," Kaylee said. "I'm glad everyone could make it tonight." She was about to ask Noah for the latest intel, but she couldn't help but notice the background behind Jade and Paige. Both had the exact same dark walnut paneled wall behind them. "Where are you?"

"Who?" Noah asked.

"Are you two together?" Kaylee asked.

Jade and Paige grinned, looked at each other, and turned their phones. The images in the circles swapped.

"We're at my house," Jade said. "In my basement."

"But the curfew!" Kaylee said.

"Relax," Paige said. "My mom's going to come get me later."

"Oh," Kaylee said.

"Any updates from your uncle?" Paige asked. "Did they figure out where Allison disappeared?"

Noah nodded. Before he could say anything, Jade asked, "Was it near Torres? Are they going to question her?"

"No," Noah said. "Allison's last signal came even further away, near the beach. My uncle doesn't see a connection to the principal. They don't see a pattern yet. Or a motive."

"Motive?" Paige asked. "Torres runs this school like a prison. Ever since Rat got here, things have gotten worse. Detentions. Suspensions. She seems to hate every student!"

"No," Kaylee said. "It's Rat."

"Why?" Jade asked.

"Just a hunch," Kaylee said. "Especially after his wrench-slapping attitude this morning."

"That's right!" Paige said. "You told us about that at lunch.

He's so weird. Maybe Rat's doing it, and Torres is protecting him."

"The cops questioned him," Noah said. "After they pinged Emily's phone near the school."

"When the hell were you going to tell us that?" Jade asked.

"I only found out about it, like, an hour ago."

"Did he have an alibi?" Paige asked.

"He said he was in the school that night," Noah said. "He walked the cops around the basement to show them a bunch of different rooms."

"But he could've easily avoided places," Kaylee said. "I went to the basement once, and it's like a labyrinth down there."

"Maybe," Noah said. "They didn't do a formal search warrant. I mean, they had no evidence to pin it on him. And he did show them around. I think the principal made him do it."

"Of course she did," Paige said. "Because they're in on it together."

Kaylee sighed and rubbed her temples. Her mind raced as she tried to connect the dots between the pinged locations, Rat and the principal. She stared at her tablet, watching the three color-rimmed circles float across the screen. The rings moved in a random pattern. At one point, they formed a triangle. At another, they made a diagonal.

"Hey, Noah," Kaylee said. "What beach was Allison's phone pinged at? Was it the one on the western side? Near where the principal lives?"

"No," Noah said. "It was the Atlantic side, somewhere near Little Pleasant Bay."

"Really?" Kaylee said. "I wonder . . . ."

Kaylee minimized the eChat app. She then launched the Maps app and split the screen to show both simultaneously. The map slowly zoomed into her location in Orleans.

"What are you doing?" Jade asked. "We can see your fingers all over the place."

"Torres lives off Rock Harbor Road," Kaylee said. She dropped a pin on the map near Rock Harbor Road and then another near the high school. "Noah, does eChat let me share my screen?"

"Look at the bottom of the chat," Noah said. "There's a little icon–"

"I see it." Kaylee hit the share button and then enlarged the map to full screen. "If you draw a line from the principal's house to the school and then keep going, where does it lead?"

"Little Pleasant Bay," Jade said. "Okay, you're freaking me out."

"That bay is a few miles wide," Noah said. "And I don't even know what part of the bay they pinged Allison's phone. It could easily be north or south of that direct line. And the same is true of Rock Harbor."

"It doesn't matter," Kaylee said. "Cast a net a mile wide across that line, and all points lead to the school in the middle."

Kaylee minimized the Map app and stopped sharing it with the chat. She couldn't help but notice how anxious Jade, Paige, and Noah looked.

"Noah, do you know where Rat took the cops?" Kaylee asked. "When he showed them around."

"No. I hear what I hear. I can't go asking questions. Look, if they catch me listening in, I'm screwed. I don't know what my dad would do to me. Or my uncle." Noah frowned and briefly looked over his shoulder. The blurred background masked what was behind him. "Why?"

"I think we need to search the school grounds," Kaylee said. "Especially the basement."

"Rat lives down there," Paige said. "How . . . how can we sneak around? Should we skip class?"

"Too risky," Jade said. "And we can't go at night. Not with the curfew."

"We go when school ends," Kaylee said. "There will still be teachers and students making plenty of noise. And that's when Rat starts cleaning the classrooms. It's the perfect cover for us to do some snooping."

"This is a bad idea," Noah said.

"I'm in," Paige said. Jade turned and looked at Paige and frowned. "Don't give me that look, Jade. Allison's missing. We've got to find her."

"And Hailey," Kaylee said. "I know she's still alive." Kaylee felt relieved Paige was on board with her plan. Noah appeared glum, and Jade still looked disappointed. "This will work. If it's just Paige and me, that's fine, but I think we should all do it together. Who's with me?

Seven

There's a Rat in the Basement

Friday, May 3rd

Kaylee, Jade, and Paige sat together for lunch in the cafeteria. Jade remained quiet, enjoying the day's featured special of fried chicken, carrots, and tater tots. Paige focused on the *SkinDeep* app on her phone, ignoring the small salad resting in front of her. Kaylee sat there, lost in her thoughts.

"I've been thinking about our chat last night," Kaylee said. "About Rat."

"What about him?" Jade asked.

"I think today's the day to check out the basement," Kaylee said.

Paige lowered her phone and frowned. The screen showed the latest enhancements to her face. She'd used the app to make her nostrils more petite and less oval. Paige shoved her phone into her skirt pocket, looked at Kaylee, and asked, "When school ends?"

"No," Kaylee said. "It's too risky. We–"

The overhead speakers popped and crackled. The din in the cafeteria lowered. A pre-recorded announcement from Principal Torres began to play.

> *This is a reminder that we have an assembly starting at 2:30 today in the gymnasium. All classes are ending early. Attendance is mandatory.*

"That's when we go," Kaylee said.

"Skip the assembly?" Jade asked. She smiled and added, "I'm in."

"You know the assembly will be about Allison," Paige said. Her eyes filled with tears. "Maybe we should go. To hear the latest."

"It's going to be the same shit as last time," Jade said. "All they want to do is scare us."

"And Rat's always at those assemblies," Kaylee said. "So, it's the perfect time."

"I suppose," Paige replied. Her phone buzzed in her pocket, and she removed it to see an eChat notification. Paige unlocked the phone and went to the app to find two messages from Dr. Ed.

> *You never answered my question*
> *Do you like who you see in the mirror?*

Paige pocketed her phone and looked up to see everyone staring at her.

"Who was that?" Jade asked. "I saw it came from eChat."

"Nobody," Paige said. She shoved a few pieces of iceberg lettuce into her mouth and stared at her plate. Paige slowly looked at Jade and said, "I'll tell you later."

"Was it Noah?" Kaylee asked. "I wonder–"

"Hey," Noah said as he approached the table. His tray held the day's special, but with a double serving of tater tots and no carrots. He took a seat beside Kaylee.

"You're late," Kaylee said. "We were just talking about Rat."

"You still want to go snooping in the basement?" Noah asked. He tore a chunk of chicken into his mouth. "When?"

"Today," Kaylee said. "During the assembly."

Noah looked around confused and then appeared disappointed. He inhaled four tots and muttered, "Why?"

"Rat will be there," Paige said. "He's always there, gawking from some corner. It's the best time for us to go."

"We'll just have to hide close to one of the basement entrances," Kaylee said. She looked across the table to see Jade and Paige nodding in agreement. The expression on

Noah's face made it clear he still had his doubts. "What, Noah?"

"Shouldn't we just let the police do their job?" Noah asked.

"You know how I feel about the cops," Jade said. "Especially your uncle."

"You can skip it if you want, Noah, but it sounds like the rest of us are in," Kaylee said.

"Let the girls handle this," Paige said with a grin. "It might go smoother."

Noah stared at his plate and stabbed one of the tater tots with his fork. He sighed and said, "All of the doors to the basement are locked." He looked around to see all three girls waiting for him to continue. "There's another entrance to the basement in the back of the library. And the library's far away from the gym. So, that's our best way to get downstairs."

"What about the key?" Kaylee asked.

"They have one at the main desk in the library," Noah said. "I know where they keep it."

"Then we're all set," Kaylee said.

"I still think this is a bad idea," Noah said. "But, I'm in."

The rest of the afternoon felt like an eternity to Kaylee. She zoned out during her American Literature class. Luckily, due to the assembly, her Advanced Algebra class was cut short. Kaylee pushed her way past her classmates and went to the library on the first floor. The door was open. She looked around to see if Rat, Principal Torres, or any teachers were nearby. Slowly, Kaylee stepped backward into the library.

The place appeared empty of both students and faculty. A dozen tables filled the center of the massive room. Surrounding them stood ten-foot-tall wooden racks of books. The carpeted floor made the room much quieter than the other school rooms. Kaylee walked over to the main desk and wondered if Noah had already gotten the key.

"Kaylee!" Jade said. Her voice came from the far end of the room. "Come to the back."

"And close the door," Paige said.

Kaylee swung the door closed and hurried to the back of the library. With the door closed, the library became eerily silent. There were three rows of shelves, all parallel with the back wall. She went to the last one and found Jade and Paige standing near the door to the basement.

"Where's Noah?" Kaylee asked.

"I bet he bailed," Jade said. "He's probably with his uncle."

Two loud knocks rang from the door to the hallway, and the door slowly opened. The noise of the students making their way to the gym filled the room, and the door quickly closed. Kaylee peered through the open shelves to see if someone had entered the room. The narrow opening limited her view, and she couldn't be sure if they were alone.

Suddenly they heard someone rummaging around at the front of the room. Papers fluttered, and drawers shuddered. Jade, Paige, and Kaylee crouched low and looked at one another with trepidation. Kaylee opened her mouth to speak, but Jade flung her hand over her face. The noise stopped. All three held their breath and waited for the door to open and the person to leave. But the room remained silent.

"Hey," Noah said as he stuck his head around the last bookcase.

Kaylee let out a short stifled scream. Jade fell backward and knocked Paige against the wall.

"Asshole!" Jade said as she stood up. She reached down and helped Paige to her feet. "Why didn't you tell us you were here?"

"I wasn't sure if you guys were back here yet." Noah raised his hand and dangled a silver key from his fingertips. "Are we ready?"

Kaylee stood up, snatched the key from Noah, and said, "Let's go." Her hand trembled as she fumbled to get the key to slide into the lock. She flipped it upside down and tried again. It still wouldn't go in. "I don't think this is the right key."

Noah gently placed his hand over Kaylee's. The trembling stopped. He turned her fingers so that the key's teeth pointed down, and then together, they smoothly pushed the key into the lock.

The door's hinges creaked in protest as Noah opened the door. Cold, damp, musty air rushed from the opening. The staircase faded into complete darkness at the bottom of the stairs. He reached for the nearby light switch, but Kaylee brushed his hand away.

"Shouldn't we be . . . discrete?" Kaylee asked. Her voice was now a whisper.

Noah nodded and took the lead, with Kaylee, Paige, and Jade following him. Jade closed the door behind her. The staircase was now pitch black. Noah stopped and waited for his eyes to adjust. A bright light appeared from behind him.

"This is stupid," Jade said as she waved her phone back and forth. The light from the phone's flashlight settled on the bottom of the staircase. "We're the only ones down here."

They reached the bottom of the stairs and stopped. Paige reached for the nearby light switch. Noah stopped her and said, "We don't know how many lights that thing will turn on. Jade's got the right idea."

Everyone turned on their phone's flashlight. Without the overhead lights, the basement felt like a mystery. Its secrets were revealed in bits and pieces as each beam of light swept across the different surfaces. A mix of fenced cages, solid walls, and assorted doorways lined the seemingly endless hallway.

"Is it just me, or does it stink down here?" Jade asked.

"It's gross," Paige said.

The tight confines of the passageway smelled like a mix of garbage and acidic chemicals. Noah led the way, stopping at each door and testing the handle. The first doorway revealed a storage room filled with paper supplies, such as stationery, pens, and pencils. The next room held an overflow of desks and chairs.

The overhead pipes occasionally rattled, and the plinking sound of water falling to the floor could be heard in the distance. Kaylee wiped beads of sweat from her brow. Her heart raced in her chest, fueled by a combination of fear and excitement. She stopped in front of a caged storage room and peered between the chain links. The light from her phone showed various tools hanging from the walls. Her eyes settled on the oversized wrench that Rat had wielded the other day.

Noah was several feet ahead of everyone else, staring at a closed door. He tugged on the handle and pressed his body firmly against the door.

"This one's locked," Noah said. He twisted the handle, but it wouldn't budge. Noah pointed at the floor. "Look." A dim light could be seen coming from the crack beneath the door. Noah pressed his ear to the cool metal door and listened for a few seconds. "I hear something."

Kaylee pushed past Jade and Paige and pressed herself between Noah and the door. She closed her eyes and leaned against the door, trying to hear what Noah heard. A low mechanical hum resonated softly, its drone broken intermittently by a slight banging sound. Kaylee looked up at Noah and said, "That tapping. Is someone banging on a pipe?"

"I . . . I can't tell."

Kaylee yanked hard on the handle, but the door wouldn't budge. She slapped her hand against the door and yelled, "Hailey! Are you in there?"

"Lower your voice," Paige said.

Kaylee went back to the caged tool room. Her breathing became short and choppy. She ignored the stench in the air as she twisted the metal handle open and entered the room. The phone's light came to rest on the oversized wrench hanging on the wall. Kaylee grabbed it and returned to the locked door.

"What are you doing?" Noah asked.

Kaylee didn't bother answering him and instead smashed the wrench against the handle.

"Are you crazy?" Noah cried. He grabbed the wrench and yanked it from Kaylee's grip. Noah ran his fingers against the broken handle before gently twisting the knob. The handle snapped off in his hand. "Great." Noah dropped the wrench onto the floor. The clang of the metal hitting the concrete rang throughout the basement.

Kaylee pushed the door open. A rush of warm air greeted her. The dimly lit room was about six feet wide and twice as deep. An old foldaway cot, covered in stained black sheets, sat in the back right corner. Across from it was a pair of laundry baskets stuffed with clothes. A school desk and chair sat just inside the doorway. Across from the desk, a small floor heater vibrated and whirred. The air from the fan caused a wall calendar hanging over the desk to ripple and smack against the wall.

Kaylee, Noah, Jade, and Paige stepped into the tiny room. Jade walked over to the calendar and held it steady. She blew a bubble and snapped the peppermint gum back into her mouth. The 2019 Cape Cod Firemen calendar showed the month of May with a shirtless buff man wearing a fireman helmet and cuddling a Dalmatian puppy. Jade looked at Paige and said, "Who knew Rat was gay."

Paige walked over to the desk and started flipping through a hardcovered notepad. Kaylee began to inspect the pile of clothes.

"This is wrong," Noah said. "You're leaving fingerprints. And we're breaking and entering. This isn't why we came down here."

Kaylee rummaged through the clothes a bit more and sighed. She said, "You're right. These things all belong to Rat. None of this is Hailey's. But there are more rooms to search."

"No, Kaylee," Noah said. "We need to leave."

"This place creeps me out," Jade said. She pushed her way past Noah and stopped. "Shit."

Kaylee looked past Jade into the darkened hallway. Rat slowly stepped into the room, holding the wrench. Kaylee screamed.

☺☹☹

Principal Torres paced back and forth in her office while Rat leaned against her closed door. Her pink heels clacked loudly against the floor. In between them sat Kaylee, Noah, Jade, and Paige. The four students appeared shell-shocked as they stared at a television mounted on the wall behind the principal. A video shot from someone's phone showed Emily Mason surrounded by Hailey, Jade, Paige, and Allison. Standing a few feet away were Kaylee and Noah. The TV's speakers loudly played out the events.

> "Why do you care?" Emily cried.
> "Because you're a liar!" Jade screamed. "You look nothing like your Instagram pics."
> "So what?" Emily said. She wiped tears from her eyes.
> "SkinDeep is for tweaks," Allison said.

"It's not to drop forty pounds," Paige added.
"I was only having fun," Emily replied. *"It shouldn't matter."*
"We don't like fakes," Hailey said. *She turned and looked at Noah and Kaylee and asked, "Right?"*

Principal Torres paused the video and glared at the four students. Her face dripped with contempt. She glanced up at Rat, still leaning against the door, and said, "You can go now, Edgar."

Jade looked at Paige and mouthed, "Edgar?"

Paige shrugged her shoulders but said nothing. Rat lowered his head, turned, and left the office, slamming the door behind him. The closed blinds rattled as they settled back into place.

"I can't tell you how many times I've thanked Brittney for recording that video," Principal Torres said. She leaned against her desk, crossed her arms, and stared at Noah, Kaylee, Jade, and Paige. "I should suspend you for what you did in the basement. But then you'd be outside. Out of my watch." The principal paused and shook her head. "It's not safe out there. Not for any of you." She sighed and added, "Noah, I can only imagine what your uncle will have to say."

Principal Torres turned around, stared at the television, and sighed. Without looking back, she said, "You need to watch what you do and where you go. Now, go wait outside. Your parents have been contacted. I hope they punish all of you."

After fidgeting with the bobby pins securing her bun, Principal Torres faced the students, raised her voice, and said, "Severely!"

Eight

Who's Left?

Monday, May 6th

Lesley's Mercedes SUV shuddered as it traversed a pothole. The wipers hummed as they swept back and forth, clearing the morning mist from the windshield. She reached into her purse and retrieved her daughter's cell phone. Kaylee took the phone and stared at the time - 8:22 a.m. The screen showed a list of missed notifications.

"You may have to wait for me to pick you up from school today," Lesley said. "I've got a showing at two out in Wellfleet."

"I can call Dad," Kaylee said.

"He's out of town. Again."

"Oh." Kaylee nervously rubbed her hands together. "Well, how about Noah?"

"I . . . I don't know."

"He's no longer a suspect, Mom. Seriously. What's wrong with you?"

"He . . . he was part of your little gang breaking into the janitor's room."

"I told you that was *my* idea! And I apologized. I'm. . . I'm sorry."

"Honestly, Kaylee, this is so unlike you."

Kaylee turned and looked out the window at what she could only assume was a mom with her two teenage girls walking together. All three were huddled beneath a bright rainbow-colored umbrella. The mom laughed as she struggled to keep the umbrella from collapsing in the wind. The joy they displayed made Kaylee think about her big sister. Would she ever see her again?

"Hailey's gone!" Kaylee shook her head and began to cry. "And now, Allison. I . . . I had to do something."

The stoplight at the upcoming intersection switched to yellow and then red. Lesley slowed her vehicle to a stop and took Kaylee's trembling hand into hers. "We both miss Hailey. But this isn't your problem to solve."

"You sound like Noah." Kaylee let go of her mom and wiped her cheeks dry. "He didn't like us going into the basement."

"He didn't? Well, maybe I *should* trust him." Lesley briefly closed her eyes as she struggled to keep from bursting into tears. "Whoever's behind this sent another note with Allison's diamond ring. This is getting so out of control. I . . . I can't lose you, Kaylee. I just can't."

"You can trust Noah." Kaylee gently placed her hand on her mom's arm. She debated telling her mother that Noah had been giving her rides since the beginning. But Kaylee didn't want to risk making things worse. "Wouldn't I be safer having him drive me back and forth to school every day?"

Lesley took several seconds before finally saying, "Okay, Kaylee. You're right. I'm sorry, I just . . . ." She tapped her fingers against the steering wheel and sighed. "I asked Detective Lane why he hadn't brought in the FBI. He said it wasn't time. Not time? Three girls are missing. Three! With notes and jewelry! I mean, what's he waiting for?"

"Maybe he wants to take all the credit."

"Maybe." Lesley frowned and added, "He seems the type."

Kaylee could see the tension hammered into her mother's face. "So, you're okay with Noah now?"

"What? Oh, yes. Yes, it's fine. Tell him I'm sorry, okay? And thank him for me, too."

Kaylee smiled. It felt good to smile, especially with her mother. Ever since Hailey's disappearance, tensions at home had become almost unbearable. Her mom would snap at the slightest mistake or issue, and Kaylee couldn't rely on her dad for help. Besides always being gone, the mere mention of his name would only upset her mother more.

Several minutes later, they arrived at Engel Academy. The rain had, thankfully, ended. Lesley pulled up to the curb and placed the vehicle in park. She looked at her daughter and said, "Text me to let me know that Noah can bring you home today."

"Sure."

"And then again, once you're home safe."

"I will."

Kaylee unbuckled her seatbelt and opened her door. She started to get out but suddenly felt her mom pull her closer. Kaylee turned and hugged her mother. They warmly held one another for several seconds, Kaylee melting in her mom's caring embrace.

"I'll be okay, Mom," Kaylee said. She kissed her mother on the cheek and exited the SUV. "I'll text you later."

Kaylee slammed the door closed, waved goodbye to her mother, and then made her way toward the school. Since sunrise, the temperature had been in the low 40s, and the blustery wind still whipped tiny raindrops across her skin. Cars clogged the parking lot as students tried to find a parking spot. A familiar exhaust rumble burbled behind Kaylee. She turned around to see Noah approaching in his red Camaro. The driver's window lowered.

"Wait for me," Noah said as he drove past Kaylee.

She decided to follow him to the far end of the lot. The wind, gusting at 25 mph, caused Kaylee's hair to whip wildly across her face. What she wouldn't give for a warm knit hat. She regretted wearing such a thin jacket and crossed her arms to try and keep herself warm. Kaylee struggled to adjust her hair as she reached Noah's Camaro. She tucked her hair behind her ears before the wind immediately whipped it away. Kaylee sighed as Noah got out of his car and frowned.

"What?" Kaylee asked.

"You've been ignoring me," Noah said. "All weekend."

"Oh! My phone." Kaylee waved her cellphone and then stared at the screen. "Part of my punishment. My mom took all my shit away. No computer, iPad, or anything."

"How did you do homework?"

"My mom would give me my laptop, but only under her supervision."

"That sucks."

"I didn't get my phone back until we got to school."

"Oh, okay. I . . . I was worried about you."

"Thanks." Kaylee felt her cheeks get flush. She looked down at her phone and began scrolling through her notifications. There were several texts from Noah and one from Jade. Kaylee pocketed her phone. "I missed a lot. Sorry. I tried to text everyone before she took everything."

Noah reached into his back seat and grabbed his backpack. He closed the door and said, "Your mom's strict."

"She's just worried. Would you believe she gave me mace?"

"What?"

Kaylee opened her bag and retrieved a small four-inch-long pink cylinder. "See. It's plastic and looks like lipstick. But it's not."

"I better not piss you off. It's bad enough that your mom hates me."

"Oh, she doesn't. Not anymore. In fact, I convinced her to let you drive me back and forth to school. I mean, like, all the time now. I never told her that you've been my secret Uber."

"What changed her mind?"

"I think she's just overwhelmed. Hailey's gone. My dad's not around. She's just got too much to handle. Oh, and I told her you were against the whole basement raid. She told me to tell you she's sorry and to thank you."

"Good."

Noah locked his car, and then he and Kaylee headed toward the school, doing their best to remain steady in the strong gusty wind. Most of the students had parked, so the traffic in the lot was thinning.

"Oh, she gave me something else," Kaylee said. "I think it's overkill, but she insisted." Kaylee reached into her pocket and retrieved a keychain with a black leather disc attached. She held it up for Noah to see. "It's an Airtag."

"My uncle did one of those for his dog."

Kaylee stopped walking and asked, "Are you saying my mom put me on a leash?"

"Well, kind of." Noah grinned and nodded toward the school. As Kaylee began walking with him, he asked, "Is there a way I could track you with that?"

"I think so." The wind blew Kaylee's hair against her face causing it to stick to her lips. "Why?"

"Maybe we get one for me too." Noah grinned as he moved Kaylee's hair away, clearing it from her face. "We can keep each other safe."

Kaylee smiled. For some odd reason, the idea of her and Noah tracking one another made her feel closer to him. "So, did you get in trouble?" Kaylee asked. "Because of the basement thing?"

"My dad was pissed. But my uncle, well, he was sort of proud of me."

"Really?"

"He thinks I might make a good cop someday."

Kaylee stopped and grabbed Noah's elbow, causing him to come to a halt. A high-pitched whine filled the quiet lot. Jade came speeding into the parking lot, her e-bike's motor whirring loudly. Her helmet was strapped to the back seat, allowing her afro to bounce in tandem with the bike's movements. When she saw Noah and Kaylee standing there, she yanked the handlebar, turned, and raced toward them. Jade slammed on her brakes, coming to a stop mere inches from Noah.

"Watch it!" Noah said.

"She's gone!" Jade cried, tears gushing down her face.

"Who?" Kaylee asked.

"Paige! Her . . . her mom called me last night freaking out because she never came home."

"Slow down," Noah said. "Where'd she go? Was she with you?"

"No." Jade took a deep breath and wiped her cheeks dry. Her voice trembled when she spoke. "Paige told her mom she had a date Sunday afternoon."

"With who?" Kaylee asked.

"I have no idea. Paige never said anything to me." The tension in Jade's body slowly uncoiled. She took several deep breaths and stared off toward the school. The three of them were the only students remaining outside. "She . . . she kept getting those messages." She looked up at Noah and added, "On eChat."

"What messages?" Noah asked.

"I don't know. She said someone was trolling her. But that stupid app deletes every text, so she couldn't show me. And she wouldn't tell me what they were talking about. Or his name. I told her to block him. Paige said not to worry, that she could handle things." Jade rubbed her bloodshot eyes and shook her head. "I swear, she almost sounded . . . intrigued by this guy."

"Do you think that's who she went to meet?" Kaylee asked.

"I . . . I don't know. When I asked her if she was meeting the troll, she said no. But . . . . Paige can be so . . . ." Jade looked at Noah and then at Kaylee. "Do you think she was taken like Hailey and Allison? Is . . . is she alive?"

☺☺☹

Paige opened her eyes and tried to get her bearings. Her temples ached as if she had a bad hangover. She was lying on her side on a musty bed. The scent of rotting trash filled the damp, cool air. Paige sat up, rubbed her eyes, and studied her clothing. Mud and grass covered the knees of her denim jeans. She pulled the sleeves of her blue knit sweater closer to her wrists and rubbed her hands together to warm her cold skin. The room was very dark, but she could make out some thick wooden support posts nearby and a staircase in the corner. She instinctively reached for her pearl necklace, but it was gone.

The faint sound of a boat's horn came from somewhere outside. Paige glanced at the stairs again. The steep staircase had an open railing, and the risers appeared warped. A small landing at the top of the stairs ended beside a closed door. She stood up and took one step toward the staircase, and stopped. A cluster of tiny red pin-sized lights positioned above the doorway clicked on. Paige squinted and tried to grasp what she was seeing. She soon realized it was an infrared camera.

The concrete floor and walls absorbed what little light came from a single overhead lamp. Wooden slats ran across the ceiling. Paige wondered if she was in a basement and, if so, what sat above her.

Something rattled from the other side of the room. Paige jumped and spun around. There was another bed, lost in the shadows beyond the support posts. Someone was sitting on the edge of the bed. The person stood up.

"Who's there?" Paige asked.

The stranger took a few steps closer, stopped, and whispered, "Paige?"

Paige's eyes widened. She still couldn't make out the person's face, but she knew the voice. Paige rushed forward and cried, "Allison!" The two girls threw their arms around each other and sobbed. "I'm so glad you're alive."

"Me too," Allison said. She ran her hands through Paige's matted messy hair and then stepped back so she could look her in the eyes. "But . . . that means he got you too."

Allison walked to Paige's bed, sat down, and lowered her head. Paige couldn't help but notice how ragged Allison appeared. The knees of her jeans were torn, mud covered her pink jacket, and her usually vibrant hair hung lifelessly. Allison's knuckles appeared bruised and scraped. Paige sat down beside her and held her hand.

"I guess you put up a fight," Paige said. She gently ran her thumb across Allison's tender wounds. Paige glanced up at the infrared camera at the top of the stairs. "Who's doing this?"

"I . . . I don't know."

Paige instinctively reached for her necklace again. Allison gently took Paige's hand into hers.

"He took my diamond ring," Allison said. "That was my grandmother's engagement ring. Remember how he sent Hailey's charm bracelet?"

"He's sending a message. To the police."

"To everyone."

"Wait." Paige sat upright and looked around the room. "Hailey. Where is she?

Nine

A Dead End

Friday, May 10th

Kaylee, Noah, and Jade walked side by side through the twin doors exiting the gymnasium. The assembly, led by Detective Rick Lane, had just ended. After a lengthy and sometimes uncomfortable discussion about Paige's disappearance, the police announced a new 6 p.m. curfew.

"Why did they have to show us Paige's bloody necklace?" Kaylee asked.

"It's to scare us," Jade said.

"Well, it's working," Kaylee said.

"Whoever's doing this has a definite pattern," Noah said. "Emily's necklace. Hailey's charm bracelet. Now Paige. My uncle thinks—"

Noah stumbled sideways from someone bumping into him. He slammed against Kaylee, catching her before she fell to the floor. He turned to see Rat walk past them, glance back, and grin.

"Asshole!" Jade yelled.

The grin on Rat's face melted away. He pointed at Jade and said, "Watch it. Bullies like you always get what you deserve."

Noah put his arm around Kaylee and guided her into a nearby alcove. Jade joined them, and Rat disappeared into the crowd. They watched the other students and faculty walk by as if in slow motion. Every other person seemed to shoot them a judgmental glance.

"What were you saying about your uncle?" Kaylee asked.

"My uncle thinks they're still alive. He said, well, um, that if they weren't then, we'd be getting . . . other things in the mail."

"Other . . . ." Jade said. Her eyes widened. "You mean like body parts?"

Noah nodded. He turned to Kaylee and said, "Sorry."

"No. That makes sense." Kaylee stared into the pack of students. A frown soon spread across her face. "Why are they staring at us like that?"

"Probably because of the way Principal Torres practically called us out as being the next victims," Jade said. "Her stupid speech about bullies not winning. What the hell? We did nothing wrong!"

"Everyone, just calm down," Noah said. "I think tensions are high all over. Even the cops are getting frustrated." Noah paused and looked across the hallway. The gym had emptied, and several faculty members were standing near the doorway. His uncle emerged, along with Principal Torres and Emily's dad. "Why does he keep coming to these things?"

"Who?" Kaylee asked. She followed Noah's gaze. "Oh. Mr. Mason. Did I tell you they wanted my mom on stage too?"

"They?" Jade asked. "They, who?"

"Torres. She told my mom she wants all the parents of the victims to be here."

"I told you," Jade said. "These assemblies are just to scare us." Jade snapped her gum, sending a hint of peppermint into the air. "Besides, I don't think we're being targeted. I don't care what Torres thinks. For all we know, she's behind this." Jade stared at Noah and added, "Or your uncle. I don't trust any of them."

"It's got to be a coincidence," Noah said. "About who's disappeared."

"No," Kaylee said. "It has to be someone who was there." Kaylee's eyes widened. She looked up at Noah and asked. "Do you think Brittney's involved? She shot the video."

"Brittney?" Jade chuckled and shook her head. "Kaylee, you're sounding desperate. That girl can barely find her way out of her locker." She glanced across the hallway and her smile instantly faded. "Shit. Your uncle's coming."

Detective Lane and Principal Torres approached the alcove. The five stood in silence for several seconds, studying one another.

"I mentioned grief counseling during the assembly," Principal Torres said. "If any of you need to talk, come to my office. We can make an appointment." She turned to the detective and said, "Thanks for coming in today."

"Of course." Detective Lane watched the principal walk away. Once she was out of earshot, he looked at Jade and said, "I was serious in there. All of you need to watch your back. Everyone in that video needs to be on alert." He stared at Noah and added, "Even you."

Kaylee glared at the detective. She couldn't understand his attitude toward his nephew. Was that meant to be a warning? He certainly didn't sound very supportive. Detective Lane didn't bother to say goodbye to any of them. He turned and walked down the hallway, forcing students to move aside as he made his way to the exit.

"Your uncle really is a dick," Jade said.

"But Noah's getting good info from him," Kaylee said.

"I guess." Jade looked around at the students in the hallway. The crowd from the assembly had thinned out. "School's over, isn't it?"

"I'm glad they held the assembly at the end of the day," Noah said. "It's been a long week."

"We need to figure out our next steps," Kaylee said.

"For what?" Jade asked. "Playing detective?" She didn't wait for Kaylee to respond. "If you think I'm going back in that basement, you're crazy."

"Maybe we were wrong about Rat," Kaylee said. "Maybe it's Principal Torres." Kaylee's eyes widened. "Oh! Or she's making Rat do it for her."

"Girl, you're seriously going crazy," Jade said.

"Torres making Rat do this?" Noah asked, shaking his head. "Why? Besides, you've got nothing to prove that."

"But–"

"No, Kaylee." Noah rested his hands on Kaylee's shoulders. "You're. . . you're not thinking clearly, okay? I know you miss

Hailey. We all do."

"And Allison and Paige," Jade added. She closed her eyes as tears welled within them. "I can't keep talking about this shit. I . . . I need to go. See you on Monday."

"Jade, wait!" Kaylee said.

Jade ignored her and stormed off down the hallway.

"She'll be fine," Noah said. He gently squeezed Kaylee's shoulders before letting go.

"I feel like we're close," Kaylee said. "The cell phone data. I mean, there's a definite line, right?"

"And don't you think the police are looking into that?"

"I . . . I guess. I just . . . ."

Noah smiled and pointed toward the hallway. The two walked in silence as they headed to the exit. Noah's feet landed with a heavy thud while Kaylee's scuffed and dragged. They paused beside the digital bulletin board.

The screen cycled through images and details of Emily, Hailey, Allison, and Paige. The police information page now showed pictures of both Detective Lane and Principal Torres as primary points of contact. Kaylee shot Noah a look of disapproval, and they both turned away and headed to the main exit.

Once outside, the cool, damp afternoon breeze welcomed them. Kaylee stopped and took a deep, cleansing breath. Being a Friday, the students with cars seemed to be in an extra rush to leave school. The parking lot had already thinned out. Kaylee caught a glimpse of several familiar faces, including Brittney, as they sped away. She couldn't help but wonder which one of them would be next. Was their circle of friends from the video being targeted? Why this school? Her thoughts were broken by the sight of her mother's Mercedes SUV arriving.

"Why's my mom here?" Kaylee asked. She grabbed her phone and noticed a string of text messages from her mom. Kaylee hadn't looked at her phone since before the start of the assembly. "Shit."

"What?" Noah asked.

"My mom's picking me up." She pointed to the curb. "See?"

"Oh. Okay. Well, see you on the video chat tonight?"

"Sure."

Kaylee slowly made her way to the curb while Noah headed toward his car. When Kaylee reached the SUV, she noticed her mom inside crying. Kaylee opened the door and asked, "What's going on?"

Lesley stared at the cell phone in her hands and said, "I just got off the phone with Detective Lane. They found Hailey's bike."

"Where?" Kaylee felt her throat tighten. She couldn't help but wonder if the location would fall within the area of the cell phone data. "Mom?"

Lesley turned to face her daughter and said, "Near Cliff Pond."

"Cliff Pond?" Kaylee frowned. The kettle pond was part of Nickerson State Park, southeast of town and far away from the line she'd drawn to connect the phone signals. "Was it . . . okay? Any damage?"

"Some hiker found it on the ground in the woods. Detective Lane said they were still studying it. What's that department? Forensics?" Lesley grabbed a tissue from the small packet resting beside her and wiped her cheeks dry. "Do you think her body could . . . could be in the pond?"

Kaylee didn't know what to say. She looked around the parking lot, searching for Noah. His Camaro sat parked far in a corner, and Kaylee couldn't tell if he was in the car or not. She then glanced back to the side of the building to see if she could see Jade near the bike rack. It was impossible to tell if her e-bike was still there. Kaylee decided she'd text both later. She hopped into the front seat and took her mother's hand.

"I'm sure she's okay, Mom. We . . . we can't give up hope."

"I got so worried when you didn't text me back." Lesley anxiously peered out the windows. "I'm just glad you're safe. My gut tells me this is far from over."

Jade stared at her reflection in the bathroom mirror. She was the only one in the restroom since the other students had already left the school. The silence felt unsettling. Jade turned on the faucet, scooped up a handful of water, and splashed it against her face. All she could think about was the image of Paige's necklace and the spots of deep red blood covering the shimmering pearls. She took a few slow breaths to try and calm herself. The buzz of her phone caused her to become annoyed. "Now what?"

Jade dried her hands across her skirt and retrieved her phone. The lock screen showed she had an eChat message waiting for her. "What now, Noah?" Jade grabbed some paper towels and wiped the water from her face. She went to the app, only to find a text from Dr. Ed. Not recognizing the name, Jade sighed and slid her finger across the blood-red pixilated message.

Knock Knock

"Who the hell is this?" Jade whispered. She went to Dr. Ed's profile but found no detailed information. Another secret text appeared.

Do you want to look like Brittney?

Jade laughed loudly and rolled her eyes. She tapped a coral-painted fingernail against the screen as she pondered wasting her time replying, and if so, what should she say. A smile spread across her face as she wrote back to Dr. Ed.

Hell NO!

Jade went to click on Dr. Ed's profile so she could block him, but the entire chat session vanished. She sighed and said, "I really hate this stupid app."

The message helped break the angst she felt. Jade took a deep breath, smiled, and left the bathroom. After grabbing a fresh piece of gum, she went outside and quickly made her way to the side of the building.

Jade unlocked her electric bike, hopped on the seat, and roared out of the school parking lot. Her eyes teared up from the wind racing past her face. Her brother's bike was heavy but maneuvered well. Today's gusty weather, however, posed a challenge. Jade struggled to keep a straight line as she made her way along Route 6A. She stopped when she reached the intersection with Main Street. A burgundy-metallic Cadillac SUV pulled up beside her, and the front passenger window slowly lowered.

"Shouldn't you be wearing a helmet?"

Jade knew the voice. She turned and glared at Principal Torres staring at her from behind the driver's seat.

"Shouldn't you still be at school?" Jade cocked an eyebrow and frowned. "I thought you worked late."

"I have an appointment." Principal Torres raised her window and took a left turn onto Main Street.

Usually, Jade would turn right to head home. Instead, she decided to follow the principal. Traffic was light, and Jade could have easily passed by the principal's vehicle, but she opted to keep a safe distance back. After a few blocks, Main Street became Rock Harbor Road. Jade remembered Noah saying that Principal Torres lived somewhere nearby. Was she heading home? What appointment could she have? Jade chuckled as she realized she was suddenly playing detective, just like Kaylee.

The Cadillac raced away, speeding across the Route 6 overpass. Jade struggled to keep pace. Soon, a few other cars passed her by, and she lost track of the principal's SUV.

Jade came to a stop at the intersection across from the bay. Boats of various sizes dotted the white-cap-filled ocean, their horns occasionally blaring. The wind whipping off the water was even worse here. She sighed and said, "This is stupid. Do Kaylee and Noah really spend all their time doing this detective shit?" Her phone buzzed. "Now what?"

Jade frowned at the eChat notification. She unlocked her phone and went to the app. The encrypted message came from Dr. Ed.

Do you like who you see in the mirror?

Jade's hand trembled with anger as she watched the message fade away. She wasn't big on playing games. Jade quickly responded.

FU
Back off or I'm calling the cops

After a few seconds, the screen displayed a message.

CHAT DELETED

Jade clicked on Dr. Ed's profile. The next screen said the account didn't exist. She glared at the screen and asked, "Did you just block me?" Jade shoved the phone into her pocket and muttered, "Asshole."

The intersection around her was empty. Jade did a quick U-turn and made her way back to the corner of Main Street and Route 6A. She continued forward and began her usual route home. The traffic thinned out considerably, and soon she found herself alone on the narrow road.

The chat with Dr. Ed bothered her. Who was this guy? Was it even a guy? Could it have been Torres? Noah? Was it the guy that Paige talked about? Or was it just some random troll? Jade's heart sank as she realized Dr. Ed could be the connection.

The e-bike's gauge showed the battery charge at 38%. Jade wondered if she had enough to get to Kaylee's house so she could tell her about Dr. Ed. Or should she go see Noah? Noah knew the most about eChat. Maybe he could figure out how to track down this Dr. Ed.

As Jade debated what to do, a vehicle slammed into the back of her bike. She tried to hold onto the handlebar, but the force of the impact was so violent that she soon found herself and her e-bike sailing through the air. Jade screamed. Panic swept through her body, her arms flailing wildly as they desperately searched for something – anything – to grab. She frantically tried to grip the bike, locking her knees against the frame. The Super73 belonged to her brother and was all she had left of him. She couldn't let go. But the violent impact was beyond her control, and the forces of gravity tore her from her beloved bike. Suddenly everything went into slow motion. Jade looked around, trying to see who'd hit her. The images became a blur – the sky, the ground, the trees, the road. Woven within her confusion, Jade could hear the squeal of a set of tires and the roar of an engine fading in the distance. Her terror and fright ended when her body smashed into a nearby tree. Blood spewed from Jade's mouth, and her world went dark.

Ten

Curfew

Kaylee flopped in her bed and stared at the television atop the walnut dresser in her bedroom. Her mother still banned Kaylee from using her phone, iPad, and laptop, leaving the TV as her only source of entertainment in her room. She grabbed the remote and flipped through the channels, but nothing she saw interested her until CNN Headline News appeared. Kaylee was stunned to see a reporter standing in front of Engel Academy.

"When did we go national?" Kaylee wondered aloud. An image of Hailey appeared on the screen. The picture was the same one displayed on the digital bulletin board at school. A lump formed in Kaylee's throat. "I know you're still alive. I'm. . . I'm going to find you."

A half-empty bag of Oreo cookies sat tucked beneath the blanket. Kaylee tossed one into her mouth, rolled from her bed, and walked to her window. The sun sat low on the horizon, casting a warm orange glow across the sky. Kaylee glanced at the nearby clock – 7:25 p.m. A cracking branch outside caused her to flinch. The wind had been vicious since she got home from school. Between the curfew and her lack of electronics, Kaylee suddenly found herself feeling trapped. She cupped her hands and pressed her face to the glass. The street looked like a ghost town. Kaylee turned on a lamp and lowered the shade. She looked around her messy room and frowned.

A pair of black sneakers, the gray socks still jammed inside them, rested outside her closet door. Kaylee grabbed them, opened the door, and dropped to her knees. Four more pairs of black sneakers covered the floor. She sighed as she collected them and organized them on the nearby shoe rack. A pair of pink and white sneakers, hidden in the shadows at the far end of the rack, caught her eye. Their bright color sparkled like a diamond lost in a darkened mine. Hailey had bought them for her last Christmas as a gift. Kaylee grabbed one and studied the pristine white stitching down the side. She'd never worn them, despite her sister's constant desire for her to brighten her wardrobe. The memory of Hailey only brought her pain. Kaylee shoved the shoe back into the corner.

Kaylee stood up, turned, and headed back to her bed. As she passed her window, the glass rang with two loud knocks. Kaylee jumped and stared at the shade. The howling wind could be heard whipping through the giant oak tree in front of her house. Kaylee cautiously stepped closer to the window and raised the shade. Her tension vanished at the sight of Noah staring back at her, smiling.

"What are you doing?" Kaylee asked as she unlocked and raised the window. The blustery wind cut across her face. "And how the hell did you get up here?"

"Your bedroom's above the covered porch. It was an easy climb."

Kaylee stuck her head out the window. Noah was crouched on his knees, his jeans using the grippy asphalt shingles to hold him in place. She thought back to the many times she and Hailey had climbed through the window to sit on the porch roof to play. Their antics always drove their parents crazy. But neither she nor Hailey had ever tried to reach the ground.

"Can I come in?" Noah asked.

Kaylee glanced back at the condition of her messy room, sighed, and said, "Sure."

Noah shoved his gangly arms through the open window and landed face-first on the floor. His entrance was far from graceful. Noah groaned as he pulled the rest of his body forward before rolling into a sitting position with his legs crossed. Kaylee closed the window and sat on the floor across from him.

"Why are you here?" Kaylee asked. "It's after curfew."

"I was worried about you. You weren't answering my text messages."

"My mom took all my stuff away. Remember?"

"Still?" Noah leaned closer. "After everything that's happened, you'd think she'd want you to stay connected with everyone."

"Right?" Kaylee leaned back against her bed. "What would you've done if I wasn't here?"

"Oh, I knew you were home."

"How?"

Noah pulled out his phone and smiled. "I can track you. Remember?"

Kaylee smiled and glanced up at the keychain with the Airtag resting next to the television. She said, "We have to get one for you."

"You still wanna keep tabs on me?" Noah grinned a playful smile.

Kaylee felt herself blush and quickly said, "We should all have one. Including Jade. Hey. Have . . . have you heard from her tonight? Did you two do a 7 p.m. video chat?"

"I haven't heard from Jade since we saw her at school. She's ignoring my text messages. She . . . really doesn't like me. Or trust me."

"That's not true. I think she's just, well, I mean, her brother . . . ."

"My uncle killed her brother, not me. Besides, her brother had a gun and was in the middle of a robbery. Is she going to hold this over my head forever?"

"I . . . I always thought Jade felt you should have taken her brother's side and not your uncle's."

"I didn't take any sides, Kaylee. I tried to stay out of it. Jade . . . Jade sees a white cop kill a Black kid, and she doesn't want to hear anything else." Noah shook his head in frustration. He looked at Kaylee and asked, "Do you know my family history?"

"No."

"Aunt Regina is my mom's sister. Her husband died before I was born. He was a cop with the Orleans police. Black. Killed in the line of duty."

Kaylee inched closer to Noah.

"She married Uncle Rick about fifteen years ago," Noah said. "Everyone looks at me weird because I've got a white uncle. Who's a cop. I mean, it's not like I had a choice."

"I don't think anyone judges you for—"

"Of course they do. Look, my uncle's tough. And I get why people think twice after what happened with Jade's family. But he loves my aunt. And my family."

The two sat in silence for several seconds. Kaylee could see the pain on Noah's face. She couldn't begin to imagine what his family life was like. Although he'd been dating Hailey these past few months, Kaylee had never spent any time with Noah's family, and she didn't even know where he lived.

"Have you explained this to Jade?" Kaylee asked.

"I tried. Her mind's made up."

"Well, it doesn't help that your uncle's so intimidating."

"I've told him he needs to smile more."

"Right?"

Kaylee grinned, and Noah smiled and laughed. Noah said, "Thanks for listening."

"Sure. I mean, why wouldn't I?"

"I tried to tell Hailey that story once, and she just cut me off. She said she didn't care about the past."

"It's obviously important to you."

Noah nodded and relaxed his shoulders. He looked around the room, taking time to study the pictures on the walls. He smiled when he noticed the Harry Potter poster. "Did you go? To the park?"

Kaylee looked up at the poster and smiled. "Yes. Have you been?"

"I loved it. It's definitely my favorite theme park."

"Mine too." Kaylee grinned. She let her mind wander, imagining her and Noah park-hopping and enjoying the rides all day and night. Her smile soon faded. "We . . . we all went as a family last summer. That was our first time there since the Harry Potter stuff first opened. That's when I got the poster. It was such a great vacation. Me. Hailey. Mom and . . . my dad."

"Where . . . where is your dad? Hailey never liked to talk

about him."

"My parents are separated. It's been a while now. It was after school started last year."

"I'm sorry."

"Dad travels for work. Mom works seven days a week selling houses. They just . . . fought all the time."

"That must have sucked."

"It did, but, I . . . I still miss having him here." Kaylee felt her eyes well up. "He comes by now and then, but if my mom's here, they just fight."

Noah gently rested his hand on hers. She looked up and smiled. He said, "I'm sure everything will work out."

"Thanks." Kaylee allowed herself to enjoy Noah's sweet touch before slowly pulling her hand away. "So, have you heard anything else from your uncle? You heard they found Hailey's bike over at Cliff Pond."

"No, I didn't. I haven't seen my uncle all day."

"That sort of kills our linear pattern with the phone locations."

"You never know. Maybe other clues will surface." Noah's eyes suddenly widened. "Oh, I didn't tell you."

"What?"

"My uncle's getting frustrated. Like, angry at everyone."

"You? Us?"

"What? No. Well yes. I mean, he's mad at the team doing the investigation. The cell phone data. The blood analysis. The mysterious letters. Forensics. They're making zero progress. Nothing."

"Oh. But you also said yes. He's mad at us?"

"He's. . . mad at you."

"Why me?"

"I mentioned some of the theories we've been tossing around. Like how you drew that line across the map trying to link the phone locations."

"And?"

"He said to stop playing cop."

"Oh." Kaylee lowered her head and sighed. "I'm just trying to help."

"I know. It's okay. He's just, well, he's the boss, you know?"

"Sure." Kaylee forced a smile. "I'm. . . I'm sure the cops will piece it all together." Kaylee allowed her eyes to focus on the contents of her closet. The pink and white sneakers sparkled in the sea of black sneakers and shoes. Her bottom lip quivered, and she added, "They have to."

"They will." Noah studied Kaylee's solemn eyes. "Hey." He reached out and took Kaylee's hands into his. "Are you okay?"

"What?" Kaylee's eyes settled on Noah's hands. His touch felt soft and caring. "Sorry. There are times when it just . . . . I try not to think about it, you know? About how everyone's going missing." Kaylee pulled her hands free from Noah's gentle embrace. "When I get stuck in my room like this, it's all I can think about. How is it all connected? What's the pattern?"

"Me too." Noah leaned back and frowned. "I know I keep saying we're not the target, but, well, it's starting to feel like we are."

"But at school, you said it was all a coincidence."

"That . . . that was to try and calm everyone down. I mean, it all leads back to the video. To us."

Kaylee wanted to make a counterargument but couldn't think of one. She nodded and said, "I . . . I know."

"We're going to be okay, Kaylee."

"I hope so. It's just the three of us."

"No. Seriously. I mean, you and me. *We* will be okay. If that viral video is the reason for all of this, we were on the sidelines. Remember?"

"I . . . I guess." Kaylee closed her eyes and replayed the video of Hailey and the others taunting Emily. She opened her eyes and said, "Does that mean Jade's next? She's the last in the group who directly bullied Emily."

"I hope not. But . . . I haven't heard from Jade since school ended."

The rhythmic thump of footsteps ascending the stairs resonated beyond the bedroom door. Kaylee and Noah both turned and looked in that direction.

"Shit," Kaylee said. "You better go."

Noah stood up, flung the window open, and jumped outside, landing with a thump. He crouched down and poked his head back into the bedroom.

"Did you drive here?" Kaylee asked.

"No."

"Aren't you worried about the curfew?"

"I'm tall enough to pass for an adult." Noah grinned and added, "You worry too much." He shimmied backward until he reached the gutter. Noah stopped and stared at Kaylee.

"What?" Kaylee asked.

"I know I've said this before, but . . . you're. . . so different from your sister."

Kaylee lowered her head and instinctively ran her fingers across her acne-covered cheeks. She then closed and locked the window. Through the pane, Kaylee watched Noah grab the roof's edge and lower himself to the corner post. He gave her a wave before disappearing below the roofline.

A knock on her bedroom door caused Kaylee to jump. She said, "Come in."

The door opened, and her mother took a cautious step inside. Lesley looked around and frowned. "Did I hear you talking to someone? Where's your phone?"

"You tell me. You took all my stuff."

"Then who were you talking to?"

"The TV." Kaylee pointed at the television on the dresser near her mother. "I was saying how there's nothing to watch and how much I wanted my phone and iPad back."

Lesley walked up to Kaylee and put her arm around her. She guided her to the bed, and the two sat down. Kaylee winced at the sound of the bag of cookies being crushed.

"I'm just trying to protect you," Lesley said. "Your friends are–"

"Being taken! Don't you think it's better that we're able to keep in touch? What if something happens to Jade or Noah, and they need my help?"

Lesley shifted uncomfortably on the bed. She frowned and reached beneath the blanket, retrieving the bag of Oreo cookies. "Maybe . . . maybe you're right." Her mother stood up and walked to the bedroom door, taking the cookies with her. "I'm sorry, Kaylee. You're right. I . . . I shouldn't keep you so disconnected from everyone. I'm just trying to protect you."

"I understand. But, me, Jade, and Noah need to watch out for one another."

"Noah's been so good at driving you back and forth to school. I . . . I'm sorry I ever doubted him."

☺☺☹

Noah stood behind the giant oak tree near the curb, staring up at Kaylee's bedroom. From his angle, he couldn't see if her mother had entered. He hoped his actions hadn't gotten Kaylee into any trouble. Noah looked around, surprised by how eerily quiet the streets were. Everyone seemed to be taking the curfew seriously – even the adults.

Noah raised his hoodie to conceal his face, walked past Kaylee's house, and turned right. He kept his head down as he walked, staring at his feet. After walking a couple of blocks, he stopped and looked up. An Orleans Police car was parked against the curb, its engine off. The black and white Ford Interceptor had no police lights on top. Instead, they were integrated into the grille and windshield. The passenger window lowered. Noah sighed and stepped closer.

"Get in the back," Detective Lane said.

Noah got into the cruiser's back seat and slammed the door shut. He stared at his uncle's eyes, glaring at him from the rearview mirror.

"So. Noah. Is Kaylee still playing detective?"

Noah looked down at his knees but didn't respond. He wasn't ready for this discussion. The engine fired to life. Noah's head slammed backward as the car pulled away from the curb. He turned and stared out the window, watching the empty streets and walkways pass by.

"Answer me, Noah."

"I . . . I think she's scared. She's convinced the group's being targeted. I'm guessing her days of snooping around are done." "Good." The cruiser came to a halt at a stop sign. Detective Lane glanced back at his nephew and added, "We don't want anyone else getting hurt, do we?"

Eleven

A Curious Little Lamb

Saturday, May 11th

Kaylee awoke, rolled to her side, and stared at the clock. She was stunned to see it was just after 11 a.m. Ever since Hailey's disappearance, Kaylee found a solid night's sleep to be highly elusive. Most nights, she found herself awake every hour or two, staring at the ceiling, her mind racing with thoughts and fears. What made last night different? Was it Noah's unexpected visit? His gentle touch? Kaylee smiled as she crawled out of bed and grabbed her frayed gray terrycloth bathrobe.

When Kaylee opened her bedroom door, she was surprised to hear voices coming from downstairs. One was definitely her mom's. The other? Kaylee quickly descended the stairs. Her heart sank when she reached the bottom and recognized the gruff voice speaking to her mother. Kaylee slowly entered the living room and stopped at the edge of the faded floral carpet.

"I was about to make your mother go check on you," Detective Lane said.

"What's going on?" Kaylee asked, trying to suppress the terror washing over her.

Her mother was seated on the couch, a box of tissues by her side. Lesley patted the empty cushion beside her. Kaylee's heart began to pound in her chest. She took a seat next to her mom and asked, "Is . . . is it Hailey?"

"No," Detective Lane said.

"It's your friend," Lesley said. "Jade."

"She's missing?" Kaylee stared at the detective. Her mind drifted back to Noah's visit last night when he mentioned he hadn't heard from Jade. "Are you sure?"

"She's. . . not missing, Kaylee," her mother said.

"Jade was involved in a hit-and-run yesterday." Detective Lane stroked his silver beard and knelt beside Kaylee. "I'm sorry to tell you that she didn't make it."

"What?" Kaylee turned and looked at her mother and then again at the detective. "I . . . I don't understand."

"As far as we can tell, she died on impact." Detective Lane briefly put a comforting hand on Kaylee's knee. He stood up and walked to the front door. "She was pronounced dead at the scene."

"Dead?" Kaylee asked. "Jade's. . . dead?" This was the first time the cops had discovered a body. Jade was the last of the group that directly taunted Emily. Was Noah right? Were they spared because they stood on the sidelines? Or was the person behind the disappearances now taking things to another level? Tears welled in her eyes as she imagined Jade riding her e-bike. Kaylee looked up at the detective and asked, "Is . . . is this the same person after everyone else?" Kaylee struggled to keep from crying. "The same one who got my sister?"

"It's too soon to say," Detective Lane said. "But I doubt they're connected. There's nothing in this accident that's even remotely close to the disappearances of the other four."

"You found Hailey's bike. Did the two bikes have similar damage?"

"No." Detective Lane spent a few moments studying his notepad. "Tell me, Kaylee, when did you last see Jade?"

"At school. After the assembly. You were there, remember? It was me, Jade, and Noah. In the hallway."

"You didn't see her after that?"

"What are these questions?" Lesley stood and took a few steps closer to the detective. "Are you trying to accuse my daughter of something?"

"No. Relax, Mrs. Jones. I'm just trying to understand where Jade was before the accident."

"Where did it happen?" Kaylee asked. "When?"

"Not far from her home. We're still trying to narrow down the exact time." Detective Lane crossed his arms and paused for several seconds. "And what about Noah?"

"What about him?" Kaylee asked.

"When did you last see him?"

"Why?" Kaylee's heart stopped. "Is . . . is Noah missing, too?"

"No. But if you two were the last to see Jade, I'd like to know when you last saw my nephew."

Kaylee looked around the room as she struggled to compose herself. A part of her was still in shock that Jade was dead. Her voice quivered as she said, "At . . . at school."

"Are you sure?" Detective Lane asked.

Kaylee nodded and lowered her head. She couldn't look the detective in the eye.

"Your nephew's a nice young man," Lesley said. "He's been taking Kaylee back and forth to school for me."

"Indeed." Detective Lane opened the front door and took one step outside. He turned back and said, "Thanks for the information about Noah. I'll let you know if we find out any more about Jade's accident."

The door slammed loudly upon the detective's abrupt exit, causing Kaylee to jump. Her mother sat beside her and put her arm around her daughter. The two held one another tightly. Kaylee immediately began to sob. She soon found herself wailing, unable to stop the tears from falling. Kaylee never considered Jade a close friend, but her death was far too much for her to handle. The weight of the disappearances had been something she could manage because they came with a glimmer of hope. Jade's death was a complete and total shock.

"It's okay," Lesley said. She kissed her daughter's head. "I'm sure what happened to Jade was unrelated. You heard him say it, Kaylee. This was a hit and run. An accident. Don't cry. Please."

Kaylee took a deep breath and found herself gasping for air. For a brief moment, she feared she might pass out. But soon, her composure returned. Kaylee wiped her tears away and looked into her mother's eyes. "This has to stop, Mom. Everyone's being taken away."

"This is, well, something none of us can prepare for. All I can tell you is it will all be over soon. The police will solve this. I . . . I know they will. But I'm worried about you, Kaylee." Lesley glanced at her watch and frowned. "I'm. . . I'm going to clear my schedule for today."

"Don't you have an open house?"

"I can get someone to cover. I don't want you home alone."

"You shouldn't miss work. I'll be fine. I . . . I just wasn't expecting to hear that about Jade." Kaylee grabbed a tissue and blew her nose. "Maybe Dad could come over?"

"He's in Phoenix."

"Oh." Kaylee snatched a few more tissues from the box and wiped her cheeks dry. "I . . . I could see if Noah could come over. Would . . . would that be okay?"

"Noah? Um, sure. Why not. Are you sure you don't want me to stay?"

"No, Mom. You should go to work."

"What about . . . well, Principal Torres mentioned a grief counselor. Maybe it's time you see one?"

"I don't need counseling. Really. I . . . I can hang with Noah today. We'll be safe here. Together."

"Okay."

Kaylee and her mom made their way back upstairs. Kaylee went into her bedroom and opened the shade. Her posters and faded wallpaper sparked to life, enveloped by the bright sunlight. Kaylee stared at the porch roof just beyond the windowpane. She smiled as she recalled Noah's visit from last night.

"Kaylee?"

Kaylee spun around to see her mom standing in her doorway. Lesley's arms were filled with Kaylee's laptop, personal iPad, and cellphone. Kaylee smiled, ran to her mom, and snatched all of her gear.

"Thanks, Mom!"

"I need to run," Lesley said. "I'll check in with you later."

"Okay."

"Text me if Noah can't spend the day with you."

"Sure."

Kaylee closed her bedroom door, flopped on her bed, and

powered up her phone. She had four new eChat messages from Noah spread across an hour. Kaylee's fingers trembled as she read each one.

U OK?

Have u heard from Jade?

Tell ur mom to give u ur phone back!

Why r u n Jade ignoring me? Please answer

She smiled, flattered by his concern. Her smile soon faded as she realized Noah may not know about Jade. Kaylee wrote back.

Did you hear about Jade?

Kaylee waited patiently to see if Noah would respond quickly. He did.

Yes! WTF
U OK?

Kaylee thought back to her breakdown in her mother's arms. She still couldn't believe Jade was gone and told Noah how she felt.

TBH no

Tears welled in her eyes again. Kaylee went to the bathroom and grabbed a facecloth. After running it beneath some hot water, she pressed it against her swollen eyes. The heat helped to bring a bit of relief. As always, Kaylee caught herself staring at her acne. She sighed and turned off the light. Kaylee returned to her bed, grabbed her phone, and read Noah's message.

Want me to come over?

☺☹☹

Many years ago, Kaylee's dad had converted the basement to a home theater room. A U-shaped black leather sectional faced a seventy-inch wall-mounted LCD television. Tiny Bose speakers, mounted to the drop-ceiling, provided the surround sound. The lack of windows ensured that you could enjoy a film in total darkness no matter the time of day.

A bowl of microwave popcorn with extra butter separated Kaylee and Noah. Kaylee kept a gray cotton blanket bundled up in a ball under her arm. She glanced at Noah to make sure he was still enjoying the movie and not playing with his phone. Kaylee grabbed the remote and hit pause.

"Hey," Noah said, obviously upset she'd stopped the film.

"So, I was right? You didn't think you'd like this."

"I never like old movies. Especially ones from before I was born."

The paused image on the screen showed Dr. Hannibal Lecter standing behind a plexiglass wall staring at the FBI's Clarice Starling.

"Silence of the Lambs is a classic."

"But why did you pick this?"

"I just told you it's a classic."

"Kaylee!" Noah took a sip of his Coke. "This guy abducts women, and the cops can't find him."

"I know, but . . . ." Kaylee shifted nervously, causing the leather cushion beneath her to squeak. "This . . . this might give us clues. Right?"

Noah sighed, shook his head, and stuffed his mouth full of popcorn. A grin slowly spread across his face, and he mumbled, "You seriously need to think about becoming an FBI agent." He washed the rest of his popcorn down with a big gulp of soda. "I think I'm going to start calling you Starling."

Kaylee laughed. "I'm serious, Noah. Think about what he said about the first victim."

"Who?"

"Dr. Lecter. The first victim was different from the others." Kaylee turned and stared at the paused image on the television. "We don't really know much about Emily."

"We never had a chance."

"Maybe we should go talk to him."

"Who?"

"Mr. Mason."

"Emily's dad?" Noah frowned and asked, "Why?"

"Maybe there's some other connection. Maybe Emily had friends we didn't know about."

"The cops have already talked with him. They have Emily's social media details, just like everyone else."

"I guess. But it couldn't hurt to go see him. Right?"

"Maybe." Noah sighed and stared at his feet. "Kaylee, my uncle doesn't like you snooping around. At all. I think we should just let him do his job."

Kaylee and Noah sat in silence. The only light in the room came from the television screen. Dr. Lecter seemed to be staring back at them.

"We never said we were sorry," Kaylee said. "About Emily."

"We didn't do anything."

"I know. It's just that, well, he's at every assembly. Emily barely had a chance at school. Shouldn't we, you know, pay our respects?"

Noah lowered his head for a bit before nodding. He picked up the bowl of popcorn separating him and Kaylee and placed it on his lap. He leaned closer to her and said, "You continue to amaze me."

"What?" Kaylee looked back at Dr. Lecter on the television. "It's the right thing to do."

The overhead fluorescent lights flicked on, blanketing the room in a harsh white light. Kaylee jumped and looked around. A set of footsteps stomped against the wooden stairs that led up to the kitchen.

"Kaylee?" Lesley asked. "Are you down here?" Kaylee's mom stopped a few steps from the bottom and cast a concerned look at Kaylee and Noah. "Am I interrupting?"

"No," Kaylee said. "We're just watching a movie."

Noah leaned back and grabbed a handful of popcorn. He smiled and nodded toward the television. "She said it's a classic."

Lesley stared at the paused image on the screen. "Why on earth are you watching *this*?" She made her way downstairs and over to Kaylee. "Give me the remote."

"Mom! No!"

"It's fine, Mrs. Jones," Noah said. "I kind of like it. I've never seen such an old movie."

"Old?" Lesley frowned. "That movie won a lot of Oscars."

"Why are you home?" Kaylee asked.

Lesley looked at her watch and said, "I told you I'd be home by four." She looked at Noah. "Did you want to stay for dinner?"

"Oh, uh, I guess. As long as I'm home before curfew." Noah turned to Kaylee and asked, "Do we have time to finish the movie?"

"Plenty," Kaylee said. "Mom, can you turn off the light when you leave?"

"Oh, I want to see the rest. It's one of my favorites. Let me go get a glass of wine. I'll be right back."

Kaylee looked at Noah and rolled her eyes. Noah suppressed a laugh as Lesley ran back upstairs. When she was gone, Noah asked, "Why the face?"

"My mom talks non-stop through movies. It's annoying."

"I'll try to shut her up." Noah winked at Kaylee. "So, were you serious about going to see Emily's dad?"

"We have to, Noah."

Kaylee scooped up a handful of popcorn and tossed it in her mouth. Noah grabbed the bowl and stood up.

"What are you doing?" Kaylee asked.

"Switch positions with me. Let me sit next to your mom. It will be easier to keep her quiet."

Kaylee slid to where Noah had been sitting. Noah sat in the middle of the sectional and placed the bowl to his side. The two were now sitting next to one another.

"What time do you want to go?" Noah asked. He reached past Kaylee to grab his Coke, causing his head to come within inches of her face.

"Um, noon?"

"Okay." Noah flashed her a smile and briefly glanced at Kaylee's lips. He then sat back and took a sip of his soda. "I'll pick you up at noon."

"What's at noon?" Lesley asked from the top of the stairs. Now barefoot, she descended to the basement. A wine glass filled with chardonnay dangled from her right hand. "Where are you going?"

"To, uh, to Noah's," Kaylee said. "For lunch."

"Right," Noah said. "Lunch at my place."

"I've got another open house tomorrow. Just be back by curfew." Lesley furrowed her brow as she studied the new seating pattern on the sectional. She sat down beside the popcorn and grabbed the nearby remote. "Noah, just ask if you have any questions about this movie. I've seen it at least half a dozen times."

"Sure thing, Mrs. Jones. But I like to keep quiet when I watch my movies. No distractions. You know?"

"Oh, sure." Lesley smiled, took a sip of wine, and hit the play button. "Me too."

The movie resumed playing, and the music filled the room. Noah turned to Kaylee, leaned close to her ear, and whispered, "Pay close attention, little Starling. You may learn something we can use tomorrow."

Twelve

Knock Knock

Sunday, May 12th

Kaylee paced back and forth in her living room, pausing every few seconds to glance at the clock on the microwave in the kitchen. The time was just past noon. Noah always ran a few minutes late when picking her up for school. After what happened to Jade, she and Noah were the only two left in the group. Kaylee couldn't help but worry something might have happened to him. Her cell phone suddenly buzzed. She looked at the screen, expecting to see a message from Noah. Instead, it was a text from her dad.

> *Hey Pumpkin. Got your message about Jade. How are you?*

Kaylee smiled. Her dad had been quiet lately, and she wasn't even sure if he was in town, in Phoenix, or somewhere else. She sent a quick reply.

> *OK*
> *It's weird*

The rumble of Noah's Camaro reverberated against the front window. Kaylee looked outside just as he pulled into the driveway. She parted the curtains and waved to him just as the phone chimed with another message from her dad.

Are you staying safe? Home with mom?

Kaylee frowned, unsure of how to answer him. Did he even know that her mom was working an open house today? She doubted he did. Her parents rarely spoke these days. Outside, Noah lowered his window, beeped his horn, and waved. Kaylee sent a quick reply to her dad.

Yes chat l8r

The chilly weather struggled to reach 50 degrees. Kaylee grabbed a thick black and white checkered coat and hurried outside to Noah's car. The car window was still down, and she smiled at his goofy grin. *Love Lies* by Khalid and Normani played from the car stereo.

"Hey, Starling," Noah said. "You ready to go play detective?"

"Stop!" Kaylee giggled, went to the passenger's door, and got into the car. "I'm not a detective." She looked over at Noah, grinned, and said, "Yet."

Noah laughed and said, "For the record, Detective Jones, I still think this is a stupid idea. And a complete waste of time."

"I'll note that in my official report." Kaylee's smile faded. "Wait. I just thought of something."

"What?"

"Where does Mr. Mason live? I never thought to—"

"Oh, I looked it up online." Noah waved his phone. "He's not that far from here."

Noah slowly backed out of Kaylee's driveway and began to follow the route on his phone's map. During the drive, they talked about what to ask Mr. Mason and what topics they should avoid. They arrived at their destination fifteen minutes later. The Mason property covered four densely wooded acres. Noah brought the car to a halt at the entrance to the driveway. Due to all the foliage, you could barely see the house from the main road. Half of the shrubs flanking the entrance were dead.

"Well, this looks inviting," Noah said. He turned to Kaylee and asked, "Are you sure about this?"

Kaylee nodded and smiled, although deep down, she felt butterflies forming in her stomach. Noah turned the wheel and slowly entered the driveway. Ruts filled the dirt-lined road, causing the car to shimmy as they drove deep into the property. The winding road finally came to a clearing. Noah hit the brakes and brought his Camaro to a halt.

Despite the expansive size of the Mason property, the home itself was relatively small. A faded white porch ran along the front of a pale blue ranch house. A black wrought-iron bench and two matching rocking chairs were perched at one end of the porch. Several shingles on the home appeared loose and rotted. Shades were lowered in each of the windows. Behind the house sat an oversized detached three-car garage with a boat and trailer parked nearby. There were no vehicles around.

"What a dump," Noah said. "It looks abandoned."

"Do you think he's home?"

"There's only one way to find out." Noah pulled up to the front of the house and parked close to the porch. After killing the engine, he turned to Kaylee and asked, "Are you ready, Starling?"

"Shut up." Kaylee chuckled and got out of the Camaro. She waited for Noah to join her near the porch steps. The warm sun helped to offset the cool temperature. "I'm kind of nervous."

"Hey, this was your idea."

Kaylee took the lead, walked up the three short steps to the porch, and then stopped in front of the door. She took a deep breath and rang the doorbell. Typically, you'd be able to hear the bell from outside the house. But all was silent. Kaylee looked up at Noah, shrugged, and rang the bell again. Still nothing. Before she could do anything, Noah rapped his knuckles twice against the aluminum screen door.

"The bell must be broken," Kaylee said. "Or he's just not home."

The snap of a deadbolt unlocking caused Kaylee to jump. Noah put a comforting hand on her shoulder. A second lock snapped. The front door's hinges squeaked as the door slowly opened. Mr. Mason stood in the shadows. The lowered shades made it hard to see inside the home. He stepped forward, looked down, and slowly pressed his nose against the screen. His pale blue eyes darted between Noah and Kaylee.

"Yes?" Mr. Mason asked.

"Mr. Mason?" Kaylee said. "I'm Kaylee. Kaylee Jones."

Mr. Mason stared at Kaylee but didn't say anything.

"We both go to Engel Academy. We . . . we sort of knew Emily."

"Oh," Mr. Mason said. He looked at Noah and asked, "And you?"

"My name's Noah."

"Jones. You . . . you lost your sister, didn't you?" Mr. Mason said to Kaylee. "I'm so sorry. I . . . I know how you must feel. Not a day goes by that I don't think of Emily." He rubbed his puffy eyes and sighed. "Why are you here?"

"We wanted to find out more about Emily," Kaylee said. "Can we come in?"

Mr. Mason turned and disappeared briefly. When he returned, he wore a black and red flannel jacket. Mr. Mason opened the storm door and stepped down onto the porch, closing the main door behind him. He motioned to the chairs and bench at the far end of the porch. Noah and Kaylee took the bench while Mr. Mason sat down on one of the rocking chairs. The sun's warm rays bathed the front of the house, including the porch seating. The cool air caused all three to cross their arms to keep warm.

"What would you like to know?" Mr. Mason asked.

"Well . . . ." Kaylee's mind went blank. Her heart raced in her chest as she struggled to remember the list of questions they'd crafted on the ride over. "Did . . . did Emily have any friends? Like, here."

"Friends?" Mr. Mason sighed. "No. We . . . we haven't been here that long." He pointed to the boat near the barn. "I've been a fisherman all my life. We were living in New Bedford before moving here."

"Why the change?" Noah asked.

"I . . . I lost my wife. And Emily, her mother."

"Oh my God," Kaylee said. She locked eyes with Noah. When the two had discussed what questions to ask Mr.

Mason, they never anticipated what he might say back. "I'm so sorry. We . . . we had no idea."

"She . . . she died of suicide." Mr. Mason's eyes filled with tears. His face appeared gaunt. The toll of so much loss in such a short amount of time weighed heavily on him. "Needless to say, I couldn't stay in that house anymore. I had an uncle in Truro who always told me to give the outer Cape a try. He said I should start a fresh life. Emily didn't want to move. I . . . I sort of forced that on her. And now my wife and baby girl are gone."

Kaylee suddenly regretted coming here. She could see the torment Emily's dad was going through as he relived the loss of his family. She gently tapped her hand against Noah's thigh. He looked down at her and raised an eyebrow. Mr. Mason was busy staring at his feet, lost in his thoughts. Kaylee nodded toward him.

"We're sorry for your loss," Noah said. "We, uh, never really got to know Emily."

"Emily always struggled to make friends," Mr. Mason said. "She could be bossy and loud." A smile spread across his face. "But she was all bark, no bite. You know?" Mr. Mason wiped his damp cheeks dry. "And she eventually got so excited about the move. I remember her telling me she was reaching out trying to make friends before we relocated."

Kaylee's mind started to replay the video of Jade and the others getting into the fight with Emily. She wondered if he even knew about the recording.

"So, she didn't have any other friends?" Kaylee asked. "Or family?"

"No," Mr. Mason said. "It was just us." He leaned back in the rocker, causing the porch planks to creak. "Why?"

Kaylee scratched her cheeks and looked up to Noah for support. He stared back, saying nothing. She knew he was thinking this was all on her now. Kaylee cleared her throat and said, "We're trying to figure out if there's a connection. Four people are missing now."

"And Jade's dead," Noah added.

"I saw that on the news," Mr. Mason said. "Such an awful accident. So, you think these are all connected? From that video?" He frowned when Noah and Kaylee looked surprised. "Oh, I've seen it. The police showed it to me." He lowered his head and sighed. "But, it wasn't the first time I'd seen it."

Kaylee's eyes widened, and the tension in her body melted. She asked, "No?"

"Emily showed it to me." Mr. Mason sank deep into the rocking chair. "She came home from school that day crying." He looked at Kaylee and then at Noah. "Were you two in that video?"

Kaylee nodded and said, "We were sort of in the background."

"Oh. I don't remember that much about it." Mr. Mason sighed and added, "That . . . that was the last day I saw her alive."

"We . . . we probably should have tried to stop the fight," Noah said.

"People can be so mean," Kaylee said. "It's that stupid SkinDeep app."

"Skin what?" Mr. Mason asked.

"SkinDeep," Noah said. "It's an app that lets you change your appearance."

"I don't think I know that one. I thought Emily said the video was on Instagram."

"It was," Kaylee said. "You don't follow Emily online?"

"Just Facebook. But, she never really posted much there."

"Oh." Kaylee fidgeted as she tried to figure out how to explain things. "Emily, well, a lot of the girls, actually, would use SkinDeep to change their looks. Then she'd post it to Instagram."

"Change her looks?" Mr. Mason asked. "How?"

Kaylee pulled out her phone and launched the *SkinDeep* app. She aimed the camera at Mr. Mason and took his picture. Kaylee stood up and knelt beside his rocking chair, holding the phone, so he could easily see the screen. Kaylee began to fiddle with the controls and instantly made Mr. Mason look twenty years younger.

"That's. . . incredible." Mr. Mason stared at the image of his younger self. He gently took hold of Kaylee's phone. "I . . . I could show you pictures of me from a decade . . . no, more than a decade ago. And they'd look exactly like this."

"You can do lots more," Kaylee said. "You can change facial features, skin tone, even your body shape."

"I had no idea." Mr. Mason looked at Kaylee and asked, "You kids do this all the time? And then show others?"

"It's an annoying obsession," Noah said. "I could never get Hailey to stop playing with that app."

"Emily . . . ." Kaylee pulled her phone from Mr. Mason's grasp. She launched Instagram. "Emily made a lot of changes. Big ones." Kaylee went to Emily's profile and began swiping through some of the posts. She paused on one with Emily sitting in the same rocking chair Mr. Mason was sitting in. Emily looked nothing like the picture the police posted about her disappearance. And she looked nothing like the girl in the video being harassed by Jade and the others. Instead, Emily appeared much thinner. Her acne was gone, and her straight short brown hair was now shoulder-length and wavy. Emily had a more delicate nose, fuller lips, and a tanned complexion.

Mr. Mason appeared dazed as he stared at the screen. "That's. . . that's *my* Emily?"

Kaylee nodded and said, "She kept reaching out to people from our school and friending them on Instagram. So, when she finally arrived, well, she looked nothing like her pics." Kaylee closed the app and pocketed her phone. "She never showed you those?"

"She told me she was making lots of friends online," Mr. Mason said. "Before the move. Even that first weekend we got here, she was so excited to meet everyone." He sighed and stared at Kaylee. "So, is that what the fight was about? That she didn't look like her pictures?"

Noah and Kaylee nodded without saying anything. Mr. Mason started to rock back and forth, causing the porch planks to creak again. The cool breeze blew some dead leaves across his feet. All three sat in silence for several seconds.

"The cops told me they were going through her Instagram account," Mr. Mason said. "I remember them showing me those pictures, but . . . I never understood they were supposed to be Emily. Maybe I was just too upset at the time. Or, maybe I didn't know my daughter as well as I thought."

Kaylee suddenly regretted showing him the pictures. She could see the disappointment on Mr. Mason's face. She thought about how she'd been sneaking around with Noah and not telling her mom. "We all keep secrets from our parents. It's. . . it's not your fault that Emily used SkinDeep and posted those pictures."

"I guess I'll never know," Mr. Mason said.

"Don't say that," Kaylee said, trying to sound upbeat. "I haven't given up on Hailey. You can't give up on Emily." Kaylee smiled briefly, but the pain on Mr. Mason's face persisted. She looked at Noah and tried to remember the list of questions they'd come up with during the car ride. Kaylee turned to Mr. Mason and asked, "Did she talk to you about the friends she made? Maybe mention them by name?"

"Not that I can remember," Mr. Mason said. His eyes widened. "Oh. Wait. There was one girl she was very excited to meet. What was her name?" After several seconds he looked at Kaylee and said, "Brittney. Do you know her?"

Kaylee looked at Noah and then turned to Mr. Mason and said, "I do."

"But I don't remember if Emily ever met her," Mr. Mason said. "Does that help you?"

"Maybe," Noah said. He smiled at Mr. Mason. "We've taken up too much of your time. We should go."

"Oh. Okay." Mr. Mason stood up. "I'm sorry I couldn't remember much more." He looked at Kaylee and smiled. "You asked me the same questions as the detective."

"See that, Starling?" Noah shot Kaylee a grin as he stood up. He turned to Mr. Mason and said, "I keep telling her she's going to end up working for the FBI. She's quite the detective."

"I'm. . . I'm sorry about the fight," Kaylee said. "I'm sorry I didn't stop it."

"That day she came home after the fight . . . ." Mr. Mason sighed and rubbed his weary eyes. "I told Emily she just needed time to make new friends. I told her there were good people out there. I . . . I wish she'd gotten to know you two." For the first time since their arrival, Mr. Mason smiled. "You seem like nice kids."

"The cops will find her," Kaylee said. "And then we can start over." She looked at Noah and added, "Both of us. And get to know Emily."

Mr. Mason nodded and led Noah and Kaylee to the front steps. He said goodbye and went inside, locking both deadbolts behind him.

Noah and Kaylee got into his Camaro. Noah fired up the engine and slowly headed back down the driveway. The car shimmied over the potholes covering the dirt road. He paused when they reached the end and said, "That was a waste."

"Not really," Kaylee said. "We were looking for a connection. I think we found one."

"We did?"

"The video is definitely the connection." Kaylee pulled out her phone and opened Instagram. "It's Brittney." She jumped to Brittney's profile and swiped until she reached the video. "She shot the video. He said Emily knew her."

"No. He said Emily was excited to meet her."

"My gut tells me they met. Why else was Brittney recording the fight?"

Noah chuckled and said, "Because she's a selfish, spoiled senior. It can't be her. Besides, don't you think the cops already questioned her?"

"They did?"

"They had to. I mean, she shot the video. She was there at the fight."

"I . . . I guess." Kaylee sighed and asked, "Do you think that means Brittney's on the list, too? Like us?"

"Gee, I didn't think of that."

"Maybe there were others standing behind us or in the background when the fight happened. I wonder who else Emily knew." Kaylee went to Emily's profile and then looked at her list of Followers. Scrolling through the profile names, she quickly found Jade and the others that had gone missing. Kaylee recognized many of the other profiles. "Emily's Instagram account looks like she connected with dozens of students."

"I guess we have a lot more detective work to do, Starling. How about we grab some lunch first?"

"Sure."

Noah pulled out onto the main road, and the car roared away. They stopped at a local deli and got some meatball subs and Cokes. They took them back to Noah's house. His parents weren't home, and they ate lunch in the living room while playing X-Box. When done, Noah brought Kaylee back to her home. Her mom's SUV was in the driveway.

"I had a fun afternoon," Kaylee said.

The front door of Kaylee's house opened, and her mother stepped out onto the porch. Lesley waved toward the car.

"I should go." Kaylee opened her door and looked back at Noah. "See you tomorrow morning for school?"

"Uber Noah will be here on time."

"Or a few minutes late."

Kaylee walked to the front porch while Noah backed out of the driveway and sped off around the corner. She unzipped her jacket as she approached her mom.

"Did you have a nice lunch?" Lesley asked. She licked her thumb and wiped the stain on Kaylee's sweatshirt. "Is that tomato sauce?" She sighed. "It's so tough to get out. I'm starting laundry soon. Go upstairs and take that off so I can clean it."

"Okay."

Kaylee followed her mom into the house. When she got upstairs, she flopped on her bed and removed her sneakers. Her phone buzzed, showing a new eChat notification. Kaylee unlocked her phone and went to the app, expecting to see a message from Noah. Her smile faded when she saw the text came from someone she didn't know – a profile called Dr. Ed. Kaylee slid her finger across the blood-red pixilated message.

Knock Knock

Kaylee watched the encrypted message fade away. She pulled up the sender's profile, but it was marked as private. As she debated what to do next, a second text appeared.

Do you like who you see in the mirror?

Kaylee frowned and instinctively ran her fingers across her

acne-covered cheek. Before she could respond, the screen went blank and displayed a message.

CHAT DELETED

The letters slowly faded, leaving only a solid white screen beneath the eChat controls. Kaylee tried to go back to Dr. Ed's profile, but it was gone. A pit formed in her stomach. She knew Noah was still driving, so she called him. Noah picked up on the third ring.

"Hey, Starling," Noah said. "Miss me already?"

"Hey. So, I just got a weird text. On eChat."

"Weird how?"

"Someone I never heard of. It's the first time someone outside of our group's texted me on there."

"Probably just some troll."

"But when I tried to look him up, the account was gone."

"That's the only downside to eChat. Everything's so encrypted and private that you can get spam and trolls without any proof. I wouldn't worry about it." Noah paused for a few seconds and added, "Unless you hear from him again."

Thirteen

Doctor Who?

Monday, May 13th

Kaylee sat on her front porch, waiting for Noah to arrive to bring her to school. The temperature sat below 50 degrees, but the wind was nonexistent. She closed her eyes and replayed the weekend's events, from their visit with Mr. Mason to the bizarre eChat messages from Dr. Ed. Kaylee never heard from the troll again and, deep down, hoped Noah was right about him. Her mind immediately drifted back to Emily.

Kaylee unlocked her phone and went to her Notes app. She'd spent last night making a list of everyone from her school whom Emily had friended on Instagram. The final tally, excluding the group from the video, ended up being 41 students. Would any of them be targeted? Kaylee wondered if she should warn them that they might be next. Or were she and Noah next in line? She didn't know what to make of Brittney's possible role. Her head ached as she weighed all the possibilities. The rumble of Noah's Camaro broke her concentration.

Noah pulled into the driveway, and the morning sun reflected off the car's windshield. The sports coupe appeared freshly washed, and the tires shined a deep oily black. He lowered the window, stuck his head out, and smiled.

Kaylee glanced over her shoulder to see her mom peering through the living room window. She waved to her, stood up, and headed to the driveway.

Noah leaned further out the window and said, "Hey there–"

"Don't Starling me," Kaylee said with a scowl. She crossed in front of his car and opened the passenger door. "It's getting old."

"Okay . . . Detective."

Noah burst out laughing. Kaylee's frown quickly faded, and she soon found herself chuckling. Once she was buckled into her seat, Noah backed out of the driveway and headed off toward the school.

"How was the rest of your night?" Kaylee asked. "I never heard from you after we talked on the phone."

"My uncle came over for dinner."

"Oh?"

"He stayed pretty late."

"Did you get good intel?"

Noah nodded and said, "And I didn't even have to hide and listen in this time. But . . . ."

"What? Is it bad news?"

"Forensics couldn't get anything off of Jade's bike. They were expecting to find paint from the vehicle that hit her."

"So, what does that mean?"

"Now he's starting to think it's just an accident. Or maybe Jade just lost control."

"That's bullshit. Jade was great on that bike."

"I told him that. But he said that there wasn't much to go on without any witnesses."

"My gut tells me it's connected to the others."

They soon arrived at school and, once inside, headed off in different directions. Kaylee found it impossible to stay focused during her morning classes. Whenever she saw someone from Emily's list of Instagram friends, Kaylee would try to get up the courage to talk to them. But every time, she would suddenly get cold feet. Kaylee lost track of how many times she walked up to someone and then walked away without saying anything. Deep down, Kaylee couldn't escape the feeling that Jade's death wasn't an accident. That their tiny group was being targeted. The list she'd created suddenly felt pointless.

When her final morning class ended, Kaylee pushed her way past her classmates to get to the hallway. The more she thought about the list, the more doubts washed over her. Everyone who vanished so far had been in the video. Were others really at risk? If so, how come none had been targeted? Kaylee stopped, moved to the side of the hallway, and watched everyone pass by. She sighed and shook her head. Deep down, she knew it had to be the video. That meant either her or Noah would be next. Kaylee kept her head hung low as she stepped back into the sea of students. As she maneuvered through two tall seniors, she accidentally plowed right into someone.

"You better watch where you're going," Rat said.

Kaylee looked up to see Rat holding a wrench. Not just any wrench, but the one he'd held when they broke into his room in the basement. Rat smiled a twisted grin, allowing saliva to drip from his overbite. Kaylee tried to apologize but found she couldn't speak. She walked around him and continued down the hallway.

The cafeteria, located downstairs, felt a mile away. Kaylee increased her pace and entered the stairwell. Her heart froze as Principal Torres rose from the lower level. The principal's ink-black hair shimmered like liquid from the overhead lights. Their eyes locked, stopping Kaylee in her tracks.

"Slow it down, Miss Jones," the principal said.

Just as she did with Rat, Kaylee said nothing and started to walk around the principal.

"Stop," Principal Torres said.

Kaylee obeyed and immediately became motionless. The principal grabbed her by the elbow and led her to the corner. Kaylee watched as other students slowly walked by and stared at the two of them.

"You seem upset." Principal Torres slowly released her grip. "What's wrong?"

"It's. . . it's nothing."

"Have you been to the counselor?"

"What? No. I'm. . . I'm fine."

"I'm losing too many students."

Kaylee stared at the principal. Principal Torres always

spoke in such a flat, unemotional tone. Kaylee couldn't tell if her words were meant as a warning or an expression of disappointment.

"I'm sorry about Jade," the principal said. "I always told her to wear a helmet." Principal Torres adjusted her bun and stepped aside. "Go on. And watch yourself."

Kaylee nodded. She headed downstairs and didn't bother to look back at the principal. The main floor was twice as busy as the second, and the eyes of the other students seemed to watch her like vultures studying their prey. She rushed past the digital bulletin board as Hailey's picture appeared on the screen. Kaylee suddenly envisioned her face on that board, followed by Noah's.

Judgment, fear, and guilt piled on her shoulders, weighing her down and slowing her movement. The chattering voices became an incoherent blur. Kaylee quickly made her way toward the cafeteria. As she turned the corner, she slammed into another person. Kaylee looked up to see Noah grinning.

"What's going on?" Noah's smile soon faded as he noticed the anxiety chiseled into her face. "Are you okay?"

"Not really."

Noah looked around the packed hallway. He put his arm around Kaylee and led her to the nearest classroom. He stuck his head inside to find the room empty. Noah grabbed Kaylee's hand and pulled her into the room.

"What is it?" Noah asked.

Kaylee suddenly burst into tears. The outpouring of emotion took her by complete surprise. She covered her face and sobbed. Noah put his arms around her and gently hugged her. Kaylee pulled him close, buried her face against his chest, and continued to cry.

"I'm sorry," Kaylee said.

"It's okay. Let it out." Noah swayed back and forth, holding Kaylee's head. A full 30 seconds passed before she finally calmed down. When she looked up at him, he asked, "Better?"

Kaylee nodded, let go of Noah, and wiped her eyes. Noah had moved them far enough into the room so that people in the hallway couldn't see them. She sighed and said, "I . . . I don't know where that came from."

"Did something happen?"

"No. Well . . . . I just . . . ." Kaylee took a deep breath. As she exhaled, she felt the stress drain from her body. "I ran into Rat and Torres. And I walked past the monitor showing Hailey and the others. I started thinking that one of us would be next." She shook her head and sighed. "Do you think I had a panic attack?"

"All I know is it's long overdue."

"What is?"

"This." Noah used his thumb to wipe Kaylee's face dry. "You've been a rock since the beginning. You lost your sister. Then Allison. And Paige. Now Jade's dead. And the whole time, you've been so focused on figuring out who's behind it all. It's amazing how strong you are."

"Oh, well, you missed my breakdown when I found out about Jade."

"What? When?"

"Your uncle came to tell us." Kaylee nodded and wiped another tear from her face. "He told me she was dead, and I . . . I just lost it."

"We're all on edge. You. Me. This whole school." Noah smiled and said, "Don't be afraid to vent."

Kaylee took a small step back and used the cuff of her blouse to wipe the rest of her tears away. She looked up at Noah and said, "I just want this nightmare to end." Kaylee gazed at the nearby doorway. She couldn't see the other students, but she could hear them. "I don't know who I can trust anymore."

"You can trust me."

"You're the only one." Kaylee smiled as she gazed into Noah's warm eyes. He was so much taller than her. She suddenly felt vulnerable but also safe, having him so close. Kaylee put her hand on his chest and said, "Noah, I—"

"What are you two doing in here?" Principal Torres's voice boomed as she walked into the classroom, her pink heels clacking against the floor. She squinted and adjusted the bobby pins in her bun. "Are you looking to get detention?"

Noah pulled Kaylee's hand away and said, "No, ma'am."

Kaylee didn't respond. Instead, she lowered her head and

followed Noah out into the hallway. Neither acknowledged the principal. She glanced back to see Principal Torres standing in the classroom doorway, arms crossed, staring at them. Kaylee looked up at Noah and said, "She freaks me out."

"Ignore her. You hungry?"

"Starving. But, let me use the restroom first."

Kaylee went into the bathroom and found Brittney standing at the sink, brushing her hair. Autumn and Summer stood silently near the exit. Kaylee and Brittney locked eyes in the mirror but didn't exchange words. Kaylee went to the furthest stall, closed the door behind her, and snapped the latch to secure the door. After several seconds, Brittney and the twins left the bathroom.

Before she could sit down, Kaylee's phone buzzed with a notification. She checked the lock screen to see she had a new eChat message waiting for her. Kaylee went to the app to find a text from Noah.

I'm standing guard outside...Starling

Kaylee felt herself blush. Her fingers froze as she tried to figure out a cute response. She couldn't deny her growing feelings for Noah. What could she write that was playful but also safe? The phone chimed, and another message appeared. A sense of dread washed over Kaylee when she saw it came from Dr. Ed.

Do you like who you see in the mirror?

"Who are you?" Kaylee whispered. She decided to ask him.

Who RU?

Dr. Ed responded. Kaylee stared at the blood-red pixilated message before slowly running her finger across the text bubble.

Do you want to look like Brittney?

Kaylee opened the stall door and peered into the bathroom to confirm Brittney was no longer there. She found it a bit of a coincidence that Dr. Ed texted her after Brittney left. Could Dr. Ed be Brittney? Kaylee decided to play along and sent a quick reply.

R u a plastic surgeon?

Kaylee's fingers trembled as she revealed Dr. Ed's response.

I can change your life
Let me help you

Kaylee surprised herself by how quickly she responded.

How?

Several seconds passed. Kaylee stared at the blank white screen. The app showed their chat was still active, and Dr. Ed hadn't deleted it or blocked her. Soon, two pixilated messages appeared.

Meet me
I can show you

"Meet me?" Kaylee watched the message vanish. "Oh my God."

Kaylee left the stall, ran to the exit, and raced into the hallway. Noah was standing across from the bathroom door, staring into his phone. He looked up and smiled.

"He's back," Kaylee said. She rushed over to Noah. "Or maybe her?"

"Who?"

"Dr. Ed. The troll from last night. I just got a bunch of text messages on eChat. He's behind the abductions. I know it!"

Kaylee held up her phone to show Noah the chat thread with Dr. Ed. The screen showed one line of unencrypted text.

CHAT DELETED

"Shit." Kaylee frantically tried to find Dr. Ed's profile, but there was no history of their chat. "This thing is way too private!" She sighed and lowered her phone. "I don't think Dr. Ed's a troll, Noah."

"What did he want?"

"He said he could make me as pretty as Brittney."

"How?"

"He said I'd have to meet him." Kaylee's pulse raced with excitement. "Don't you see, Noah? He's asking me to meet in private. I bet he did this with Hailey and the others. Remember Paige told Jade she met some troll on eChat?"

"That's right. But, did Hailey ever mention him?"

"No."

"What about Allison?"

"No, but . . . ." Kaylee's excitement faded. She lowered her head and sighed. "You think I'm being stupid."

Noah gently took hold of Kaylee's chin and made her look up at him. He said, "Of course not. What's his profile?"

"I . . . I don't know. The entire chat's gone. Can I search for him?"

Noah nodded. He grabbed Kaylee's phone and did a general search for profiles containing "Dr. Ed." A lengthy list of results appeared and included anyone with that series of letters in the account name, profile name, or any other field. He handed the phone to Kaylee.

"Shit." Kaylee frowned as she began to scroll through the results. "That list goes on forever."

"He probably has his profile locked as private, anyway," Noah said. "If he does, it won't show up on the search. It was worth a try." Noah paused and scratched his chin. "The next time he texts you, just block him. But you have to do it before he erases the chat."

"No. No way."

"Why not?"

"I want to see where this leads. The text came right after Brittney saw me and left the bathroom. So, maybe–"

"Kaylee . . . ." Noah groaned and shook his head.

"What?"

"You're . . . relentless." Noah smiled and added, "Let me know if you hear back."

"Of course."

"And . . . don't do anything stupid."

Kaylee spent the rest of the school day barely paying attention to her teachers. The rest of her focus remained on her phone, tucked in her skirt pocket. School policy required all phones to be off while in class, but Kaylee decided to keep hers on vibrate. Every little buzz sent a chill down her spine. She could never check her phone during class, but she would immediately look to see if Dr. Ed had contacted her once class ended.

Brittney and Kaylee crossed paths a few more times. As always, Brittney barely acknowledged Kaylee. Kaylee began to doubt Brittney could be Dr. Ed. The timing of the text in the bathroom had to be a coincidence. Meaning Dr. Ed had to be someone else. But who? The end of the school day came, and, much to Kaylee's disappointment, she never heard from Dr. Ed again.

As Kaylee left the school, she walked past Principal Torres. Kaylee could feel the principal's piercing eyes judging her. The panic attack from earlier, along with the messages from Dr. Ed, had Kaylee's nerves thoroughly wound. Fear no longer filled her body. She clenched her fists and spun around. Kaylee walked up to Principal Torres and asked, "Why are you so mean to us?"

"Excuse me?" Principal Torres appeared taken aback.

"You . . . you treat us all like . . . criminals!"

"I don't think I like your tone, Miss Jones."

"Well, the feeling's mutual!"

Kaylee turned and hurried to the exit. The principal did not call out or pursue her. She found Noah waiting for her just outside the main entrance. His smile faded as she got closer.

"Hey," Noah said. "Are you okay?"

"No. Torres." Kaylee turned and looked back through the glass doors. Principal Torres stood motionless behind the glass, her eyes glued to Kaylee. "I kind of told her off."

"You what?" Noah's eyes widened, and he started to laugh. "Why?"

"I'm just sick of her attitude." Kaylee briefly closed her eyes and shook her head. "I . . . I want to check something. I'm sure your uncle already looked, but . . . . Let's take the long way."

Kaylee quickly raced down the front steps.

"Long way?" Noah frowned as he followed Kaylee. "What long way?"

Kaylee didn't answer. All students were required to park along the front or left side of the building. Once Kaylee got to the bottom of the stairs, she turned and went in the opposite direction. She led Noah around the far side of the school, past the bike racks. Multiple signs indicated this section of the parking lot was reserved for the faculty and visitors.

"Are we walking around the entire building?" Noah asked. "What are you looking for?"

Kaylee, filled with confidence, marched along the cars facing the school. The principal, vice-principal, and a few others had parking spots that flanked the side entrance to the building. The lot, lined with towering pine trees, ran to the sporting fields behind Engel Academy, adjacent to the main gym. Kaylee stopped when she got to the backside of Principal Torres's Cadillac.

"What are you going to do?" Noah asked. He grinned and added, "Key her car?"

"No." Kaylee looked up at the second-floor windows. They were the only ones that overlooked this part of the parking lot. Thankfully, nobody was watching them. Her eyes settled on a camera perched high above the keypad-secured side entrance. She shrugged, walked to the front of the Caddy, and stopped. Kaylee's eyes widened. She looked at Noah and said, "I knew it."

Noah walked to the front of the SUV and said, "Shit."

Just below the driver's side headlight assembly, the bumper was dented and scraped. The dent was minor. Most of the damage appeared cosmetic. Multiple black streaks ran up and down the bumper, and some gouged the paint.

Noah knelt down and ran his fingers across the damage. He said, "It looks like someone tried to wash off most of it." He looked at Kaylee and asked, "You think this is from Jade's bike?"

"This can't be a coincidence." Kaylee took a picture of the bumper and forwarded it to Noah's phone. "You need to show this to your uncle. He's got to question Torres about Jade. Or did he?"

"I can't remember. I . . . I don't think so." Noah stood up and glanced at the security camera pointed at them. He said, "We should go."

They remained silent as they walked back to Noah's car on the opposite side of the building. As they drove away from the school, they began to spitball different theories. If Torres ran Jade off the road, why would she show up at work with her damaged car? Could the principal be Dr. Ed? What if Rat was behind it all and had borrowed the Caddy? Has Detective Lane questioned Rat and Torres about their whereabouts when Jade was killed?

They had more questions than answers by the time they reached Kaylee's house. Dua Lipa's *New Rules* played quietly from the car stereo as Noah pulled into the driveway. He parked the car and then killed the music and the engine.

"You're going to show your uncle the pic, right?" Kaylee asked.

"Sure."

"And tell him about Dr. Ed?"

"Well, there's not that much to tell him. You need to get screenshots next time."

"Oh! That's a good idea. But, those messages fade so fast." Kaylee stared out the window, lost in her thoughts. "Can't they search all the profiles named Dr. Ed?"

"We did that. They'll see the same thing." Noah sighed and lowered his head. "My uncle's just going to tell us to stop playing cops."

Kaylee pulled out her phone and frowned when she saw the lack of notifications on the lock screen. She said, "What if he never contacts me again?"

"Did you say anything to scare him off?"

"No. No, I . . . I never answered him." Kaylee shoved her phone into her pocket, opened the door, and exited the vehicle. "Let me know what your uncle says."

"I will."

"Oh, and Noah . . . ." Kaylee felt her stomach churn slightly. She leaned into the car and said, "Thanks for today. In . . . in the classroom. When I lost it."

Noah grinned, leaned toward her, and said, "Anytime."

Kaylee smiled, closed the door, and took a few steps backward. The Camaro's engine roared to life. Noah backed the car out of the driveway and gave Kaylee a quick wave before driving away. The tires squealed as he turned the corner and disappeared.

Confidence filled Kaylee as she made her way up the walkway. She paused to look up at her bedroom window. A smile spread across her face as she remembered the night Noah climbed the porch to check on her. So what if they were the last two? They had the trackers. They had a possible lead with this Dr. Ed person. The fears that had consumed her earlier suddenly felt premature. Kaylee ran up the front stairs and began to fumble for her house keys. The phone in her pocket buzzed. She retrieved it and stared at the screen's eChat notification. Kaylee went to the app to discover that the blood-red pixilated bubble waiting for her came from Dr. Ed.

Do you like who you see in the mirror?

Kaylee took a deep breath to calm herself as she sent her reply.

Who ru?

Kaylee stared at the screen and waited for Dr. Ed's reply. A message appeared.

CHAT DELETED

The alert soon faded, leaving eChat's blank white screen behind. Kaylee sighed and said, "Shit. I forgot to get screenshots." The driveway and streets were empty of cars. The wind, gusting at over 20 mph, caused the air to feel rather cold. Kaylee grabbed her keys and alternated her gaze between the Airtag and the eChat app. "I know it's you. You've got my sister." Kaylee pocketed her phone and unlocked her front door. She said, "Now I just need to figure out who and where you are.

Fourteen

Brittney

Friday, May 17th

Kaylee stood outside the door to the science lab, her face buried in her phone, studying Hailey's Instagram profile. Her sister somehow had amassed over five thousand followers. Kaylee sighed, knowing she had less than fifty. Noah emerged from the classroom and quietly looked over her shoulder.

"What are you doing?" Noah asked.

"Oh," Kaylee said. "Hey. Um, I was just going through old posts."

"Any luck?"

"No. I told you I've spent every night building a worksheet listing all the Instagram followers that Hailey, Allison, Paige, and Jade had in common."

"I still can't believe you did all that." Noah pointed toward the end of the hallway, and he and Kaylee began to walk. "How many are there?"

"I have no clue. I mean, it's endless. I gave up when I hit a hundred that matched." Kaylee paused and waited for Noah to stop walking. When he looked back, she asked, "Has your uncle done this yet?"

"Done what?"

"Have the cops tried to cross-check their Instagram followers?"

"Probably. I can ask him."

"Thanks." Kaylee resumed walking with Noah by her side. "I keep wondering if this Dr. Ed person is in there somewhere. He has to be."

"If someone's stalking people on Instagram, they wouldn't use a legit account."

"Finsta?" Kaylee shook her head and sighed. "Shit. I didn't think of that."

"The same goes for Dr. Ed on eChat. That's gotta be fake." Noah glanced down at Kaylee and asked, "Have you heard from him today?"

"No. He's been silent since Monday."

They reached the end of the hallway and paused at the stairs. Principal Torres stood there, almost as if she were waiting for them. Kaylee and Noah ignored her and descended to the first floor. When they entered the cafeteria, Kaylee stopped. Brittney walked past her and Noah, lunch tray in tow. Brittney went to the middle of the room and sat with Autumn and Summer.

"What?" Noah asked.

"Remember how Dr. Ed asked me about Brittney?"

"We talked about this. She's not Dr. Ed."

"I have an idea."

Kaylee hurried across the cafeteria and stopped beside Brittney's table. Although the table could easily hold six or eight people, Brittney, Autumn, and Summer were the only three present. The twins glared at Kaylee, their eyes filled with disgust at being interrupted.

"What?" Brittney said, keeping her attention on her lunch.

"I need to talk to you," Kaylee said. She scowled at the twins and said, "Alone."

"Excuse me?" Autumn asked. "This is our table, and we—"

"Now!" Noah said.

Kaylee spun around, surprised to see him standing there. Several students sitting nearby stopped what they were doing and looked over at Noah. The twins looked at Brittney for approval before grabbing their trays and leaving.

"Who are you to talk to me like that?" Brittney asked Noah, her nostrils flaring in anger.

"Like I need your permission," Noah snapped back.

"This won't take long," Kaylee said, her stern tone eerily similar to the principal's. She took a seat beside Brittney and smiled. "I want to know if the rumors are true."

"What rumors?" Brittney refused to look at Kaylee and focused on eating her salad.

"That you had work done. On your face."

"You sound like Allison." Brittney slammed her fork onto the table. "Why do you care?"

"Because Allison, Paige, and my sister are gone. And Jade's dead."

Brittney sighed, pushed her tray away, and stared at Kaylee. The frustration on her face subsided. She said, "I'm sorry about your sister. This . . . this whole serial stalker curfew thing is just . . . scary. But what's that got to do with me?"

"You shot the video."

"The one with Emily?" Brittney glanced at Noah. "What about it?"

"Everyone in the video is being targeted," Kaylee said.

"I know." Brittney glanced around the cafeteria, pausing every now and then to look at different people she knew. "Everyone knows." She faced Kaylee and said, "It's just you and Noah left."

"We know." Kaylee briefly looked up at Noah. "I have a hunch." She leaned closer to Brittney. "I think the stalker is online."

"Online? Like, Instagram?"

"Yes, but I think the link is SkinDeep."

"SkinDeep?" Brittney rolled her eyes and pulled her lunch tray closer. "I don't use that stupid app."

"I know." Kaylee looked up at Noah for support. He smiled and nodded toward Brittney. "Someone contacted me. A doctor. I got the impression he was your plastic surgeon."

"Are you looking for an upgrade?" Brittney looked over at Kaylee and chuckled. "To what? Look like me? As if."

"He said—"

"Just stop." Brittney lowered her voice and glared at Kaylee. "Not that it's any of your business, but my mom paid for me to get plastic surgery last summer. It was minor. Okay?

And it wasn't cheap. Trust me, you couldn't afford it."

Kaylee felt speechless. The anger and pride on Brittney's face signaled she was telling the truth.

"What did you have done?" Noah asked.

"Just some small changes to my nose and cheekbones. They were subtle. The doctor's the best in Boston." Brittney smiled, briefly turned her head, and jutted out her chin. "Didn't you notice?" She stopped posing and darted her eyes between Noah and Kaylee. "After summer break."

"Not really," Noah said.

"I did," Kaylee said. "So, what's your doctor's name? Was it Dr. Ed?"

"Never heard of him. My doctor's a woman. And I'm not telling you her name. Now leave me alone!"

Kaylee stood up and led Noah to the wall on the far side of the cafeteria. They passed the twins, who immediately returned to Brittney's table. The three girls quickly huddled together, whispering and shooting angry glances at Noah and Kaylee.

"Well, that was fun," Noah said. "And kind of pointless."

"Not really," Kaylee said. "I mean, she admitted she had work done. And Dr. Ed said he helped Brittney. But if she's telling the truth – and I kind of believe her – then that means Dr. Ed's not her doctor. So, he must be related to her. He knew she had work done."

"Maybe. But, I mean, the rumors about her plastic surgery started last year when school began. And Brittney loves to brag that she doesn't need SkinDeep. She posts that all over social media. Constantly."

"And?"

"All I'm saying is that this Dr. Ed person is kind of stating the obvious. You said you thought she had surgery, right? So you could go online and troll people by saying you're Brittney's doctor."

"I . . . I guess." Kaylee sighed and lowered her head.

"Take a step back, Kaylee. If Dr. Ed really is following everyone online, he could be anyone."

"But he acted like he knew me. I know all of my Instagram followers. There aren't many."

"Good point." Noah crossed his arms and furrowed his brow. "Maybe it's guilty by association?" The look on Kaylee's face indicated she couldn't understand him. He said, "In the video with Emily, everyone was talking about SkinDeep."

"So?"

"So that means anyone that's seen the video knows Allison and the rest used the app." Noah smiled with pride. "Don't you get it? If Dr. Ed really is behind all of this, and he's targeting everyone in the video, he just has to assume they all use SkinDeep." Noah scratched his chin and added, "Maybe I should become a detective."

"So, what you're saying is Dr. Ed could be anyone and not even be online." Kaylee rubbed her temples and sighed. "We're back to being nowhere."

Kaylee felt her stomach growl. She turned and headed toward the lunch line, with Noah following close behind. They spent their lunch sitting together away from others. Kaylee tried to keep her eyes on Noah but often glanced over at Brittney and the twins. Although they were well out of hearing range, Kaylee knew they were talking about her.

"Ignore them," Noah said.

"She thinks just because she's pretty, she can have an attitude," Kaylee said. She stared at her hamburger and fries and sighed. "They all do."

"At least you got her to admit she had work done. She's been denying that all year. Good job . . . Detective." Noah grinned and suppressed a chuckle. "When I ask my uncle about the Instagram list, I'll also ask him to look into Brittney's doctor. I mean, it couldn't hurt, right?"

"Thanks." Kaylee shoved her plate of half-eaten food away. "Any more news about Jade's accident?"

"No. But he still thinks it's unrelated."

"And he bought the principal's alibi about her SUV?"

"Torres told him someone hit her car at the grocery store while she was inside shopping. They said the material on the bumper isn't a match with Jade's bike."

"Well, even if Torres isn't involved, I don't think Jade's death was an accident." Kaylee snatched a cold french fry from her plate and tossed it into her mouth. "I . . . . I have to believe the others are still alive. I have to."

☺☺☹

Allison pulled her knees closer to her chest and leaned forward, burying her nose into her denim jeans. The stench coming from the pile of trash beneath the stairs made her light-headed, and her finger still had the scars from the diamond ring ripped from her hand. She looked at Paige sitting beside her, cupping her nose with her hands.

"Do you think he'll get the trash today?" Allison asked. "Or turn the heat on? It's so cold in here."

"Who knows." Paige looked at the wooden floor-to-ceiling posts in the middle of the room. Multiple four-inch-long black metal handles were screwed to various sections. There were no windows to allow natural light into the room. A single dim overhead light cast a dull yellow tint across everything. "I just hope he doesn't tie us up again. Every time he comes down here to clean up, he ties us to a post. What does he want?"

"Who knows. He never says anything."

"Or she."

"Right?" Allison scooted to the edge of the bed and looked around the dimly lit room. "We were fools for meeting Dr. Ed."

"I thought it'd be safe at the football field. Wide-open. Daylight."

"Me too."

"I . . . I think Dr. Ed's a woman." Paige instinctively reached for her missing pearl necklace. "When she grabbed me, her arms felt thin."

"Really? I think it's a guy. That voice. I mean, it's disguised, but . . . it's deep. Too deep for a woman."

"You're probably right." Paige moved closer to Allison and allowed her head to rest on her shoulder. "He said he could change my life." She looked around the damp cold room and added, "He was right."

Every movement the girls made caused the red lights on the infrared camera at the top of the stairs to illuminate. Just below the camera hung an old Pioneer car stereo speaker screwed to the wall. The speaker suddenly crackled and then emitted a steady stream of static. A voice began to speak.

"Stay away from the door." There was a mechanical sound to the voice as if it were run through an audio processor. "I'm coming in."

A series of locks snapped open, and the rusty brass doorknob beneath the locks turned. As the door opened, the hinges creaked loudly. A masked figure appeared at the top of the stairs, holding a tray of food. The person looked around but said nothing and lowered the plastic tray onto the top step. The tray had three peanut butter and jelly sandwiches, some napkins, a jug of water, and three paper cups. The stranger left and closed the door.

Allison slid off the bed and went to the top of the stairs to get the tray. She sighed and said, "PB and J again."

"I'm sick of this!" Paige started to cry. "It's the same thing every day! I hate carbs."

"You need to eat, Paige. Seriously."

Allison brought the food downstairs and placed the tray on the bed beside Paige. She sat next to Paige and put her arm around her.

"I'm sorry," Paige said. "I just can't take this."

"It could be worse," Allison said. "The food's not great, but at least he feeds us." She pointed at an open door at the far end of the room. "We've got a bathroom, too. And, well, he hasn't harmed us."

"Not yet." Paige wiped her tears away and sat up. She grabbed one of the sandwiches, stared at the stale-looking bread, and took a nibble. "But you're right. At least we're still alive."

"We have to stay strong." Allison held one of the sandwiches close to her nose. The scent of peanut butter and grape jelly brought welcome relief from the trash pile across the room. Allison took a bite of the sandwich and said, "Don't give up hope."

"I haven't." Paige pointed to a bed on the other side of the room where a figure lay motionless beneath a tattered navy blanket. "But what about her?"

Fifteen

Detective Starling

The branches of the oak tree that stood on the Jones's front lawn sprawled over 60 feet wide. The tangled branches swayed and banged against one another in the dark night's heavy wind. The only lit window in the front of the house was Kaylee's bedroom above the porch.

Kaylee stared at her phone's lock screen. The time read 10:45 p.m. She'd recently updated the image to one of her and Hailey from last Christmas. They both wore matching Santa hats with their names spelled out in silver glitter. Kaylee placed the phone beside her and stretched out on her bed, resting her head on a pillow. She closed her eyes and replayed her discussion with Brittney from lunchtime. Brittney said her plastic surgeon was a woman from Boston. How could Dr. Ed be Brittney's doctor? What if Dr. Ed was nothing more than some creepy troll just feeding off the fears sweeping the Cape? At least she got Brittney to admit she'd had plastic surgery. Noah was right about that.

A smile spread across Kaylee's face as she recalled Noah coming to her defense, bellowing at the twins to leave. Her phone chimed. Kaylee opened her eyes and checked the screen to find a notification from eChat. Kaylee slid back, propped herself against the walnut headboard, and went to the app. Her heart paused when she saw the message waiting for her was from Dr. Ed. Kaylee slid her finger across the blood-red pixilated text bubble.

Knock Knock

Instead of replying, Kaylee lowered her phone. She sighed and said, "What did Noah tell me to do?" Her eyes widened. Their chat was active, so Kaylee clicked on Dr. Ed's profile. There was no information other than the words "Private." His picture, location, number of friends, or anything that might help explain his identity were missing. Kaylee took a screenshot anyway, thinking it may come in handy for the police. She then sent a quick reply.

Hello

Kaylee knew it was a useless response. But she needed time to think. What questions should she ask him? She needed to figure out a way to get him to at least give a hint to his or her true identity. A message from Dr. Ed appeared.

I know you use SkinDeep to change your looks

Kaylee quickly took a screenshot of his message before it disappeared. The eChat app gave the user only a few seconds to read a text before erasing it. Dr. Ed's message gave her pause. Kaylee hated the *SkinDeep* app and rarely used it. Was Noah right? Was Dr. Ed just making assumptions based on what happened in the video? She decided to play along with him.

It's the best!

Kaylee felt empowered as her mind began to construct a plan of attack. She didn't wait for another text from Dr. Ed, and instead, she sent him a few more messages.

Do I know you?
Do you go to my school?
OMG RU Brittney?

A half-empty rolled-up bag of potato chips rested on the

nightstand. Kaylee pried it open and began to much on some chips. Her screen remained silent and blank. She grinned, hoping she'd given Dr. Ed something to think about. An encrypted reply soon appeared.

I can get rid of your acne

Kaylee's heart paused. She dropped her chips and instinctively ran her fingers across her face as anger slowly filled her body. Part of her wanted to lash out at him, but she reminded herself to stay focused. Her goal was to figure out if Dr. Ed was the one who had taken the others. Does Dr. Ed know me? Did he know the others? Kaylee took a deep breath and responded.

Did you help my sister?

The question was a risky one to ask. If Dr. Ed had abducted Hailey, he'd probably block her. Then again, if Dr. Ed was indeed the bad guy in all of this, would he be so stupid as to go after two sisters? Kaylee began to second guess every decision she'd made lately. Dr. Ed's reply appeared. With a trembling finger, Kaylee revealed his response.

I'm here 4 u Kaylee

"Damnit!" Kaylee said, frustrated he wasn't taking the bait. She quickly took a screenshot of his message before it faded. Kaylee munched on a few more chips as she tried to think of what to say. She sighed and said, "I wish Noah were here." Another blood-red text bubble appeared.

Do you like who you see in the mirror?

Kaylee stood up, went to the bathroom mirror, and let her eyes settle on her pock-mocked cheeks. A solitary tear emerged from Kaylee's right eye and traversed down her face, the snaking path dictated by her pimples. "No," she whispered. Kaylee glanced at her phone, the eChat screen now blank. Anger filled her veins. "Who the hell are you?" The phone soon chimed with another text from Dr. Ed.

Interested?

Kaylee went back to her room and collapsed on the bed. Her thoughts of entrapping Dr. Ed vanished, replaced by years of taunting and mockery about her looks. She mumbled, "What the hell am I doing?"

A noise outside the window broke her concentration. Kaylee jumped up and ran to the window, hoping to find Noah there. She snapped the shade up, cupped her hands to her cheeks, and pressed her face to the windowpane. There was no one on the roof. The branches of the oak tree waved and cracked, backlit by a nearby streetlamp. Kaylee sighed, lowered the shade, and went back to her bed. The lock screen on her phone showed the picture of her and Hailey. She buried her pain and remembered what she had to do. Kaylee went to the eChat app and sent her reply.

Yes
Will it hurt?
I don't know u
I'm scared

The crackling branches made her think of Noah's smile through her window. How she wished he were sitting beside her right now. Kaylee's phone chimed. She slowly revealed the new encrypted message from Dr. Ed.

You'll never look at yourself in the mirror the same way

Kaylee quickly snapped a screenshot and saved the photo. As the message faded away, she wondered if this type of chat had happened with Hailey, Paige, and Allison. And what about Jade? Or was all of this unrelated? She decided to try and get a bit more information out of him.

RU a doctor?

Where's ur office?

Her messages were undoubtedly another risk. Was this person trolling her, or for real? Kaylee suddenly had a dreadful thought. What if Dr. Ed was actually Brittney just toying with her? Kaylee told herself she had to see this through. Dr. Ed soon replied.

I ask the questions

"Damn." Kaylee ran her fingers through her hair before quickly snapping a screenshot. The message faded. "Okay, Dr. Ed. I'll play along," Kaylee said as she sent her reply.

I'm interested

Kaylee shoved a handful of chips into her mouth. She found it difficult to swallow. Her throat had become dry, and her heart pounded in her chest. The eChat screen suddenly flashed a message she did not want to see.

CHAT DELETED

"Shit!" Kaylee stared at her phone, somewhat dumbfounded. The eChat app returned to its home screen with no record of her ever having a conversation with Dr. Ed. "I have to tell Noah."

A loud knock on her door caused Kaylee to scream. The door opened, and her mother stuck her head inside. Lesley looked around confused and asked, "Are you okay? Why'd you scream?"

"Sorry." Kaylee's eyes darted between her mom and her phone. "I was watching a scary video."

"Am I going to have to take that thing away from you again?"

"No, Mom. It's fine."

"Well, it's late. I'm going to bed. I've got showings all morning."

"Okay."

"Any plans this weekend?"

"No. Not . . . not yet."

"Well, remember the curfew."

"I will."

Lesley left, leaving the door open. Kaylee wondered if Noah was awake. Kaylee grabbed the now empty bag of chips and her phone and went downstairs to the kitchen. The entire first floor was pitch black, and the wind howled as it buffeted the living room windows. Kaylee hurried into the kitchen and turned on the overhead light. After tossing the bag into the trash, she went to the fridge and grabbed a can of Diet Coke.

Kaylee opened the door to the basement and turned on all of the lights. She went downstairs and flopped on the sectional. The howling wind could barely be heard down here. Her favorite gray cotton blanket sat curled up in the corner of the couch. Kaylee draped the coverlet around her, cracked open her soda, and sent an eChat message to Noah.

U up?

Kaylee held the blanket close to her nose. She could still make out Noah's scent from when they watched *Silence of the Lambs*. She smiled as she thought of him calling her "Starling." Noah soon responded.

sup?

Kaylee wrote back.

Dr. Ed contacted me
I told him I'm interested

The fear and trepidation Kaylee had felt while chatting with Dr. Ed had been replaced by joy. She was so thrilled to be sharing this news with Noah. Kaylee took a swig of soda while waiting for his reply. The screen dimmed, and the phone rang loudly. Noah was calling her.

"Hey," Kaylee said.

"What did he say?"

"It was like last time. But he told me he knew about my acne."

"So, he knows you? Or maybe he just sees you online."

"Maybe. He also said he knew I used SkinDeep. Except I don't. I never post altered pics online."

"Did you tell him that?"

"No."

"So, how'd you leave things?"

"I said I was interested."

"And?"

"And that's where it ended. He closed the chat."

The line stayed silent for a few seconds, and then Noah finally said, "Weird. Did . . . did he say anything else? Anything that might tell you who he is?"

"Not really. Oh, but I got a few screenshots. I'll send them to you to give to your uncle."

"Good job . . . Starling."

Kaylee giggled, and Noah laughed loudly.

"So what now?" Noah asked.

"I assume he's going to get back to me about meeting him."

"And then?"

Kaylee paused and took a sip of soda. She knew what Noah was thinking. He would tell her to get the meeting address and give it to the cops. Deep down, she knew he was right. Kaylee said, "Let's wait and see what happens."

"Meaning what?"

"Well, I may never hear from him again."

"But if you do? And he wants to meet?"

"I . . . I don't know." Kaylee pulled the blanket tighter around her body. "Don't worry, Noah. I won't do anything stupid."

"Like breaking into Rat's place in the basement?"

Kaylee found Noah's tone to be stern and a bit judgmental.

"Meaning what?" Kaylee asked somewhat defensively.

"Meaning you've said that before. Just . . . . Let me know the minute you hear from him."

"Okay."

"I mean it, Kaylee."

"I will! Chat tomorrow."

"Later."

Kaylee stayed up until two in the morning, watching a couple of old rom-com movies in the home theater. She slept until almost noon and now found herself in the kitchen debating if she should have breakfast or lunch. Music from a nearby Bluetooth speaker played *Shallow* from the movie *A Star is Born*. The front door opened, and her mother came inside.

"Did you just wake up?" Lesley asked. She slammed the door closed with her foot and walked over to the kitchen.

"No." Kaylee opened the refrigerator and started getting cold cuts and condiments out to make herself a sandwich. "Are you home for the rest of the day?"

"No. I have another appointment in an hour." Her mom began looking around, confused. "Shit. I left my bag in the car." She quickly spun around and went back to the hallway. When she opened the door, Noah was standing there. Lesley screamed. "You scared the crap out of me."

"Sorry, Mrs. Jones," Noah said.

"Kaylee's in the kitchen."

Noah let Lesley pass him by. He entered the house and closed the door behind him. Kaylee stared at him from the kitchen.

"What are you doing here?" Kaylee asked.

"I showed my uncle the screenshots."

"And?"

"He said you need to stop playing detective."

"Maybe he's mad I'm doing a better job than the cops. I was just making lunch. Want a sandwich?"

"Sure."

Noah entered the kitchen and walked over to Kaylee. Packages of ham, cheese, and turkey were stacked on the counter, along with jars of mustard, mayo, and ketchup. Kaylee opened the pantry, grabbed a loaf of Wonder Bread, and tossed it at Noah. After catching it, he spun around and pretended to spike the loaf as he placed it on the counter. Kaylee rolled her eyes in response.

"Did your uncle say anything else?" Kaylee asked.

"Like what?"

"Like he'd look into it."

"No."

Kaylee frowned and began opening the package of cheese. She stopped and looked at Noah and said, "I wonder if Jade was right."

"About what?"

"Your uncle."

"C'mon. My uncle isn't behind all this." Noah chuckled, but his grin faded when he noticed the serious look on Kaylee's face. "You think my uncle's Dr. Ed?"

"Maybe. Dr. Ed could be . . . anyone. Right? Isn't that what you said?"

"Yes, but . . . . We don't even know if he's connected to any of this. He could just be some troll."

"No. He asked to meet."

"And then went silent."

"I'm going to hear back from him." Kaylee snatched the loaf of Wonder from Noah. "I know it."

"Kaylee . . . ." Noah stepped closer to Kaylee and pulled two slices of bread from the package. He stacked pieces of ham, turkey, and cheese onto one of the slices. Noah shook his head and said, "You're impossible."

The front door opened, and Lesley came inside, carrying a large leather handbag in one hand and her cellphone in the other. She was speaking into the phone in a calm but perky tone. Kaylee called it her "work voice." Lesley waved to the kids and walked to her office at the back of the house.

"We just need to be prepared, Noah," Kaylee said. "For anything."

"So, Detective Starling, what are you thinking?"

Kaylee opted to build a simple ham and cheese sandwich. She spread a huge dollop of mayonnaise across the American cheese, squished the top piece of bread over it, and took a bite. Kaylee looked at Noah and said, "Simple. We plan a trap."

Sixteen

The Trap

Sunday, May 19th

Kaylee picked at a plate of waffles drenched in butter and maple syrup. Typically, Sunday breakfast was her favorite weekly meal. Her mother would often take the time to whip up something special. But, with her mom running late, Kaylee found herself eating frozen waffles. She glanced at her phone resting on the table beside her plate. The time was 12:15 p.m.

"I'm going to be late," Lesley said. She grabbed a banana from a fruit bowl and shoved it into her purse. "This open house runs until four." Lesley stopped and shook her head as she looked around the room. The tension on her face melted.

"What?"

"It's. . . been almost a month now." Lesley's lower lip began to quiver. "I don't understand why the cops have no new leads. Nothing!"

A part of Kaylee wanted to tell her mother what she'd been doing to try and track down Hailey's abductor, but she knew she couldn't. Instead, Kaylee reached over and rested her hand on her mom's arm. Lesley looked down and smiled at her daughter.

"I talked to the chief of police," Lesley said. "I told him they needed to get the FBI."

"What did he say?"

"He said Detective Lane's been pushing back hard, saying

149

he just needs more time. The chief told me he's pulling in the state police. I . . . I guess that's progress." Lesley smiled and ran her fingers through Kaylee's hair. "So, what are you going to do today? Will you be spending it with Noah? You two seem to be together quite a bit these days."

"What? Oh, uh, no. I haven't heard from him. I've got homework. Lots of tests tomorrow."

"Okay." Lesley filled a travel mug with coffee, turned off the coffee maker, and placed the almost-empty carafe into the sink. "I'm sorry to leave the kitchen such a mess."

"I can clean things up."

Lesley kissed the top of her daughter's head, grabbed her mug and purse, and left the house.

Kaylee picked up her phone and went to the eChat app. She sent Noah a message.

Still nothing from Dr. Ed

Dr. Ed's silence bothered Kaylee. She made it clear she wanted to meet. Why the delay in responding? Was he really just some troll? Was he, perhaps, Brittney? Kaylee's phone chimed with a message from Noah.

Maybe that's a good thing?

Kaylee frowned and tossed her phone onto the table. The plate of waffles, despite the homey scent of maple and cinnamon, suddenly looked unappetizing. Kaylee sighed and threw the remains into the trash. She spent the next half hour cleaning the kitchen. Her mind, however, remained ever focused on her phone, waiting for it to chime with a message from Dr. Ed.

The following two hours passed by slowly. Kaylee did have some major tests to prep for, but she couldn't focus. She spent the day flopped on the couch in the home theater in the basement. Kaylee alternated between doing homework, watching television, and texting with Noah. When her phone chimed at 2:32 p.m., Kaylee assumed it was Noah again. She went to the eChat app to find a message from Dr. Ed. Her finger trembled as she revealed the encrypted message.

Knock Knock

Kaylee had spent the entire day waiting to hear from him. Now she found her mind to be a blank void. Fear and adrenaline took over, flooding her with doubt. She sighed and said, "What do I do now?" Kaylee reminded herself that Dr. Ed may have taken her sister, and there was no way she could back down now. She sent a reply.

Been waiting to hear from you

A blood-red pixilated text bubble from Dr. Ed materialized on the screen.

Are you ready to meet?

Kaylee instinctively ran her fingertips across her acne-covered cheeks. Deep down, she absolutely wanted to change her face. She could hear her mother's voice, telling her that her pimples would eventually go away. Part of her wondered if this guy was the real deal. Could he change her? She thought of Hailey, Allison, and Paige. And Jade. So much loss. Kaylee knew what she had to do and sent her response.

Where and when?

Knots formed in Kaylee's stomach. She took her phone upstairs to the kitchen and opened the pantry doors. Stacks of chips, crackers, and cookies lined the two middle shelves. Kaylee grabbed a bag of salt-and-vinegar kettle potato chips and tore the top open. Before she could toss any into her mouth, her phone chimed with Dr. Ed's response. Two messages waited for her.

4pm on the school football field
Come alone

Kaylee quickly took a screenshot of the message. Seconds later, an all too familiar message flashed on the screen.

CHAT DELETED

Kaylee stared at her phone, a small grin spread across her lips. Part of her felt proud that she'd captured the details and had a plan to meet him. She had no intention of meeting him. But, the trap was laid. Her phone chimed again with another eChat message. This one came from Noah.

Anything?

Kaylee exhaled, tossed some chips into her mouth, and started to type a reply. She canceled out of it and opted to just call Noah. There were too many details to discuss.

"What's going on?" Noah asked.

"Dr. Ed just contacted me."

"And?"

"He said to meet at the school at four. The football field."

"Four?" Noah sounded shocked. "Like in ninety minutes?"

"That's what he said. And he said to come alone."

"Figures. Wait. You didn't say yes, did you?"

"He didn't give me a chance. He deleted the entire chat."

"But Kaylee, you aren't seriously thinking of going, are you?"

"No! I took screenshots for your uncle. Hold on." Kaylee sent Noah the pictures of her chat with Dr. Ed. "Can you send these to him and tell him about the meeting at the school?"

"I'm on it."

"Do you think he'll listen?"

"I don't see why not." Noah paused for several seconds. "These are good pics, Kaylee. I'm sure the cops will go check it out."

"Make sure he knows Dr. Ed's expecting me. Alone. The cops have to be discreet."

Noah laughed.

"What?" Kaylee sighed, confused by his reaction.

"I'll make sure the Orleans Police Department follows

Detective Starling's detailed instructions for the ambush."

Kaylee giggled and soon laughed loudly. Her body shook with relief as the tension slowly left her body.

"I'll let you know what he says," Noah said. "Later."

Kaylee's phone remained silent for the next ten minutes until a single chime rang out. An eChat notification appeared on the lock screen. She went to the app, somewhat relieved to see the blood-red encrypted message came from Noah.

Cops will be there

Kaylee sighed and collapsed onto a kitchen chair. She had no idea if this Dr. Ed was the person behind the disappearances or just some troll. Kaylee didn't care. Weeks, days, hours, and minutes of worry and fear evaporated from her body and dissipated away. Everything now rested with the police. All she had to do was wait. She sent a quick thank you text to Noah, grabbed her chips, soda, and phone, and went upstairs to her bedroom.

The sense of calm Kaylee felt downstairs proved to be short-lived. Her eyes darted between the time displayed on her phone, iPad, and clock on her nightstand. She found herself anxiously waiting for the time to change. Each passing minute seemed to take longer than the last. Instagram, TikTok, and YouTube weren't the time-sponges she needed. As the hour ticked past four o'clock, Kaylee felt beads of sweat form on her brow. She exchanged several eChat messages with Noah, asking for updates from his uncle. But Noah never had any news to report. At 4:38 p.m., Kaylee got another eChat message. This one came from Dr. Ed.

I said to come alone

Kaylee felt her throat close. Saliva drained from her mouth, causing her tongue to become dry. Her hands trembled as the message faded away. Before she could respond, the screen went blank.

CHAT DELETED

Tears ran down Kaylee's face as she frantically called Noah.

"Hey," Noah said. "I still haven't heard from my uncle, but–"

"He knows!" Kaylee sobbed and struggled to catch her breath. "He just sent a text. He knew the cops were there!"

"What? Are you sure?"

"Yes!"

"What did he say?" Noah waited several seconds as Kaylee cried continuously. "Kaylee? Want me to come over?"

"No." Kaylee took a deep breath and wiped her tears away. "No. I'm. . . I'm okay."

"My uncle's calling. Let me call you back."

"Tell him–"

Noah ended the call before Kaylee could finish. She tossed the phone onto her bed, went to the bathroom, and flicked on the vanity light. Kaylee walked to the sink and stared at her reflection. Bloodshot eyes looked back at her. She felt like a failure. He went! Dr. Ed went and waited for her. And he escaped the cops. How? Kaylee imagined Dr. Ed taking Kaylee's disobedience out on Hailey and the rest. Assuming they were still alive. She didn't know what to think anymore. Her phone chimed from the other room. Kaylee went to her bedroom and stared at the screen. There was an eChat message waiting for her. She prayed it was Noah. The app showed the pending text came from Dr. Ed. Tears ran down Kaylee's face as her trembling finger slid across the blood-red text bubble.

I'm disappointed Kaylee

Kaylee gazed at the message. Confusion and guilt washed over her. Kaylee felt lost, unsure of what to say or do. The encrypted text faded away, replaced by an all too familiar notification.

CHAT DELETED

Fear enveloped Kaylee. A chill ran down her spine as she

dreaded she may have just sentenced her sister to certain doom. She shook her head and tried to work through what the message could have meant. It could have meant anything. He was disappointed. So what? Maybe he never really went to the school? Did the cops?

Kaylee lowered the phone and closed her eyes. Her head ached, and her mind was a jumble of cloudy, conflicting thoughts. Suddenly the doorbell rang, causing her to jump. Kaylee sat terrified, unable to move. Two loud knocks slammed against the downstairs door. With her phone close by her side, Kaylee rushed downstairs. As she approached the door, she could see the Orleans police car in front of her house. She opened the door to find Detective Lane glaring back at her.

"Hi," Kaylee said.

"Hi? Is that all you've got to say?" Detective Lane crossed his arms and took a step forward, stopping in the middle of the doorway. His black coat whipped from the wind coming from behind him. "I told my nephew that you two needed to let us do our job. Now, I gave you the benefit of the doubt that maybe this Dr. Ed person was the real deal. It turned out to be a waste of our time."

Kaylee felt incredibly intimidated as she stared up at the cop. His raspy voice dripped with anger. She slowly lowered her head and stared at his boots. Bits of grass and mud from the football field clung to the soles.

"Do you have anything to say?" the detective asked. "Well?"

Kaylee stared at her phone and sighed. She looked up and said, "I . . . I think he was watching you."

"Excuse me?"

"He texted a little while ago and said he told me to come alone. So, I mean . . . ."

"We combed that entire field. The perimeter. The bleachers. The school buildings. We found nothing." Detective Lane snatched the phone from Kaylee's hand. "Let me guess, he sent it on that app that deletes messages?" Kaylee nodded as the detective returned the phone. "Can I offer you another theory? Maybe this is just some online troll messing with you. Maybe you're being played. Maybe, just maybe, you should stop trying to be a cop."

Detective Lane turned and walked out onto the porch. He took a deep breath, looked back over his shoulder, and said, "I can't wait to tell your mother about this."

Kaylee slammed the door closed and ran upstairs to her bedroom. She collapsed onto her bed and sobbed into her pillow. Conflicting thoughts filled her mind. What would her mother say? Was Dr. Ed just a troll? Did he really have Hailey? Who was he? Kaylee's phone rang. She sat up and smiled, seeing the call came from Noah.

"Hi," Kaylee said. She rubbed her sniffling nose.

"Hey," Noah replied. "You okay?"

"No. Your uncle just left." Kaylee struggled to keep from crying. "Did you hear?"

"He said they found nothing. What did he tell you?"

"He . . . he told me to stop playing detective."

"I told you he's pissed, Kaylee. Whenever I try and–"

"I heard back from Dr. Ed."

"What?" Noah sounded genuinely shocked. "When?"

"Before your uncle got here. Noah, I told your uncle that I thought Dr. Ed was watching them, but he told me to stop. He . . . ." Kaylee couldn't contain her emotions and began sobbing heavily. "I'm. . . I'm sorry."

"Don't apologize." Noah waited for Kaylee's breathing to calm down. "What else did Dr. Ed say? Anything?"

"Just that he was disappointed. And then he deleted the chat. Noah, I . . . I don't know what to do."

"Let me come over."

Kaylee glanced at the time and sighed. "My mom will be home soon. Shit."

"What?"

"Your uncle said he's going to tell my mom what I did." Kaylee shook her head, frustrated in how everything had unfolded. "Don't come over, Noah. It's just going to be a shit-show."

"Okay, well, call or text me later."

"Sure."

"Hey. Kaylee?"

"Yeah?"

"It's going to be okay."

"Thanks."

☺☺☹

Kaylee finished loading the dishwasher and turned on the power. The unit shimmied and hummed as the wash cycle began. The clock on the nearby microwave oven read 6:48 p.m. Her mother had texted her around five, saying she had a last-minute showing and wouldn't be home until after seven. Kaylee waited for her to say something about Detective Lane, but her mom never did.

The house phone rang. Kaylee checked the caller ID and smiled when she recognized her dad's cellphone number.

"Hey, Dad."

"Hi, Pumpkin. I was just checking in. You didn't answer your phone."

Kaylee looked around, somewhat confused. She said, "Oh, I left it upstairs."

"Really? You always seem to have it glued to your side. Are you okay?"

Kaylee paused, unsure of how much to confide in her dad. She sighed and said, "I've. . . been better."

"You've been through so much. Your sister and your friends. And the one who got killed riding her bike. I've been thinking about you. Worried."

"Thanks, Dad."

"I left a message with the detective to get an update. Do they have any leads?"

Kaylee looked around the empty kitchen and tried to collect her thoughts. She wondered if she should tell him about Dr. Ed and the botched meeting at the football field. Dread washed over her as she pictured Detective Lane returning her father's call and telling him what she'd done.

"They, um, thought that they did." Kaylee clutched the phone and wandered into the living room. "But it was a dead end."

"Really? That's too bad. Look, I'm sure they will catch him. This can't go on forever, right?"

A lump formed in Kaylee's throat. She knew she and Noah were the last two from the video. Is that how this would all end? How could she even explain everything to him? Where to begin? Kaylee walked to the living room window, parted the curtains, and stared outside at the empty street.

"Pumpkin?"

"Sorry, Dad, I'm just . . . thinking."

"Is your mother with you?"

"No. She's working."

"Well, I don't like the idea of you being home alone."

"It's okay." Kaylee headed back into the kitchen. "I'm. . . . I'll be okay."

"You've always been the strong one." He paused as if waiting for his daughter to acknowledge him. "I'm back in town. I'll be here for a few days before I head out again."

"Oh. Okay. Will you be coming by?"

"I'll definitely see you soon. Bye, Pumpkin."

"Bye, Dad."

After returning the phone to its base, Kaylee turned on a few of the downstairs lights. It wouldn't be dark for another hour or more, but seeing the lights on gave her a sense of safety. Kaylee went upstairs. As she entered her room, her phone chimed from the bed. The screen showed one new eChat message waiting for her. Kaylee stared at the message and hoped it was Noah. She launched the app. Her eyes widened when she saw the text was from Dr. Ed.

Knock Knock

Once again, Kaylee found herself confused and scared. Part of her never wanted to hear from Dr. Ed again. That last message had a finality that seemed to bring an end to this nightmare. The message faded away. Kaylee stared at her phone, unsure of what to say. Another blood-red pixilated bubble appeared.

Care to try again?

"Shit." Kaylee's hand trembled as she watched the text

vanish. She waited to see if Dr. Ed would terminate the entire chat session. Several seconds passed, but the chat remained active. He wanted a response. Kaylee glanced at her iPad and considered texting Noah to ask him what to do. She ran her hand through her hair and began to look around the room in confusion. Her eyes settled on the Harry Potter poster. The memories of that vacation and the joy she felt with her sister gave her strength. Kaylee immediately sent a single-word reply back.

Yes

Kaylee felt nauseous. What am I doing? Who is this person? Dr. Ed avoided any discussion about her sister or the others. Was Detective Lane right? Was Dr. Ed just toying with her? The cops had looked everywhere. Maybe Dr. Ed was never there and just took a guess? Every scenario blurred her mind. A series of blood-red pixilated bubbles soon appeared.

8pm at the football field
Come alone
I mean it

Before Kaylee could respond, the screen went blank. Dr. Ed had wiped their entire chat clear. Again. Kaylee realized she forgot to take screenshots of the exchange. Would it have made a difference? Would Detective Lane listen this time?

The eChat screen flashed again, showing a new encrypted message. This one came from Noah.

U OK?

Kaylee immediately called him.

"What's going on?" Noah asked. "What'd your mom—"

"He texted me again. Dr. Ed." Kaylee waited for Noah to respond, but all she could hear was the sound of him breathing. "Noah? Did you hear me?"

"Yes. I . . . I don't know what—"

"I'm meeting him."

"What?" Noah's voice cracked as it went up a couple of octaves. "No! Absolutely not!"

"I'm doing it with or without you."

"You're crazy. You hear me?"

Kaylee flicked on her speakerphone and dropped the phone on her bed. She snatched her backpack from the floor and yelled, "Are you in?"

"Just stop."

"Either way, you have to tell your uncle. But I didn't get screenshots this time. It's up to him if he wants to believe me or not."

"You're not thinking this through. Would you please–"

"Look, Noah, Dr. Ed's either some troll or the guy who abducted my sister. If it's a prank, the joke's on me. But if Dr. Ed is behind all of this . . . ." Kaylee sighed and looked at the Harry Potter poster again. "This could be our one chance to find Hailey."

"I . . . I understand. But let me talk with my uncle."

"Okay, but make sure he understands they have to stay hidden. Dr. Ed's watching that place. I told him that, but he didn't want to hear it."

A car door slammed loudly from the front of the house. Kaylee ran to her window and could see the back of her mother's SUV parked in the driveway. She grabbed the phone and turned off the speaker. She said, "Shit. My mom's home. I . . . I have to go."

"Wait. What . . . what time are you supposed to meet him?"

"He said to meet at the school. The football field." Kaylee waited for Noah to say something. "Eight o'clock."

"And you're really going to do this?"

"I have to." Kaylee eyed her house keys sitting on the bureau. She snatched them and looked at the Airtag resting inside the black leather sleeve. "You can track me, Noah. Remember?" She flung the keys next to her backpack. "I'll be okay. But, I'd . . . I'd rather not do this alone."

Downstairs, the front door opened and then closed with a slam. Kaylee could hear her mother's footsteps enter the kitchen and her keys rattle as they slid across the kitchen counter.

"Noah?"

After several seconds, Noah said, "I'll be at your window at 7:30."

"Really?" Kaylee felt her body uncoil. She smiled and said, "Thanks."

Kaylee ended the call, went to her closet with her backpack, and grabbed the closest pair of black sneakers. The pink and white ones from Hailey beckoned from the shadows. Kaylee smiled as she exchanged her old faded black sneakers for the colorful ones. Her mother's feet stomped on the stairs and grew louder as she reached the top floor. Kaylee flung the shoes and backpack inside the closet and closed the door. Her mother knocked twice against the bedroom door.

"Come in," Kaylee said.

Lesley entered and looked around the room. She said, "I heard voices."

"I was on the phone with Noah."

"Oh." Lesley frowned as she studied the messy bedroom. Her eyes settled on the keychain with the embedded tracker. "I wish we'd had that for your sister."

Kaylee followed her mother's stare. She walked over and grabbed the keys from the bed and said, "I feel safer with this, Mom. You'll always be able to find me. No matter what happens."

Seventeen

Field of Nightmares

Kaylee tip-toed downstairs from her bedroom and went into the kitchen. The clock on the microwave showed the time to be 7:25 p.m. She went to the pantry, grabbed a package of Oreo cookies, and then snatched two bottles of Diet Coke from the fridge.

"Where are you going?" Lesley asked.

Kaylee screamed and dropped the cookies onto the floor. She turned to find her mother standing in the living room with her arms crossed. Kaylee said, "You scared me!"

"What's with all that food? And why two sodas? That's a lot of caffeine at this hour."

"I've got tests tomorrow." Kaylee couldn't make eye contact with her mom because she hated lying to her but felt she had no choice. Kaylee took a handful of napkins from a nearby dispenser and said, "I will be cramming the rest of the night."

"Why didn't you do that today while I was working?"

"I . . . I had other homework to do." The barrage of questions rattled Kaylee. She wondered what Hailey would do to redirect their mom. "Dad called today."

"He did?" Lesley lowered her arms and allowed her shoulders to droop. "When?"

"Like a few hours ago." Kaylee grabbed the cookies from the floor. "He's back in town. Said he wants to see me."

"Oh."

"He's worried." Kaylee scooped the soda and napkins into her arms. "You know. With everything going on."

"Well, I'm. . . I'm glad he's checking in on you."

"Me too." A part of Kaylee wondered if her mom really was glad. She remembered Hailey telling her that their separation was most likely permanent. "Maybe he will bop over tonight."

Lesley nodded but didn't say anything.

"Can you, like, not bother me the rest of the night?" Kaylee asked.

"So, you're going to study and then go to bed?"

"No. I just mean I don't want you breaking my concentration. I need to focus."

"If you . . . ." Lesley turned and looked at the front door. She glanced back at Kaylee and asked, "Did you hear that?"

"Hear what?"

Lesley walked to the front door, unlocked it, and stepped outside onto the porch, allowing cool air to waft into the house. Kaylee stayed in the kitchen and waited. Lesley walked to the front step and looked around the empty street. The gray overcast sky and the setting sun only added to the dreary look of the nearby homes. Lesley gave one more cautionary glance around the property before coming back inside.

"Sorry," Lesley said. "I thought I heard someone on the porch."

"I really need to be alone," Kaylee said as she headed to the stairs. "Okay?"

"Fine. I'll be in my office if you need anything."

Kaylee hurried upstairs, clutching the cookies, sodas, and napkins. She entered her bedroom and used her foot to slam the door closed. After dumping everything onto her bed, Kaylee went to the window. She pressed her face to the glass, frowned, and said, "Where are you?"

Kaylee snapped the lock open and raised the window. She stuck her head outside and found Noah sitting to the side, leaning against the house.

"Are you ready?" Noah asked.

Kaylee motioned him inside. Noah's entrance was much more graceful than last time. Kaylee smiled and said, "I need to get my sneakers. My mom's in her office, so we will need to avoid that corner of the house. Where'd you park?"

"I'm like two blocks away."

Kaylee nervously looked around her room. The reality of her plan to meet Dr. Ed began to weigh heavily on her. Emily, Hailey, Allison, and Paige were missing. The cops kept getting evidence to prove they'd all been taken. And Jade was dead. She raised her hand to her face and stared at Noah.

"What?" Noah asked.

Kaylee's fingers came to rest on her nose ring. She said, "Dr. Ed always takes something. Remember?"

"I do." Noah nodded and gently pulled Kaylee's hand from her face. "It's not too late to change your mind."

"We have to, Noah." Kaylee squeezed Noah's hand. "I have to."

Kaylee grabbed her backpack and tossed the cookies, sodas, and napkins inside. The dresser was covered in pens, papers, and scattered money. Kaylee opened the top drawer, retrieved her mace, and jammed it into her jeans. She sat on the bed, grabbed her house keys, and waved the tracker at Noah. Kaylee smiled as she laced up her pink and white sneakers.

"Are those new?" Noah asked.

Kaylee nodded and grabbed a heavy gray fleece coat. She walked over to Noah and said, "A Christmas gift from Hailey."

"They're going to get muddy on the football field."

"It's okay." Kaylee's smile faded as she stared out the window.

"What?" Noah asked. "I told you we don't have to do this. We can–"

"I've never climbed down from here."

"Oh." Noah grinned and said, "It'll be fine." He grabbed Kaylee's backpack from the bed. "Just follow me."

Noah effortlessly climbed through the open window and flung her bag from the roof. He turned around and held his hand out for Kaylee. She cautiously took hold of Noah and awkwardly made her way out onto the porch.

The cool air, hovering around 55 degrees, helped Kaylee to focus. She closed her bedroom window. When she turned around, Noah was already at the corner of the porch.

"It's easy," Noah said. "Just watch."

Kaylee's body tensed as she saw Noah slip off the side of the porch and disappear from view. She dropped to her knees and crawled backward. The rough asphalt roof shingles dug deep into her palms. Soon enough, Kaylee felt her left foot slam into the gutter. "Where are you?"

"I'm on the ground. Just lay flat and drop your legs over the corner. Your knees will fall to the post. Trust me."

Kaylee sighed. In all of her planning to lay a trap for Dr. Ed, she never imagined her biggest challenge would be leaving her house. She briefly closed her eyes and took a deep breath. Kaylee's arms trembled as she shimmied to the edge and allowed her legs to drop past the gutter. But, just as Noah had said, her knees soon found the post.

"Now, just keep your legs locked on the post and lower yourself," Noah said. "Use one of your arms to grab the top of the post. Slide down a bit. Then grab hold with your other."

"Okay." Kaylee held her breath. The corner of the roof dug deep into her stomach. Her arms shook with fear as she latched onto the post and let gravity control her descent. Within seconds, Kaylee found herself at ground level. Her knees trembled as she struggled to get her balance. "Holy shit. I can't believe I've never done that before."

"I told you it was easy." Noah grabbed Kaylee's backpack and flung it over his shoulder. "C'mon. We gotta get to the school."

They crossed the street to keep a safe distance from Kaylee's home and avoid her mom's office. It took a few minutes to get to Noah's car. During the drive, they finalized their plan to get Kaylee onto the football field with Noah a safe distance away. When they eventually reached the school, Noah pulled to the side of the road and stopped. About half of the parking lot was visible from the main road, and there were no vehicles anywhere. *Finesse* by Bruno Mars wafted from the car's stereo. Noah and Kaylee said nothing as they stared at the school grounds.

"It's not too late to back out," Noah said as he turned off the music.

"No." Kaylee turned to Noah and said, "We've come too far to give up." She glanced at her phone. The screen showed the time to be 7:50 p.m., and there were no new notifications from Dr. Ed. "Still nothing. Maybe he won't show."

"Maybe." Noah looked out his windows, his nerves on full display. "Or maybe he's already here."

"Right." Kaylee took a swig of Diet Coke and placed it back into the backpack, resting between her feet. She opened the car door. The cool nighttime air enveloped her. "Find a dark place to park and then get into position." Kaylee ran her hand across her pocket and allowed her fingers to trace the outline of the keys jammed inside. "Did you want to check the tracker?"

"I checked it from outside your window earlier. It's working."

"Oh. Good." Kaylee tried to ignore the butterflies now dancing in her stomach. "Hey, have you heard from your uncle? Are the cops coming?"

"Let me check." Noah dug his cellphone from his pocket and stared at the lock screen. He turned to Kaylee and smiled. "My uncle wrote back."

"It took him long enough."

Noah's smile faded as he read the message to himself. He sighed and said, "He said to stop playing cops."

"What?" Kaylee's heart raced. "So they aren't coming? Shit!"

"Let me try calling him."

"What's the point?"

"I'll tell him we're here. At the school." Noah dialed his uncle's cell phone. "He'll have to come."

"Fine. But I'm not waiting."

"What?" Noah ended the call. "Why?"

"Because, Noah, we have to know if Dr. Ed's the real deal or not." Kaylee pulled her keys from her pocket and ran her thumb across the Airtag. "Whatever happens, you can track me." Kaylee got out of the car and slid her phone and keys into her pocket. "Text me when you get in position."

Kaylee, aided by the wind, slammed the door closed and watched Noah head off down the road. Walking onto the school property so late at night with nobody around felt odd. An overhead streetlamp flickered to life as Kaylee crossed the parking lot. The sky would be totally dark soon. Sunset, this time of the year, came around eight. The roar of Noah's

Camaro faded away, leaving nothing but the sound of the wind howling through the pine trees.

Engel Academy appeared ominous, with only a handful of windows illuminated across both stories. Kaylee wondered if Rat was busy working late or, worse, watching for her. The broken clock on the bell tower showed the time to be a few minutes before midnight. The streetlights in front of the school were the only two working, and both sides of the building remained dark. Kaylee hoped the lights were on timers and would come on soon.

Kaylee zipped up her jacket and headed to the right side of the school. There were a few white maintenance vans parked near the side entrance. She recognized them as always being there. Otherwise, the place seemed deserted. The towering pine trees lining this side of the complex shrouded the building in dark shadows. Kaylee paused as she walked past the security camera. A set of red infrared LEDs flicked on in the area surrounding the camera's lens. Her eyes widened, and she wondered if this was how Dr. Ed knew the cops had come earlier. Who at the school had access to the feed? Torres? Rat? Was she being recorded?

The long building and row of pine trees created a tunnel effect causing the wind to intensify. Kaylee's collar rippled against her neck as she approached the rear of the school. She stopped and looked back to see if anyone was following her. The lot remained empty. Kaylee lowered her head and continued forward.

The football field was part of a complex of three connected areas – one for football and soccer, another for baseball, and a third that the school would use for various other activities. Only the baseball and football fields had bleachers. Kaylee glanced at the support beams beneath the stands as she made her way onto the football field. She immediately began to look around, wondering if Dr. Ed was somewhere in the shadows. Her heart pounded in her chest as she reached the fifty-yard line.

The wind gusts this evening were brutal. Kaylee shoved her hands into her jeans, resting one hand on her phone and the other on her mace. She retrieved her phone and confirmed there were no messages from Dr. Ed. Kaylee sent Noah a regular text instead of eChat so they'd have a record of their conversation should anything bad happen.

> *In position*
> *wya ??*

As she waited for him to respond, Kaylee kept looking all around. The far ends of the field were wide open. Bleachers lined the long sides of the playing field. Huge posts with floodlights anchored the corners of the field, but all were dark. Was Dr. Ed already here? There were so many places to hide. Noah responded.

> *Hid the car a few blocks up*
> *Running back now*

Kaylee remembered the camera on the side of the building. She sent Noah a warning and recommended he come in from the other side. He responded with a thumbs up. The blustery wind caused the branches of the towering pine trees to sway and crack. Kaylee's hair whipped across her face, blinding her eyes.

The fading light made distant parts of the school grounds challenging to see. A figure appeared from behind the bleachers near where she had entered the field. Her body tensed up. But once the person's arm briefly waved above their head, she knew it was Noah. She didn't bother to acknowledge him, in case Dr. Ed was watching her. Noah soon disappeared from sight. Another text from Noah chimed on her phone.

> *Anything?*

Kaylee looked around again, sighed, and wrote back.

> *No*

Noah positioned himself deep beneath the bleachers. The

long rows of stadium seats became drenched in darkness as the sun dropped below the horizon. He sat in a crouched position, his knees close to his chest and his cellphone in his hand. Noah turned off the ringer. As he did, the phone began to buzz with an incoming call. The ID showed "Uncle Rick." Noah declined the call and sent a quick message to his uncle.

Can't talk
RU here?

As he waited to hear back, he sent a text to Kaylee.

I'm under the bleachers

Kaylee fought the wind as she nervously walked in circles in the middle of the field. After a few minutes, her phone chimed with a text from Noah.

Been texting with my uncle
He's mad af

Kaylee sighed, relieved that Detective Lane had finally responded. She wrote back to Noah.

And???

A huge gust of wind caused a branch in a pine tree at the far end of the field to crack. The sound caused Kaylee to jump. The soft chime of her phone indicated another message from Noah.

Asked him to come
Waiting to hear back

"Waiting?" Kaylee glared at her screen. Part of her wanted to write back to Noah to vent about his uncle being completely useless. Part of her wondered if they should leave. Kaylee looked down at her pink and white sneakers and thought of Hailey. She knew they had to see this through.

The next several minutes felt like an hour to Kaylee. Noah remained curled up in a ball beneath the bleachers while Kaylee paced back and forth along the fifty-yard line. The occasional roar of a car engine, or a cracking branch in the nearby forest, would cause both to pause. Yet, the football field remained empty. Every minute or so, they would text each other for a quick status check. The floodlights on the football field remained off. By 8:15 p.m., complete darkness blanketed the school grounds.

High up in a tree behind the end zone, a small camera kept watch over the entire area. The camouflage-colored silicone skin encasing the assembly made the unit disappear into the foliage. During the daytime, the battery-powered camera was nearly impossible to see. As night covered the area, a circle of tiny red LED infrared lights surrounding the lens sparked to life, activating the camera's night vision. Unbeknownst to Kaylee, the cellular-linked unit captured and transmitted every movement she made.

Kaylee's nerves had long since settled. She walked in circles, staring at her bright sneakers softly glowing in the darkness. Kaylee found herself becoming frustrated. She texted Noah.

> I can't even
> Prank?

Noah nodded in agreement as he read her message. Before he could respond, he felt cold metal against the back of his neck. A soft click rang out near Noah's ear. Having spent many days at a shooting range with his uncle, Noah knew the sound all too well. Someone had just cocked a revolver's trigger into place. Noah held his breath and waited.

"You shouldn't be here." The muddy voice of the person holding the gun was barely above the sound of a whisper. "Should you?"

Eighteen

Midnight Already?

Kaylee tried to see beneath the bleachers, but it was nothing but shadows and beams. Standing in the middle of the football field made her feel vulnerable. She looked at her phone and then back at the stadium seats. The screen showed the time to be 8:17 p.m. Kaylee expected to at least see the light from Noah's phone. She sent him another text.

Well?

The faulty clock on the school's tower groaned and creaked as the big hand snapped forward. Both hands now pointed straight up, causing the dormant belfry to come to life. The single bronze bell, tuned to "F Sharp," rang out, shattering the silent skies.

Kaylee screamed and looked up. From this far behind the school, she could only see the spire atop the bell tower. Panic washed over her, and her body began to tremble. Kaylee decided she'd had enough and should get Noah and leave. The bell tower continued to ring. Her phone suddenly chimed with a new eChat notification. She went to the app to find an encrypted text from Dr. Ed. Kaylee stared at the shimmering blood-red text bubble. Her finger shook as she revealed the message.

I said come alone

Kaylee broke out into a full sprint toward the bleachers. Her heart pounded in her chest as her feet slammed hard against the grassy field. Dirt and grass flung from her sneakers as she raced back to Noah. The school bell continued to run through the countdown to midnight. She ran to the backside of the stand and turned on her phone's flashlight. Noah was nowhere to be found. Kaylee took a deep breath and stepped beneath the bleachers. She searched for any sign of Noah having been here but found nothing. Questions flooded her mind. Should she call out his name? Should she hide? Run? Where did he park?

Tears welled in Kaylee's eyes as she emerged from the dark underside of the bleachers. She quickly made her way back toward the front of the building, passing the maintenance vans and the side entrance. Suddenly the belfry went quiet. The silence caused Kaylee to stop. With the clocktower no longer ringing, the only sound remaining was the rushing wind and the snapping pine branches. She reached into her pocket and pulled out her mace. Seeing the small pink canister made her think of her mom. Kaylee knew what she had to do and called her mom's cellphone. After three rings, her mother answered.

"Why are you calling me from your bedroom?" Lesley asked.

Before Kaylee could respond, someone behind her jammed a sock into her mouth and across her nose. A gloved hand squeezed Kaylee's hand tight, forcing her to drop her phone. The cellphone fell to the pavement but didn't lose the connection. Her mom's voice could repeatedly be heard calling Kaylee's name.

Kaylee struggled to breathe. The person holding her from behind was too strong, and she couldn't break free. The sweet disinfectant scent from the chloroform-soaked sock caused Kaylee to gasp and choke. Within seconds, she felt herself become lightheaded. As consciousness faded, the last thing Kaylee felt was her body being lowered to the ground and someone's hot breath sliding across her neck.

☺☺☹

When Kaylee awoke, she found herself slumped on a musty-scented bed. She tried to sit upright but felt dizzy and quickly collapsed against the pillow. Bile rose in her throat. Nausea was an unfortunate side-effect of being drugged by chloroform. Kaylee took a few breaths and slowly pulled herself upright. The memory of the abduction flooded her thoughts. She ran her fingers across her face, surprised to feel her nose ring was still there.

"She's awake."

The voice came from across the room.

Kaylee rubbed her eyes and asked, "Who's there?"

"Hey," Allison said as she knelt beside Kaylee's bed. "How are you feeling?"

"Allison?" Kaylee's lightheadedness made it hard to remember what had happened. "Where . . . where are we?"

"I don't know." Allison sat next to Kaylee and put her arm around her. "It's going to take time for your head to clear."

Kaylee looked around the dimly lit room. Her eyes widened when she saw Paige sitting across from them.

"Paige?" Kaylee asked.

Paige stood up and walked over to Kaylee and Allison. Her gait was unsteady, and she appeared thin and tired. Paige sat on the other side of Kaylee and allowed her shoulders to slump. Her eyes remained focused on the floor. Paige sighed and said, "Hey."

"Hey." A smile briefly appeared on Kaylee's face. She rubbed her head and looked back and forth between Allison and Paige. "Is . . . is it just us?"

"No," Paige said.

Paige pointed at the far end of the room, past the staircase. The bathroom door opened, and a backlit figure emerged. Kaylee's mind was in a fog. She leaned forward and struggled to piece together who she was seeing. Kaylee's eyes widened, and she burst into tears.

"Hailey!" Kaylee stood up and immediately started to lose her balance. Hailey rushed to catch her, and the two embraced. "Oh my God, you're alive."

The two sisters sobbed and held one another. Still weak from being drugged, Kaylee found herself using Hailey to keep her upright. Soon, the arms of Paige and Allison were around them. The four girls hugged and cried, their hands gripping one another tightly.

As Kaylee's head began to clear, she let go of Hailey. The group separated and sat down together on the nearby bed. Kaylee wiped her cheeks dry and then took her sister's hand into hers.

"I'm so glad to see you," Kaylee said to her sister.

"I'm not," Hailey said. "I was hoping he wouldn't get you."

Kaylee looked around the softly lit room. Her eyes, now fully adjusted, could see two other beds, the posts in the middle of the room, and the staircase. The scent of rotting trash only made her nausea feel worse.

"Is Noah here?" Kaylee asked.

"Noah?" Hailey shook her head. "No. Why?"

"We . . . we set a trap." Kaylee's eyes widened. She reached into her right pocket, but it was empty. Kaylee then checked her other one. Desperation consumed her as she frantically searched the rest of her pockets. "Shit. It's gone."

"What, your phone?" Hailey asked.

"My keys." Kaylee's heart raced. "I had a tracker on my keychain. Mom got it for me so she can find me. So can Noah."

"Why is Noah tracking you?" Hailey asked.

Kaylee stared blankly at her sister. She turned to Allison and asked, "Did I have any keys when he brought me here?"

"No," Allison said. "He takes all our stuff." Allison ran her fingers through Kaylee's hair and smiled. "But that was smart thinking to bring a tracker."

"Thanks."

"Maybe . . . maybe he just thinks it's a regular key chain," Allison said.

"It's Dr. Ed, right?" Kaylee asked. "He's the one behind this?"

"We all fell for it," Paige said as she nodded. "We were all so stupid."

"But Noah and I figured it out." Kaylee squeezed her sister's hand and then slowly stood up so she could face the other three. "We've been trying to connect the dots. We knew it was our group being targeted."

"The video, right?" Allison asked.

"Right." Kaylee nodded. "When Dr. Ed contacted me, I had a hunch he might be the one. Have you seen him? Is . . . is it Rat?"

"He never shows his face," Hailey said. She pointed at the doorway at the top of the staircase. "He just knocks twice and then comes in with food and supplies."

"Or other girls," Paige said. She looked up at Kaylee and asked, "How's Jade?"

"Jade?" Kaylee's heart sank. "You . . . you don't know, do you?"

"Know what?" Paige asked.

The overhead speaker crackled and hissed. A muffled, mechanical voice said. "Stay away from the staircase."

Kaylee spun around, somewhat confused by the cryptic announcement. After several seconds, two loud raps rang against the door. She watched the door slowly open, followed by Noah emerging through the doorway.

"Noah!" Kaylee cried. "Are you okay?"

Noah stood there, his head hung low and his hands behind his back. He refused to make eye contact with anyone.

"What is it, Noah?" Hailey asked.

"Did your uncle come?" Kaylee asked as hope filled her chest. "Are you here to save us?"

Noah looked at Kaylee, sighed, and said, "No."

Nineteen

The Basement

Kaylee stared at Noah standing at the top of the staircase. His head remained slumped toward his chest, and he avoided eye contact with everyone. Noah's body swayed as if he were fighting against a strong wind. The dim lighting made it difficult for anyone to see him clearly. Kaylee squinted as she tried to focus on Noah's face. Her eyes widened when she noticed blood smeared across his forehead.

"Are you okay?" Kaylee asked.

A shadowy figure appeared behind Noah. The stranger's gloved hands gripped Noah's shoulders and shoved him. Noah tumbled forward, rolling sideways down the stairs. The rickety staircase creaked and shuddered with each tumble. His hands were tied behind his back, making it impossible for Noah to stop himself. Hailey screamed and ran to the bottom of the staircase to help him. Noah groaned as he crashed against her, causing them to collapse against the cold, damp concrete floor. The door at the top of the stairs slammed shut, and the lock on the door snapped closed.

"Noah!" Hailey put her arms around Noah and helped him sit upright. "Are you okay?"

"Do I look okay?" Noah said. "Can . . . can you untie me?"

Kaylee watched her sister untie the rope wrapped around Noah's wrists. Once his arms were free, Kaylee walked over and knelt by his side. Up close, Noah looked to be in rough shape. A small gash above his right eye dripped blood down his dirt-covered face. His hands, although free, were severely scraped, and his jeans were torn.

"Can you stand?" Kaylee asked.

Noah leaned back and wiped the blood from his face. He stared at his blood-soaked fingers and shook his head in disbelief. He briefly looked around for someplace to wipe his hands dry before giving up and dragging them across his jeans. Noah crossed his left leg beneath his other one and put pressure on his right foot. He smiled, stood up, and then tried to stand on both feet. He immediately howled and lifted his left foot.

"What is it?" Hailey asked.

"My ankle," Noah said. "I . . . I think it's twisted. Maybe broken."

Kaylee immediately put her arm around Noah and tucked her head beneath his armpit. Hailey took the other side, and together they helped him hop across the room. Noah groaned as they made their way over to the nearest bed.

"Is everyone okay?" Noah asked. He flopped onto the bed and wiggled toward the back to rest his head against the wall. "Anyone else hurt?"

"I'm just a little light-headed," Kaylee said as she leaned against the nearest post.

"We're fine," Hailey said. She sat next to Noah and held his hand. "Just some bruises. He's never been that violent with us."

"So, it's definitely a he?" Kaylee asked. "Are you sure?"

Allison nodded and said, "Definitely. Why?"

"For a while, we thought it might be Principal Torres," Kaylee said.

"Oh, it's not her," Hailey said as she leaned her head against Noah's shoulder. "He's a lot taller than her. And too strong."

Noah looked at Hailey and asked, "Is it just the four of you?" Noah frowned as Hailey nodded. "Where's Emily?"

"She's not here," Paige said. "We asked him once about her, and he wouldn't answer." Paige went to the other bed and sat down. She looked at Noah and said, "So I guess it's just Jade who's left. You guys set a trap, right? Was Jade in on the plan?" When Noah didn't answer, Paige turned to Kaylee and asked, "What were you saying before Noah came in? You said something about Jade."

Kaylee and Noah looked at one another for a long time. Noah closed his eyes and leaned his head against Hailey's. Kaylee took a deep breath and said, "She had an accident. On her bike."

"Is she okay?" Paige asked. She instinctively reached for her neck, her fingers grasping for her missing pearl necklace.

"She . . . she ended up in the hospital," Noah said. "That's the last we heard."

"Oh," Paige said. The tension on her face faded, and a half-smile emerged. "Okay. I guess she's safe there."

Kaylee felt a sense of relief. She could only imagine how Allison, Hailey, and Paige would react to hearing that Jade was dead. The side effects from the chloroform were finally wearing off. Kaylee no longer felt like vomiting. She looked around the dimly lit room again. The odor coming from the pile of trash wasn't the only odd smell in the room. There was something else. Something she couldn't quite figure out. Was it rotted fish? Seaweed? Maybe it was just the after-effects of being drugged.

"Where are we?" Kaylee asked. "This doesn't seem like the school basement."

"Not even close," Noah said. "That guy kept a bag on my head until he shoved me through that door. But I glanced back just before getting to the top of the stairs. I don't know where we are, but it's not the school."

"Maybe it's a part we've never been to," Allison said. She was now sitting with Paige, and the two were holding hands. "Rat's got to be the one behind this."

"Or not," Paige said. She looked at Noah and asked, "What if Jade was right? What if it's your uncle?"

"Seriously?" Kaylee asked. "He just threw Noah down the stairs."

"Did you get a look at him?" Paige asked. "When he grabbed you."

"No," Noah said. "I was hiding under the bleachers at the school. Kaylee and I were waiting for Dr. Ed to arrive. Someone put a gun to my head."

Kaylee looked at the gash on Noah's forehead as blood

continued to trickle from the wound. She stood up and walked to the bathroom, grabbed a handful of toilet paper, and returned to the bed. Hailey snatched the paper from Kaylee's hand and began to tend to Noah's wound.

"It can't be Detective Lane," Kaylee said. She watched with what she had to admit to herself was a bit of jealousy as her sister cleaned Noah's face. "He knew what we were planning."

"What do you mean?" Allison asked.

"Well, Dr. Ed asked me to meet him at the school at four. We told his uncle, and so the cops went." She looked at Noah and added, "We thought they'd catch him."

"You set that up?" Allison asked. When Kaylee nodded, she added, "Wow. I wish I'd thought of that."

"Kaylee, that's amazing," Hailey said. A proud smile spread across her face. "So, what happened?"

Kaylee sighed and said, "They didn't find anyone. Then Dr. Ed asked again for tonight at eight."

"Did the cops come again?" Hailey asked as she stared at Noah. "Your uncle?"

"No," Noah said. "My uncle thought Dr. Ed was just some online troll." Noah closed his eyes briefly and groaned. "I texted him from the football field. He got really mad. Then Dr. Ed grabbed me. So maybe . . . maybe when my uncle doesn't hear from me, he'll come looking."

"Dr. Ed took your phone," Kaylee said. "Didn't he?"

Noah nodded and looked at Kaylee. She could see the mix of fear and disappointment in his eyes.

"So the cops weren't there?" Allison asked. "Do they even know you're here?"

"The tracker," Kaylee said. "If my keys are here in the building, my mom can find us. I called her just as Dr. Ed grabbed me." She turned to look at Hailey. "Mom thought I was upstairs in my room. I'm sure she's already called the cops, and they're coming."

"Unless Dr. Ed tossed your keys away with your phone," Noah said. "Remember how the phones were all in different locations?"

"I . . . I didn't think of that." Kaylee's brief sense of hope quickly faded. "Shit."

"Noah, I hate to say this, but . . . maybe your uncle is Dr. Ed," Paige said. "Maybe when you told him where you were he came and grabbed you."

"No," Noah said, his eyelids heavy with exhaustion. "It . . . it can't be him."

"I'm with Paige," Allison said. "You said Dr. Ed asked you to come a second time. Your uncle knew about both attempts. And, I mean, Dr. Ed's tall like your uncle. Maybe . . . maybe Jade was right about him."

Kaylee felt her eyes well with tears. She looked to Noah for support, but he was no longer looking at her. Instead, Noah had his bruised and bloody head resting against Hailey's. How many times had he told her to stop playing detective? How many times had he told her this was a bad idea? Deep down, she knew it wasn't a bad plan. Detective Lane was supposed to be the failsafe. Why didn't he come when Noah told him they were at the school? Or did he get there too late? A knot formed in Kaylee's stomach. Were Allison and Paige right? What if the reason the cops never came was because Detective Lane really was Dr. Ed? Had Jade been right all along? She looked at Noah's battered face. Could his uncle really hurt him like this?

The overhead speaker hummed and then crackled with static. A muffled voice said, "I'm coming in. Stay away from the stairs."

Kaylee went and sat beside Noah, folding her legs back and tucking her muddied pink and white sneakers beneath her. The bedsprings squeaked loudly, breaking the uncomfortable silence in the air. She glanced at Hailey, sitting on the opposite side of Noah, holding his hand. Kaylee slid her trembling hand against his thigh. Her shaking stopped when Noah gently rested his hand on top of hers.

Two loud knocks emanated from the door at the top of the staircase. The hinges creaked as the door opened, and Dr. Ed stepped inside and said, "Knock, knock." A black ski mask with slits for the eyes and mouth covered his face and neck. Dr. Ed wore a navy one-piece coverall, heavy-duty construction boots, and black leather gloves. He practically vanished into the dark shadows at the top of the stairs. The motion-sensor camera above his head flickered with each movement in the room. His right arm held several loops of thick rope, and a Smith & Wesson revolver dangled from his other hand. The wooden staircase creaked as his weight shifted. He walked to the top step and, in a muffled voice, said, "Now that you're all here, we can finally begin."

Kaylee stared at Dr. Ed, studying his build. His height. His muffled voice. Was it Rat? Was it Detective Lane? Who was he?

Twenty

Hello, Doctor

Kaylee's heart pounded in her chest. During all of her theorizing and plotting to find Dr. Ed, she never once believed she and Noah would fall into his trap. The man in black looking down at them had terrorized the town for weeks. She felt like a fool for thinking she could outsmart him. Her plan to expose and capture him had failed. Seeing him at the top of the stairs, holding that gun, made the reality of the situation come crashing down around her. She'd never felt this terrified in her life. Noah's gentle touch brought her little comfort. Kaylee flipped her hand over and grabbed his hand. He looked down at her, his face covered in blood, and frowned.

"It's going to be okay," Noah said softly.

Dr. Ed shoved the revolver into his pocket and then began to unspool the rope from his other hand. The heavy-duty cord was split into ten separate three-foot-long pieces. One by one, he flung a bundle down to the ground below, each landing with a dull thud against the damp concrete floor. Soon, the ten bundles were in a small pile in the middle of the room. Kaylee allowed her eyes to wander from the ropes to the metal cleats screwed to the nearby wall. Her mouth went dry as she feared what came next.

"Pick up the rope," Dr. Ed said. He pointed the revolver at Kaylee. "Now!"

Kaylee looked at Noah and then at Hailey. She let go of Noah's hand, stood up, and slowly walked to the pile of rope.

Kaylee dropped to one knee and grabbed the top bundle. The rope felt damp in her hands. She held it closer to her face and inhaled. The scent coming from the cord was the same fishy scent she'd smelled earlier, only more intense.

"Now, tie your sister to one of the posts," Dr. Ed said, his voice gruff and hoarse. He waited several seconds, but Kaylee remained motionless. "Do it!"

Kaylee glanced at Allison and Paige sitting on the opposite side of the room and then back at Noah and her sister. She counted the days and weeks that had passed since Emily's disappearance. So many nights had been spent worrying and wondering if everyone was still alive. Why hadn't he hurt any of her friends? Why the gun? None of this made any sense. Confusion replaced Kaylee's fear.

"No," Kaylee said softly. She dropped the rope and stood up. "Who are you? Why are you doing this? You owe us–"

"I owe you nothing!" Dr. Ed descended two steps, stopped, and aimed the gun at Noah. The rickety staircase creaked beneath his weight. "Do it, or I'll shoot the boy."

"What?" Hailey cried. "You already threw him down the stairs! Leave him alone."

Kaylee looked at her sister and said, "He's bluffing. If he–"

The blast from the gun echoed off the walls, causing Kaylee to drop into a crouched position. The room's tight confines and solid walls only amplified the boom. Allison and Paige cried out in terror. Hailey screamed as Noah recoiled and covered his ears. The bullet hit the wall a foot away from Noah's head, shattering the concrete.

"Next time, I won't miss," Dr. Ed lowered his arm slightly and aimed directly at Noah's chest. He glared at Kaylee and asked, "Am I clear? Detective?"

Kaylee stared at Dr. Ed in disbelief. Was that Detective Lane behind the mask? She slowly turned and faced Noah, but he would not look back. How does Dr. Ed know the nickname Noah gave her?

"It's. . . it's okay," Hailey said. She kissed Noah on the cheek, slid off the mattress, and walked over to Kaylee. Hailey gave her sister a half-smile and added, "Just do what he says."

The two went to the nearest post. Hailey turned and stood

against the beam, wrapping her arms around the post behind her. Kaylee took one of the bundles of rope and began to loop it around her sister's wrists.

"Tighter!" Dr. Ed took another step down but kept his gun aimed at Noah. "I want her locked against that post."

"I'm sorry," Kaylee whispered into Hailey's ear.

Kaylee redid the rope around Hailey's wrists, but this time made it much tighter. When finished, she walked around to the front of the post and looked at her sister. Kaylee wanted to burst into tears. So many weeks were spent wanting to save Hailey, and now she found herself shackling her.

Hailey gave her sister a supportive smile. She glanced down at Kaylee's feet and said, "Nice sneakers."

Kaylee grinned, but only briefly. She looked up at Dr. Ed and frowned. Their captor remained perched in the middle of the staircase. Detective Lane was an imposing man, but Dr. Ed seemed smaller. Or was it the distance? Was the dim lighting playing tricks on her mind? Could the man on the staircase be Rat? Had she and Noah ever joked about being detectives in front of him? Maybe something was said during one of the meetings in the principal's office? Kaylee felt lost. At this point, did it even matter who was behind the mask?

"Now do her feet," Dr. Ed said. He waved the gun at Noah. "Don't make me ask twice."

Kaylee grabbed another bundle of rope and quickly tied her sister's ankles against the beam. She did her best to make it appear she was making the knots tight while keeping the loops somewhat loose. When she was done, she stood up and crossed her arms.

"Now do the others," Dr. Ed said.

Kaylee looked at the pile of rope and then at Noah. Where was this leading? What would he do when she was the only one left? Would he tie her up? Kaylee stared at the gun in Dr. Ed's gloved hand. Does he plan to kill them all?

Paige leaned closer to Allison and whispered, "I've never heard him talk this much. He usually only talks to us through the speaker."

"I know," Allison said as she tried not to move her lips. "Do you recognize his voice? Is . . . is it Noah's uncle?"

"You two!" Dr. Ed took another step down the stairs and stopped. "No talking!"

Kaylee briefly closed her eyes and repeated Dr. Ed's words to herself. His muffled voice became hoarse when he yelled. Was it Noah's uncle? Her gut told her it had to be. If so, there was no way he'd actually shoot his nephew. Kaylee took a cautionary step toward the staircase. She took a deep breath and said, "I'm not tying up anyone else until you tell us why you're doing this."

Dr. Ed raised his weapon, aimed it at Noah, and fired. The revolver's blast echoed off the dense walls causing everyone to scream. The bullet took a chunk out of Noah's left calf. Noah immediately howled in pain as blood splattered against the blanket and started pooling beneath his leg. Kaylee ran to the bed, grabbed the edge of the blanket, and began applying pressure to the wound. Her eyes widened as her hands slowly became drenched in blood.

"Mouth off at me again, and the next shot kills him." Dr. Ed pointed the revolver at the pile of rope and then at Noah. "Move, Kaylee."

Kaylee looked at Noah, tears running down her face, and said, "I'm sorry." Noah's eyelids were heavy, and he appeared to be in a state of shock. Kaylee pulled his hands toward his wound. "You have to keep pressure on this, Noah. Okay?"

Noah raised his heavy eyes, looked at Kaylee, and nodded.

Kaylee pried herself away from Noah's side and went to the pile of ropes in the middle of the room. She wiped tears from her face, leaving behind streaks of Noah's blood. Kaylee didn't have a mirror, but she could imagine her acne now stained with Noah's pain due to her pride and stupidity in calling Dr. Ed's bluff. Would Noah die because of her arrogance?

Resignation replaced fear, and Kaylee fell into a trance and followed Dr. Ed's instructions. Paige and Allison cried as Kaylee tied them to the other posts. Kaylee couldn't believe what was happening. Would everything end here? Where were the cops? She took her time, hoping they would be rescued from this nightmare. What if her mom had called Detective Lane? What if Detective Lane was Dr. Ed? She remembered how her mother didn't like Detective Lane, so maybe there was a chance her mom called the chief of police or even the FBI. Thinking of the FBI reminded her of all the times Noah had called her Starling. How she so regretted playing detective. As each second passed and she secured each knot, what little hope Kaylee had left vanished.

There were now four bundles of rope on the floor. Two for Noah and two for her. She grabbed two of them and knelt beside Noah. The pool of blood beneath Noah had gotten larger. Blood soaked the mattress beneath Noah's leg. His hands trembled as he applied pressure on his wound. Kaylee thought he looked ready to pass out.

"He's too injured," Kaylee said. She looked back at the masked man on the stairs. "I don't think he can stand. The blood. It's . . . ."

"Just tie his hands together," Dr. Ed said. "Tightly."

"Can I use one of the ropes to try and stop the bleeding?"

Dr. Ed waited several seconds and then slowly nodded. Kaylee slid one of the ropes beneath Noah's injured leg and quickly made a tourniquet. Her hands shook the entire time, the blood smearing across her fingers.

"Maybe instead of a detective, you should be a doctor," Noah said. His voice sounded thin. Weak. He managed a brief smile before whispering, "Dr. Starling."

Kaylee shook her head but couldn't smile back. She stared at the blood covering the bed and her hands and realized she was to blame. Kaylee sighed, got another piece of rope, and gently tied Noah's wrists together. She made sure Noah could still move his hands. When done, she placed his hands on the rope around his injured leg.

Dr. Ed descended the stairs, keeping the gun aimed at Noah. He then pointed it at Kaylee and said, "Your turn. Come over here."

Kaylee found it hard to stand, her legs buckling under the fear of what Dr. Ed had planned for her. Kaylee gave Noah one last look before turning to face Dr. Ed. She looked around at Allison, Paige, and Hailey. All three were quietly sobbing, unable to move. Guilt wrapped itself around Kaylee like a heavy wet blanket. She wiped her tears away and walked over to the last two bundles of rope.

"That's far enough," Dr. Ed said.

Kaylee stared at the masked stranger who called himself Dr. Ed. She could now see that his eyes were pale blue. Who was he? What color eyes did the detective have? He seemed shorter than Noah's uncle. Was this Rat? What color eyes did Rat have? She couldn't remember.

Dr. Ed pointed at the wall with the cleats and said, "Move."

Kaylee went to the wall and stopped. Dr. Ed slid the revolver into his pocket, bent down, and picked up the rope. He walked over to Kaylee and dropped one of the bundles at her feet. She stared at the rope resting on the pink and white sneakers her sister had given her. The once pristine shoes were now covered in mud, grass, and blood. Noah's blood. Kaylee looked over at Noah. His eyes were barely open. She wondered how much blood he'd lost.

Dr. Ed unwound a bundle of rope and grabbed Kaylee's left wrist. She ignored him and remained fixated on Noah. Kaylee's eyes widened as Noah's closed. Suddenly, Noah went limp and collapsed onto the bed.

"No!" Kaylee screamed. Anger instantly raged throughout her body. She spun around and grabbed the front of Dr. Ed's mask, jamming her fingers into the eye openings. Dr. Ed stumbled backward in shock. As he did, Kaylee made a fist and ripped his mask off. She stared at their abductor's face and cried, "Mr. Mason?"

Twenty One

Deep Wounds

Kaylee gazed at Mr. Mason in disbelief. Emily's father was Dr. Ed? Her panic from being captured faded as her mind filled with confusion and questions. Slowly, she tried to connect the pieces of the puzzle together. The text messages. The cell phone location data. Suddenly none of that mattered. There was really only one question front and center. Why?

Everyone else in the room remained silent. Kaylee's fingernail had managed to nick Mr. Mason's upper lip. He wiped the blood away and licked his lips. Mr. Mason's eyes slowly surveyed Hailey, Allison, Paige, and Noah before settling on Kaylee.

"Turn around," Mr. Mason said, his voice no longer disguised. He grabbed Kaylee's shoulders and shoved her against the wall. "You've just made this a lot more difficult. For all of you."

Kaylee winced as Mr. Mason bound her wrists together behind her back. The knots dug deep into her flesh, immobilizing her hands. Kaylee spun around and asked, "Why?"

"As if you don't know."

Mr. Mason grabbed her by the throat and flung Kaylee toward the bed. She stumbled and crashed against Noah, causing him to awaken. Kaylee stared at Noah's blood-covered hands and bloodied jeans and felt guilt wash over her. She pulled herself upright and turned to face Mr. Mason.

"Where's Emily?" Kaylee asked.

Mr. Mason removed his leather gloves and used one to wipe the blood on his face. He licked his lips and spat on the floor. "My daughter's dead."

Kaylee couldn't believe what she was hearing. Both Emily and Jade were dead? She looked at Noah, but he appeared unconscious again. She turned to face Allison, Paige, and Hailey. The four exchanged glances before Hailey looked at Mr. Mason and said, "You killed her. Didn't you?"

"Me?" Mr. Mason shook his head in disgust and stepped closer to Hailey. "No. You did." He angrily glared at Allison and then Paige. His voice gruff, Mr. Mason then whispered, "All of you."

Hailey looked over at her sister and shook her head. Kaylee shrugged her shoulders and stared at Emily's dad. Mr. Mason took a few steps back, turned, and began to pace across the floor. His heavy boots scuffed against the damp concrete. When he reached the staircase, he stopped.

"Emily, she . . . ." Mr. Mason briefly lowered his head. He looked up but did not turn around. "Emily killed herself."

Allison and Paige both gasped. Kaylee felt her eyes well with tears. Her mind raced with something to say. Instead, she just yanked her arms behind her back as she tried to loosen her bonds. The knots, however, were far too tight. Hopelessness slowly enveloped her.

"It was that video," Mr. Mason said. He turned around. Tears ran down his cheeks. "You bullied my little girl. Bullied her! Harassed her about her looks. Why?" He took two steps forward and bellowed, "Why?"

Hailey, Paige, and Allison all lowered their heads and looked away. Kaylee glanced at Noah beside her. His breaths were short and shallow, but his eyes were now open. Barely.

"I'll never forget that day of the fight," Mr. Mason said. "Emily came home in tears. I asked her what had happened. She just kept saying how much she hated moving here. She hated her new school." He moved closer to Hailey. "She hated her new friends." Mr. Mason turned to Kaylee and said, "She hated *me* for making us move here."

Mr. Mason turned and sat on one of the lower steps, resting

his face in his hands. The wooden stairs creaked as he swayed back and forth. He said, "She showed me the video of what happened. I . . . I tried to tell her things would get better. But, I . . . I . . . ." He looked up at Kaylee. "My wife always knew how to comfort our daughter. Emily told me to just leave her alone."

Kaylee closed her eyes and remembered the conversation she'd had with Mr. Mason at his house when he told her and Noah about his wife's suicide. Her eyes darted around the room. Is that where they were? Was this his house? So, when she and Noah came to visit him, were their friends close by? A boat's horn blared far in the distance. Kaylee tried to recall if Mr. Mason's home was close to the ocean. She couldn't remember.

"I left her alone that night," Mr. Mason said. "When I went to bed, I went to check on her. And that's when I found her." A single tear ran down his face. "She was in the bathtub. Dead. Her wrist slit open."

Mr. Mason stood up and slid his right hand into his pocket. He said, "That video. All of you taunting her. I . . . I couldn't believe how you all treated her. All because she changed her looks in that SkinDeep app." He glared at Kaylee and said, "Oh, I'm well aware of all those apps you kids use. You were so easy to track." His eyes filled with tears. "Why did you have to be so mean?"

Mr. Mason crossed the room and stopped beside Hailey. He stared at Kaylee as he pulled his hand from his pocket and opened his palm, revealing a folded, straight-edged razor. The cherry wood handle's worn finish contrasted with an inset of turquoise and nickel metal. He said, "She used my razor to take her life. All she wanted to do was to fit in. To be accepted."

"I'm so sorry," Kaylee said, her voice soft and trembling. "I . . . I don't think any of us–"

"Sorry? Sorry won't bring my daughter back." Mr. Mason flicked the razor open, exposing the polished steel blade. "She was my world. When my wife died, Emily was all I had. And you took her from me. Your bullying took her!"

Kaylee stared at the razor and said, "But we never–"

"Never what?" Mr. Mason yelled. "Never meant to hurt

her? Bullshit! Words can hurt. I watched that video so many times. What is it with your generation being so obsessed with your looks? You're addicted to those stupid apps like SkinDeep to make yourself different. Better. In my eyes, Emily was perfect." Mr. Mason took a deep breath and added, "Just like my wife."

Mr. Mason stared at the razor now dangling from his grip. The steel edge glistened in the dim overhead lighting. He held the blade close to Hailey's face and slowly waved it back and forth. Hailey's eyes widened, and she immediately began to whimper and shake.

"I can't bring my baby girl back," Mr. Mason said. He pressed his chin beside Hailey's ear. "But, I can be sure that from now on, whenever you look in the mirror, you'll remember what you did." He pressed the corner of the blade against Hailey's cheek. "Do you like who you see in the mirror?"

Hailey screamed as the blade pierced her skin. Blood oozed from the incision and slowly ran down her cheek.

Mr. Mason made an inch-long gash, withdrew the blade, and rubbed the bloody edge along his sleeve. He looked at Allison and then Paige and asked, "Who's next?"

Kaylee stared at the blood running down her sister's face. Hailey continued to scream and cry, her body shaking against the beam pinned behind her. Allison and Paige wept with their heads hung low. Allison desperately yanked her arms back and forth as she struggled to free her wrists. Mr. Mason inspected the incision he'd made on Hailey's cheek. For a brief moment, his eyes glazed over, almost as if he was second-guessing his actions. Mr. Mason turned away and looked at Kaylee.

"Stop!" Kaylee said. She edged closer to Noah. "Please. You can't do this."

"Why not?" Mr. Mason looked at the razor and said, "I . . . I have nothing now." He looked at Kaylee and began to walk toward her. "I'm sorry, but it's too late."

"It's never too late," Kaylee said. Her mind raced to come up with something, anything, to say to stop him. "Remember when Noah and I came to see you? Remember what you said?"

Hailey stopped crying, raised her head, and stared at Noah and Kaylee sitting together on the bed. Allison and Paige did the same. Mr. Mason stared at Kaylee, lost in his thoughts.

"You said things might have turned out different if Emily had just met the right people." Kaylee searched Mr. Mason's face for any sign of hope. Any sort of connection. "She wanted to make friends. What would Emily say if she saw what you were doing?"

"What would she say?" Mr. Mason shook his head and sighed. "We'll never know, will we? And for that . . . ." He licked his blood-covered lips and raised his razor, pointing the gleaming blade at Kaylee. "You all have to pay."

The door at the top of the stairs burst open and slammed against the wall. The sound of the doorframe shattering caused Kaylee to scream. Splinters of wood flew through the air and fell to the floor far below. Detective Lane entered with his gun aimed at Mr. Mason.

"Stop right there," Detective Lane said. "Drop the blade and raise your hands over your head. Now!"

Mr. Mason's eyes widened. He opened his palm and let the razor fall to the floor. The steel blade briefly rang when it hit the concrete before snapping back into the cherry wood handle. Mr. Mason slowly started to turn around to face the detective. As he did, he raised his right hand but slid his left into his pocket.

"He's got a gun!" Kaylee cried.

Mr. Mason yanked the revolver from his pocket, spun around, and began blindly firing at the top of the stairs.

Twenty Two

Time to Heal

Kaylee screamed as the sound of gunfire echoed off the concrete walls. Detective Lane crouched down low, and the wall behind him became riddled with bullet holes. The detective raised his gun and fired a single shot. The bullet ripped across the air and went straight through Mr. Mason's abdomen, causing him to fall to the ground and drop his revolver. Tears of pain ran down their captor's face as he cried out and clutched his stomach.

Detective Lane glanced at his shoulder. One of the rounds discharged by Mr. Mason had clipped the corner of his jacket. Luckily, that was the only bullet that hit him. The detective stood up and glanced at the other bullets lodged into the wall. He kept his gun aimed at Mr. Mason as he descended the stairs.

Kaylee jumped from the bed and kicked Mr. Mason's revolver toward the staircase. She looked up at the shattered doorway. Four other officers, including two state troopers, came into the room brandishing flashlights and guns and followed the detective downstairs. Kaylee immediately ran back to Noah to check his tourniquet. With her hands bound behind her, she couldn't apply any pressure to the wound.

One of the cops walked past Detective Lane and knelt down next to Mr. Mason. He rolled him over, removed his handcuffs, and began stating the Miranda warning.

"Is everyone okay?" Detective Lane asked. He kicked the razor away from Mr. Mason and then checked on Hailey, carefully inspecting her wound. "Are you hurt? Any other injuries?"

"I . . . I don't know." Hailey cried and tugged on her bound wrists wrapped around the post. "How bad is my face?"

"You'll be fine," Detective Lane said.

"I need help," Kaylee cried. "Noah!"

Detective Lane walked over to the bed with Kaylee and Noah. He inspected the tourniquet and then untied Kaylee's bound wrists. Kaylee yanked her arms free and applied additional pressure to Noah's injury, but he appeared unresponsive.

Two officers began tending to Allison, Paige, and Hailey to remove them from their bonds. The other put on a pair of gloves and surveyed the revolver and razor Mr. Mason had been using. Detective Lane sat beside his nephew and gently put a comforting arm around him. Noah slowly opened his eyes and smiled.

"He's lost a lot of blood," Kaylee said. "Will he be okay?"

Detective Lane pulled back Kaylee's hand to inspect the wound. Blood slowly oozed from the gash in Noah's leg. He frowned and began to apply pressure to the injury. Detective Lane turned to the closest officer and said, "Get the paramedics down here. Fast." He then looked at Kaylee and said, "I've seen worse. Besides, Noah's young and strong. He'll be okay."

"I . . . I did the best I could," Kaylee said.

Detective Lane stared at the tourniquet, turned to Kaylee, and asked, "You did this?" He smiled when Kaylee nodded.

Now free from their ropes, Allison and Paige sat on another bed with Hailey. They did their best to comfort her as she kept her palm against her bloody cheek.

Three paramedics entered the room. Two were carrying a stretcher. A female EMT came downstairs and immediately began to check on Hailey. Kaylee watched as her sister cried hysterically as the paramedic attempted to clean the small incision on her face.

Mr. Mason groaned as another officer pulled him to his feet. They waited for the other paramedics to bring the stretcher downstairs. Mr. Mason kept his head hung low and said nothing as he was escorted upstairs. Emily's father struggled to keep his balance, his blood still oozing from his abdomen. Kaylee felt a sense of relief once he disappeared through the doorway. The infrared camera at the top of the stairs continued to blink.

"You take care of my nephew," Detective Lane said to the nearest paramedic. "He's lost a lot of blood."

The EMT nodded and then knelt in front of Noah. Detective Lane stood up and motioned Kaylee to move. Kaylee gently squeezed Noah's hand before stepping away. Another paramedic joined the first one. They set about moving Noah to the stretcher and putting a better tourniquet on his leg.

"Are you hurt?" Detective Lane asked Kaylee. He took her bloodied hands into his and began to inspect them. "Did he cut you?"

"What?" Kaylee's eyes were fixated on Noah and the paramedics. "No. I'm. . . I'm fine." She watched them move Noah to the staircase and then turned and looked at her hands. "This is Noah's blood."

The paramedics carefully carried the stretcher upstairs. All four girls stopped what they were doing and watched. The open doorway allowed fresh air to waft into the room, helping to remove the stale stench of rotting food from the trash beneath the stairs. The cool, damp salt air brought a feeling of clarity to Kaylee.

"You did the right thing, keeping pressure on the wound," Detective Lane said. His eyes studied the bloody bed. "Using the rope as a tourniquet might have saved his life."

"How'd you find us?" Kaylee asked.

"Your mom called 911."

"So, the tracker led you here?"

"No. We found your keys at the school next to your busted phone."

"Oh." Kaylee lowered her head. Confusion enveloped her, and she looked up at Detective Lane and asked, "So then, how–"

"We've been keeping an eye on Mr. Mason ever since he reported Emily as missing."

"Really?"

"You never rule out the parents." Detective Lane scratched his beard as he looked around the room. "And your theory about Dr. Ed being the connection had me curious."

"So, were you at the school tonight?"

"No. Instead, I sent a couple of officers to watch Mr. Mason. Deep down, I didn't think he'd end up being that Dr. Ed guy. Especially when nobody showed up at four at the football field. But when my guys lost track of him, I got worried. That's when your mom called and told us about your call to her and the tracker's location. The state police went to the school, but they were too late. It felt like too big of a coincidence that we lost track of Mr. Mason at the same time you went missing. That's when we came here."

"Where's here?" Kaylee looked around the room. A boat horn blared in the distance. "His house?"

"No. Although I sent men there, too. This is the basement of Mr. Mason's business. He runs a small fishing charter at Little Pleasant Bay. When we arrived, we saw his truck. And then heard someone screaming." He glanced at the mattress soaked with his nephew's blood and sighed. "I just wish we'd gotten here sooner." Detective Lane put a comforting hand on Kaylee's shoulder. "I'm sorry I doubted you."

Thursday, May 23rd

The next four days were a blur for Kaylee and Hailey. Their mother kept them home from school and canceled all her appointments to be with them. Hailey's cheek now had four tiny stitches covered by a small band-aid. Hailey had remained distraught since coming home from the hospital. Kaylee, however, felt nothing but relief. Well, that, and concern over Noah. His few text messages from the hospital had all been brief and cryptic.

Steam rose from a pan of lasagna resting in the middle of the table, the scent of garlic and ricotta cheese filling the room. Kaylee looked around the dinner table. Hailey, sitting to her left, appeared lucid staring at her dinner plate. Their mother poured herself a second glass of merlot. Directly opposite from Kaylee sat her dad. Stephen had canceled his business trips to be home with his family.

"I really think you should stay home tomorrow," Lesley said. "I've already cleared it with the school."

"I've missed too much," Kaylee said. "Besides, it's only one day. We can get our assignments, and then we've got the three-day weekend for Memorial Day." She turned to her sister and asked, "Right, Hailey?"

Hailey cupped her hand over her cheek and said, "I'd rather wait until these stitches are out."

"I agree with your mother," Stephen said. "School work can wait. You need time to heal." He glanced at Lesley and added, "We all do."

The doorbell rang, surprising everyone. Kaylee stood up, but her mother motioned her to sit down. Lesley said, "Let me get it. I swear, if it's another reporter, I'm going to scream."

Kaylee took another helping of lasagna. Hailey pulled out her phone and checked her lock screen. She sighed and said, "Still no word from Noah." Hailey looked at Kaylee and asked, "Why is he ignoring me?"

Kaylee shrugged and turned to look at the hallway. Her mother opened the front door and said, "Detective Lane. What a surprise."

Kaylee and Hailey shoved their chairs back and ran to the hallway. Stephen took his time to join them. Detective Lane entered and nodded to both girls. Lesley led the detective to the living room. She took a seat on the couch with her daughters while Detective Lane remained standing. Stephen went and stood next to Lesley, resting a comforting hand on her shoulder.

"I just brought Noah home and thought I'd stop by," Detective Lane said.

"Noah's out of the hospital?" Hailey asked. "How is he?"

"He's on crutches and in a bit of pain. But the doc's got him on some meds for that. I think he'll be fine." The detective removed his hat and ran his fingers through his tousled hair. "I also thought you might have questions about today's press conference." He spent a few seconds studying the confused stares looking back at him. "Have you seen the news?"

"No," Lesley said. "I'm just so tired of hearing about it all. It's like every cable news channel has descended on Cape Cod. We can't step out of the house without being questioned." She stood up, walked to the front window, and peered between the curtains. "I'm surprised they aren't out there right now." As she walked back to the couch, she said, "News vans have been in front of the house all week."

"Well, they should all be leaving soon," Detective Lane said. "There really won't be any new information for them after today."

Hailey looked around for her phone but realized she'd left it at the table. She asked, "What happened?"

"Mr. Mason's going to make a full recovery," the detective said. "He confessed to abducting you two as well as Allison, Paige, and Noah. He also admitted to running Jade off the road. He says he never intended to kill her."

"And what about Emily?" Kaylee asked.

"He still claims she killed herself." Detective Lane sighed as he put his hat back on his head. "We exhumed her body from his property earlier today. The autopsy will reveal how she died. But my gut tells me he's telling the truth. In any event, his fate now lies with our justice system." He scratched his beard and stared long and hard at Hailey and Kaylee. "How are you two doing?"

"They've been through a lot." Lesley, now wedged between her daughters, took them by their hands. She looked at her husband and said, "We all have."

"Thank you again for saving our children," Stephen said.

"If I can be of any service, you know how to reach me," Detective Lane said. "I strongly recommend you two girls seek trauma counseling. Perhaps even for the entire family." He walked to the door, opened it, and said, "Take care."

Friday, May 24th

Many of the students filtering into the front entrance of Engel

Academy briefly glanced at Kaylee, Hailey, Allison, and Paige. The four girls stood at the top of the stairs facing the parking lot. The metal detectors behind them randomly beeped. The friends remained stone-faced and refused to lock eyes with any of the other students. At least until Brittney, Autumn and Summer walked by them. Kaylee glared at Brittney and waited for her to finally look away.

The tension in Kaylee's body melted when she saw Detective Lane's cruiser pull up to the curb. The passenger door opened, and Noah emerged, gently hopping on his right foot. After retrieving his crutches from the back seat, he waved goodbye to his uncle and awkwardly made his way up the stairs.

"I was worried you weren't going to make it," Hailey said. She waited for Noah to reach the top step and then gave him a hug. "Did the doctor say you should be back in school so soon?"

"No," Noah said. He struggled to balance his weight between the crutches and Hailey's grasp. "But it's just one day." He glanced at Kaylee and said, "It's good to see everyone again. In a, uh, better setting."

"Don't remind me," Paige said. She waited for Hailey to let go of Noah and then let her eyes settle on Hailey's stitches. "We were lucky to make it out alive."

"But we did," Kaylee said. "And that's all that matters." She looked around them and noticed they were the only ones left outside. "We should get inside."

"Hailey," Noah said. "Can I talk to you?"

"Sure," Hailey replied.

Kaylee headed to the front door with Allison and Paige close behind her. The twin doors opened. Principal Torres and Rat were standing there waiting for them. The three girls stopped just before the threshold.

"Welcome back," the principal said. "If any of you need to leave early, just let me know. I also have a counselor available today if necessary."

"Oh, uh, thanks," Kaylee said.

Allison and Paige didn't bother to acknowledge the principal. As the three girls passed Rat, the janitor lowered his head and looked away.

"They keep pushing counseling on us," Allison said. "I just want to forget it ever happened."

"Me too," Paige said. She turned to Kaylee and asked, "See you at lunch?"

"Sure," Kaylee replied. She watched Allison and Paige walk away before softly saying, "Bye."

Unsurprisingly, Kaylee found it impossible to focus on any of her classes that morning. Her teachers were very sympathetic and supportive as they assigned her missed material to study over the long holiday weekend. By the time lunch arrived, Kaylee had regretted coming to school. She already had enough work to fill most of her free time.

Allison, Paige, and Hailey were already seated at a lunch table when Kaylee entered the cafeteria. She grabbed two slices of pizza and a Diet Coke and headed over to join them. As she got closer, she could tell something was wrong. Her sister's face was flush, and her eyes red.

"What's going on?" Kaylee asked. "I haven't heard from any of you all morning."

"It's Noah," Allison said.

"Noah?" Kaylee looked around the lunchroom in confusion. "Is he okay?"

"No!" Hailey cried. "The asshole dumped me!"

"What?" Kaylee studied her sister, unsure of how to respond. "When?"

"This morning." Hailey grabbed a napkin and blotted her eyes. "He gave me the let's be friends speech." She then picked up her phone and used the front-facing camera to inspect her face. Hailey slowly ran a fingernail across her stitches. She looked at Paige and asked, "Do you think it's because I'm disfigured?"

"No," Paige said. "That's barely going to leave a scar."

"You think?" Hailey opened the *SkinDeep* app and took a selfie. She quickly adjusted the controls to blur her stitches until her cheek looked flawless. Hailey showed Paige the image and said, "I'm going to tell my mom she has to fix this. She *has* to!"

"Wow, I didn't know SkinDeep could remove that type of

scarring," Paige said as she unlocked her phone and launched the app.

"You just told me it wasn't that bad!" Hailey sighed, took another selfie, and began to adjust the photo. "I have to get rid of this."

Kaylee stared in disbelief as Allison took a selfie and then began to play around with the image in the *SkinDeep* app.

"Hey," Noah said.

All four girls looked up, somewhat startled by his sudden appearance.

"Hi," Kaylee said, a smile spread across her face. Her smile faded when she realized she was the only one to acknowledge Noah.

"Can I join you?" Noah asked.

"We were just leaving," Hailey said. She stood up and stared at Allison and Paige. "Right?"

The two girls gathered their trays and collected the rest of their belongings. Hailey looked at her sister and asked, "Are you coming?"

Kaylee's eyes darted between her plate of food, her sister, and Noah. She said, "I haven't even started eating yet."

"Fine." Hailey left her half-eaten lunch on the table, grabbed her school-issued iPad, and stormed away with Paige and Allison in tow.

Noah sat down beside Kaylee and groaned. He fidgeted until he was able to slide his injured leg into a comfortable position. Noah looked at Kaylee and said, "So much for being friends."

"She's really upset," Kaylee said.

"I hoped she would have calmed down by now."

"I only just found out." Kaylee took a sip of soda and fidgeted in her seat. "I . . . I texted you earlier. Never heard back. I wasn't sure if–"

"What? Oh. Sorry. I haven't been using my phone today." Noah tapped his hand against his crutches. "It's been kinda nice."

Hailey, Paige, and Allison were now seated on the far side of the cafeteria, their table adjacent to one with Brittney, Summer, and Autumn. All six were staring at Noah and Kaylee and whispering and pointing.

"She thinks you dumped her because of her stitches," Kaylee said.

"Oh, I know. That was the first thing she said to me."

Kaylee took another sip of soda to quench her dry lips. She couldn't help but notice that Noah didn't seem all that upset. "Did you?"

"Did I what?"

"Dump her because of her face."

"No." Noah shook his head and sighed. "I thought you knew me better than that."

"Sorry. I just . . . ." Kaylee lowered her head. She couldn't help but feel awkward sitting alone with Noah while the others watched. Kaylee glanced at her pizza and realized Noah hadn't brought a tray over. "Are you hungry?"

"Sort of. The pain killers from the doc are messing with my stomach."

"Well, I have two slices if you want one."

Noah smiled, nodded, and scooped up a piece of pepperoni pizza. He took a small bite and said, "Thanks." Grease from the cheese pooled in the corner of Noah's mouth and ran down his cheek. He grabbed one of Kaylee's napkins and wiped his chin dry. "We never really clicked."

"Who?"

"Hailey and I." Noah looked across the cafeteria at Hailey, Allison, and Paige. All three were now showing each other pictures from their phones. He sighed and said, "No offense, Kaylee, but your sister's kind of shallow."

Kaylee took a bite of pizza and didn't respond. How could she? She knew Hailey could be self-absorbed, but she was also her big sister. And her friend. Kaylee struggled to think of something to say.

"I was planning to end things before all of this started," Noah said. He took another small bite of pizza before returning the slice to the plate. "I just didn't want to put it off any longer. I mean, we've got the long weekend. I knew she'd want to hang out. I . . . I had to end it. I guess there's never a good time, right?"

"I guess."

Noah pointed to his crutches and said, "It's going to be a while before I can be your Uber."

"Oh, that's okay. We got the Lexus back from the shop. Hailey drove us today." Kaylee paused and added, "In *her* car."

Kaylee looked around the cafeteria and felt dozens of eyes watching her and Noah. What did it look like, with just the two of them sitting there? She suddenly lost her appetite. Kaylee grabbed a few napkins and nervously wiped her lips. Some of the napkins slipped from her grasp and fell to the floor.

"So, what are you doing over Memorial Day weekend?" Noah asked.

"Oh, uh, I don't know. I mean, with everything that's happened, we haven't really talked about it. Probably homework. I've missed a lot." Kaylee looked at the napkins on the floor and sighed. "You?"

"My uncle wants to throw a huge cookout. I think the cops who saved us will be there. The EMTs, too." Noah waited for Kaylee to say something. When she didn't, he asked, "Want to come over?"

"Oh, uh, I, um . . . ."

Noah bent over, groaned, and grabbed the napkins from the floor. He placed them on Kaylee's thigh. When she went to take them, he slowly took her hand into his and said, "I'd really like you there."

Kaylee stared at Noah's hand on hers. She thought back to every gentle touch they'd shared since they started their crazy adventure to figure out who was stalking their school. She smiled and said, "I guess." Her cheeks became flush as she gently pulled her hand away. "Thanks."

"Well, thank *you*, Kaylee."

"Me? For what?"

"Saving my life."

"Saving . . . ." Kaylee shook her head and stared at her plate. "It was my fault we got captured. Mine. I should have listened to you and never played detective. Looking back . . . I was so stupid. What was I thinking?"

"Don't say that. It worked. My uncle and the cops came. We got the bad guy. You planned the trap for Dr. Ed."

"Well, you sent the screenshots to your uncle. And you

texted him from the bleachers. And, I mean–"

"Stop, Kaylee." Noah leaned closer. "If you weren't . . . *you*, who knows how things would've turned out. Hailey, Paige, and Allison all let themselves get caught. They never told anyone about Dr. Ed. You connected the dots. Give yourself some credit."

Kaylee glanced at the crutches leaning against the table and said, "But you got shot."

"And you made sure I didn't bleed out." Noah turned and grabbed his crutches. He used one to help pull himself upright. "It could have turned out way worse."

"I guess."

Noah winced as he wedged the crutches beneath his armpits. Once he got comfortable, he asked, "So was that a yes, before? Are you in?" Kaylee's blank stare made him frown. "For the cookout this weekend."

"Oh. Uh . . . ." Kaylee glanced over at the table her sister, Paige and Allison had been sitting at. All three were gone. She looked up at Noah and said, "Sure."

"Great." Noah looked around the cafeteria. His smile slowly faded. "This entire school's been through hell. You know?"

"You don't have to tell me. I think you and I suffered the most." Kaylee's eyes settled on Noah's crutches. "Especially you."

"I'll be okay." Noah smacked his hand against his thigh. "Time heals all wounds. Right?" He smiled and added, "Besides, with everything that's happened, I feel like the long weekend can be a big reset button, you know? I mean, we all need a fresh start. Don't you think?"

Kaylee nodded but didn't say anything.

"Can I walk you to class?" Noah asked.

"Sure." Kaylee stared at her half-eaten lunch. "I'll meet you in the hallway."

"Don't keep me waiting . . . Detective."

"Detective?" Kaylee grinned and said, "I thought you told me to be a doctor."

"Doctor. Detective." Noah took a few steps away, turned, and said, "I'm just glad you're coming to the cookout. A fresh start. Right?"

"Right." Kaylee felt herself blush as she watched Noah leave the cafeteria. She pushed her tray away and retrieved her phone from her pocket. After unlocking the screen, Kaylee swiped until she found the *SkinDeep* app. She stared at the lime-green square with the offset white "SD" letters and sighed. Kaylee pressed the icon until the phone gave her the option to delete the app. Without the slightest hesitation, Kaylee removed *SkinDeep* from her phone. Watching it vanish from her screen filled Kaylee with joy. She looked at Noah waiting for her in the hall and softly said, "To a fresh start."

Acknowledgements

Skin Deep started life as an episodic story on Kindle Vella. The Amazon platform requires each chapter, called an episode, to be between 500-5000 words. Vella stories are meant to be read online via an app. So, most readers would read a short episode on their phone. The first three episodes are free, and if you want to read more, you have to pay for each additional chapter. These constraints resulted in tight-knit chapters, many with a cliffhanger ending.

The Vella platform targets young adults. Therefore, when crafting *Skin Deep*, I needed to dial back the clock and channel my inner teenager. I decided to approach the story as a Scooby-Doo or Nancy Drew episode. Even the unmasking of Dr. Ed harks back to those cartoons when Shaggy or Velma would pull the mask off the bad guy.

My last novel, *Dawn of Eve*, tilted my writing away from horror and toward thriller. I think *Skin Deep* moved me closer to a mystery thriller. I had a lot of fun trying to misdirect readers as to Dr. Ed's identity. Maybe I will do more of these in the future.

I also loved linking bits and pieces into the Tallow Series universe. Did you catch all of them?

About the Author

MJ Howson was born and raised in Providence, Rhode Island. An avid reader of thriller and horror stories, MJ always planned to one day write a book. This dream was the typical "someday" ideal. During his 20s, he wrote his first manuscript and began the hunt for an agent. Feedback came back as, "We love your writing style, but look for new material." Before he could continue, his day job soon took up all of his free time.

After a successful career in IT, MJ finally decided to pursue his dream of being an author. The advent of print-on-demand and e-books made this goal something he could somewhat easily follow. The publishing world continues to advance with episodic platforms such as Kindle Vella, where *Skin Deep* first began.

MJ adopted the tagline "The Terror is Real" as the focus for his first series of horror/thriller books. Escapist, paranormal, and supernatural stories are always good for a scare. However, the tales that run the risk of being able to come true are the ones that will really haunt you.

You can connect with MJ via his website. From there, you will find links to his different social media accounts and his blog.

mjhowson.com

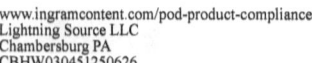